STARSHIP ROMANTASY

KIRENAI FATED MATES BOOKS 4-6

(INTERGALACTIC DATING AGENCY)

TAMSIN LEY

Twin Leaf Press

Cover by The Book Brander

Paperback version
ISBN-13: 978-1-950027-72-9

Twin Leaf Press
PO Box 672255
Chugiak, AK 99567

Dear reader,

Alien worlds mean alien words!

You should easily understand what everything means in context, but I've also provided a glossary in the back of the book to give you more information about some of the terms, plus a bonus section with descriptions of the quirky alien races you may encounter in this series.

Now kick back and get ready for a wild, sexy, and sometimes hilarious ride on board the Starship Romantasy.

Happy reading!

Tamsin

TAZHIO

I FINALLY GET THE COURAGE TO GO AFTER A HOT GUY, ONLY TO END UP STRANDED WITH HIM ON A HOSTILE ALIEN PLANET.

1

TAMARA

*D*o aliens ever get motion sick? I can't stop the thought rolling around in my head as our limo turns down the palm-tree-lined street leading to the spaceport. My stomach roils, despite the prescription patch my sister, Suzanne, affixed behind my ear. I got through a commercial flight and a car ride, but I dread boarding the space shuttle that will transport us to the cruise ship waiting in orbit.

I stare out the window and chew my nail, my other hand clutched in Beanie's fur. My six-pound chihuahua is laid back, as usual, a ball of heat on my lap. My sisters tried to talk me out of bringing him along, but this entire escapade is so far outside my comfort zone, I'm worried even he won't provide enough emotional support. *Why did I let them talk me into this?*

Suzanne grabs my wrist, pulling my hand away from my mouth. Her red-gold hair falls in a perfect swish over her

3

forehead, and her green eyes are compassionate. "Stop it, Tamara. You're going to ruin your manicure."

I curl my fingers into my palm to hide the chipped red paint. I'm not really a mani-pedi kind of person, but my sisters insisted I had to dress up to travel first class. After several hours of travel, I'm feeling anything but classy. And we haven't even made it into space yet. My green peekaboo blouse keeps slipping off my shoulders, and the stretchy waistband has rolled uncomfortably down under my belly. I wish I'd put my foot down about the clothes. Or put my foot down about this entire trip.

But I've never been good at standing up for myself.

All three of my sisters chatter excitedly about their upcoming plans, but I'm barely listening until my twin sister, Jennifer, nudges my knee. "I said, let me see your phone."

She's sitting across from us with her back to the driver. The enormous case containing her astronomy equipment rests on the seat beside her. She's dreamed of going to space since we were kids, and is the main reason I couldn't say no to the trip.

"Why do you want our phones?" Our younger sister, Bethany, clutches the sparkly case of her phone against her chest. As usual, she looks stunning in her flouncy yellow sundress, her wavy auburn hair freshly cut and styled. Our little sister is outgoing, loud, and always looks like she's about ready to go on TV—which makes sense because she hosts a popular television cooking show.

Jennifer wrestles Bethany's phone out of her grip. "I'm installing an app that will let us document any spatial events or anomalies."

I hand my phone over without a word. I know better than to argue.

"I'm not going on this cruise to spend my time gathering data for you." Suzanne tries to snatch her phone back, but Jennifer bats her hand away. "The only research I want to do is which alien has the tightest abs."

"Chill," Jennifer says. "I'm amping up our Bluetooth signals so the phones will stay tethered, even without cell service. That way, we can keep track of each other while we're fending off horny aliens."

"God, I hope they're horny." Suzanne sighs. "I've swiped nothing but duds on Bumble lately." Newly divorced with both kids off to college, Suzanne's a free agent for the first time in nineteen years. Another reason I can't say no to this trip.

I, on the other hand, have zero desire to meet eligible men, let alone alien men, not with my track record. My last boyfriend gave me the "it's not you, it's me" speech, then promptly moved in with another woman. Other than the mandatory parties we're to attend, I plan on holing up in my room with Beanie and my latest embroidery project.

Bethany leans over my lap to peer out the tinted window. "I see the shuttle!"

"Whoa." Suzanne crowds in, her elbow pressing me back against the seat. "Those are aliens!"

I squirm and shove her off me, feeling nauseous. "You're making me sick."

"Really, Tamara?" Bethany backs off. "Are you ever going to let that go? It was a million years ago."

Suzanne pushes aside my hair to check behind my ear. "Is the patch not working?"

"Stop." I shrug her hand away. "I just need space."

Memories of my tenth-grade trip to Europe still haunt me. I'd embarrassed myself by barfing all over the flight attendant's shoes. Afterward, the other kids ridiculed me mercilessly, and for the rest of high school I was called the vomit queen.

I roll down the window, and muggy air that smells like hot pavement blasts me in the face. Ahead on the tarmac, I see something that looks like an enormous purple rosebud resting on its side. My throat tightens.

One side of the ship is rolled open to form a ramp, and three broad-shouldered men wearing white uniforms wait at the base. Their skin is blue, just like in the Hallmark movies. It seems like every television show has featured a blue alien hero since an alien prince came to Earth looking for a mate last year.

The limo rolls to a stop about thirty feet from the ramp. Before the driver can get out to open our door, Suzanne flings it open and clambers out with Bethany right on her heels. Jennifer opens the door on our side, tugging her case from the seat.

I take my time gathering Beanie back into my purse and putting on my sunglasses. I can't believe I'm doing this. Teeth clenched, I step out of the limo onto the tarmac, heat permeating the thin soles of my sandals. My mouth goes dry as I look up at the big alien ship. The lavender surface sparkles slightly in the sunlight and has ribbed veins like an actual rose petal. *How can this possibly be strong enough to go into space?*

Suzanne is already strolling up the ramp, grinning like a Cheshire cat and chatting with an alien carrying two of their over-sized suitcases. Another alien has hoisted Jennifer's enormous astronomy case from the car while Jennifer flutters around like a worried mother hen. I'm struck by how similar all the blue guys seem to appear, a bit like blue Ken dolls in matching white uniforms.

Bethany looks toward me, eyes hidden behind gold-mirrored designer shades. "Ready?"

I nod but remain rooted in place as my sister strolls toward the ramp without me.

The limo pulls away, too, leaving me standing sentinel on the tarmac with the sun beating down on my head. Sweat rolls down my cleavage and sticks my shirt against my back. Beanie is probably cooking alive in my purse. Swallowing my impending terror, I move toward the waiting ramp.

A baffle wall just inside the open hatch blocks my view of the shuttle's interior, but I can hear cheerful chatter from inside. My sisters are too excited to notice I'm missing. *If I don't get on, will the shuttle leave without me?*

I pivot, taking a wistful look at the hangars surrounding the airfield. I see a couple of guys standing in the shade against one wall, smoking. Even though I don't smoke, I'm tempted to go ask them for a puff, just for an excuse to delay boarding.

"Are you ready?"

I jump at the sudden deep voice, catching my purse before it slips completely off my shoulder. Poor Beanie whines as he's jostled inside. A tall blue man in a white uniform stands on the shuttle ramp watching me intently. He looks less human than the ones who helped my sisters, with eyes that are slightly too big for his chiseled face, but he's dressed in the same white one-piece uniform. His deep blue hair is lustrous and thick, shorter along the sides and curling against his collar in the back.

His gaze lowers to my purse, and nervous guilt rocks through me. The cruise line hadn't asked about paperwork for Beanie, and I figured it was better to ask forgiveness than permission, especially since some facilities don't consider emotional support dogs true service animals. Now all I can think is that my sisters will kill me if Beanie gets us banned from the trip.

The alien steps forward and reaches for my purse. "Allow me to assist."

I adjust my purse under my arm protectively, and Beanie whines again. The alien frowns and draws his hand back.

"It's a service animal," I assure him. "He doesn't bite, I promise."

The alien moves sideways, keeping his gaze on my bag. His muscles are quite evident under his uniform, and I can't help wondering if he looks human under his clothes. I bite my lip, my heart beating faster as he shifts his gaze back to mine. The moment his midnight blue eyes meet mine, I'm swept by a moment of vertigo, and my thundering heart goes into overdrive. *Holy shit, the TV shows didn't do their alien heroes justice.* To be fair, the shows only had access to human actors painted blue, but damn, if a real Kirenai ever took to the screen, he'd be an immediate superstar. I've never felt this kind of attraction to a man in my life, let alone one I just met.

"The pattern is a remarkable likeness." His voice feels like heavy silk settling over my skin.

I blink dumbly at him a moment, trying to make sense of his comment. "Um, what?"

He gestures toward my purse. "I've never seen this type of artwork before."

I look down at it, realizing he must mean the embroidered image of Beanie. "Oh! Thank you. I sell custom embroidery on Etsy."

"You made it?"

"Yes." I automatically fumble inside the bag for one of my cards and hold it out. "If you're interested, let me know. I can work from a picture."

He glances down without taking it. "Perhaps another time." He gestures toward the hatch. "We are running behind schedule. Please follow me."

Disappointment floods me as he strides up the ramp without looking back, and I kick myself. *He was just being polite.* No way a hot guy like him is interested—not in me or my embroidery. At least he didn't kick me off the trip because of Beanie.

I hurry up the ramp, towing my suitcase behind me. Inside the shuttle, the alien ducks through a round doorway which immediately spirals closed behind him. In the other direction, the passenger area is lined with plush red chairs, some obviously not proportioned for humans.

One of the blue alien stewards urges me down the aisle. "This way, miss. May I take your suitcase? We're about to take off."

I gulp, suddenly realizing who I was talking to down on the tarmac. *The pilot.* The pilot himself came to make certain I got on board. Now I feel like everyone is looking at me, judging me for making them late. *Great start to the trip.* I relinquish the handle of my suitcase, spotting Suzanne and Bethany sitting next to each other near a window. Jennifer is hovering behind the porter who's manhandling her massive telescope case down the aisle at the back.

A whooshing sound heralds what I assume must be the ramp furling closed, and the floor begins to vibrate softly. My stomach lurches, and I flail one hand to support myself against the nearby wall, fighting back the vivid memory of my tenth-grade trip. *Do not vomit.*

The steward puts a hand to my elbow. "Are you all right, miss?"

Afraid to open my mouth, I nod fiercely and plop down in the nearest seat. The sunlight streaming through the window slices across my face as the shuttle pivots. *We're moving.* Terror grips my heart, and I search for a seatbelt. There are none. Don't these aliens have safety protocols? I squeeze my eyes shut, breathing slowly through my nose.

Beanie wriggles free of the bag, settling on my lap. I stroke his shoulders and rump, not sure if he's calming me or the other way around at this point.

Someone takes a seat next to me, and I crack one eye to see Jennifer looking at me with a raised eyebrow. "Patch still not working?"

I make a sour face. "I'm super sensitive, all right?"

Jennifer sighs. "Okay, sorry. But if you're going to sit there with your eyes closed, can I at least have the window seat?"

Clenching my teeth, I push to my feet and let her swap. "I hope you know how much you owe me for all this."

"I know, I know. Thanks." Jennifer turns and presses her face to the window.

I sit stiffly in the other seat and squeeze my eyes shut, forcing myself to keep my touch gentle as I pet Beanie's back. If I manage to finish this cruise without embarrassing myself again, it will be a miracle.

TAZHIO

The copper-haired female feels like it's put my compass off balance. I stare at the flight controls, feeling like I'm stuck in a tailspin. *Pull yourself together.*

It seems that the rumors about human females are true, and I want her, bad. But the crew has been instructed not to involve themselves with the humans. The Intergalactic Dating Agency takes pride in its success rate and screens guests to ensure there is at least one genetically viable match on board for each paying guest—not shuttle pilots like me.

I fire up the engines and focus on getting us free of the planet's gravitational pull. Soon the joy of flying once more captures my attention, and I take us on a full turn around the *Romantasy* to give the passengers a view of the cruise ship before they board. The habitat ring reflects the golden light from this solar system's intense sun, and I'm tempted to make a flyby of the control module in the center just for fun. But we've fallen behind schedule, so I resist and deposit this batch of passengers before heading back to Earth for the next round.

All day long, I stay in the cockpit and let the stewards and porters handle the incoming females. I can't risk being distracted again. But it seems it's too late for that. I keep picturing the copper-haired female's pale freckled cheeks and gray eyes, the way her blouse hugged her curves in all the right places. She seemed hesitant, furtive, and guilty—not usually the qualities I look for in a female companion. Yet the tangle of feelings roiling in my chest feels like navigating a spatial anomaly without a map.

After I'm done shuttling passengers, I return to my quarters and look up her picture on the shuttle manifest. I know I shouldn't, but I can't stop myself. Her name is Tamara Bloom. She's here with three siblings—imagine having three! Her cabin is on the third tier, inner ring. *I'll need to avoid that area of the ship.* Not that I have reason to go strolling through the passenger decks.

Yet my legs are aching to go for a walk down that corridor at this very moment.

Trying to focus on anything but her, I begin a post-check of the shuttle's comm array. Shuttle maintenance isn't my favorite thing—I much prefer flying, but I need something to do. Across the bay, several mechanics crack dirty jokes about lubing hydraulics. The sex talk turns my mind back to Tamara.

What the kuzara *is wrong with me?* I met the human once, and briefly, yet the moment our eyes connected, my matrix sparked with desire. *The last thing I need is a female distracting me from my job.*

I'm staring sightlessly at a receptor panel embedded in the hull with a spanner clutched uselessly in one hand when a familiar voice calls my name. "Tazhio, you ready?"

I look up and spot a Kirenai heading my direction across the shuttle bay floor. *Kiozhi?* He's shaped like a human wearing black-and-white Earth clothing.

Unlike me, Kiozhi is a guest on the *Romantasy.* He's one of the most eligible bachelors in the galaxy and a longtime family friend. But he's as comfortable among the mechanics as he is with his billionaire buddies, and he side-steps a mechanized cart trundling across the deck before coming to a stop beside me. He frowns at the tool in my hands. "What are you doing down here? The party's already thumping up on the observation deck, and you promised to be my 'wing-friend,' remember?"

"I think you mean wingman," I correct the human term. I only remember it because it refers to flying.

"Oh, right." He smooths the lapels of his suit jacket. "I'm glad you remember this stuff, Tazhio. Let's get going."

The last thing I want to do is go mill around a hundred human women who might drive me out of my mind. "Sorry, I can't make it. I need to make sure this shuttle is ready for tomorrow's excursion."

"Isn't that their job?" Kiozhi motions toward the mechanics. "You promised you'd have my back. The females are accustomed to males with wingmen, and I plan to be exactly what they desire."

I shake my head and smirk, thinking of the scores of women I've seen on my friend's arm. "I don't think you'll have any trouble getting a female without me."

Kiozhi scowls. "Tonight is different. I'm supposed to have an actual, viable match right here on this ship. You have to come with me and keep me on track so I can find her. You owe me that much."

"*Kuzara*," I swear. I do owe my friend for bailing out my family's art gallery during the last recession. "Fine. But after tonight, we're even, okay?"

"Sure we are." Grinning, Kiozhi leads the way to the maintenance lift.

Crew members aren't invited to social events, but Kiozhi is rich enough to get what he wants, and he wants me there. I change into a fresh uniform, and a few minutes later, we're standing shoulder-to-shoulder among hundreds of people on the *Romantasy's* vast observation deck. A nebula is visible through the translucent ceiling, bathing guests in a shifting rainbow of light. From the stage in the center, a band plays an upbeat tune, and the floor teems with human females in all manner of dresses, from short and slinky to long and elegant.

The air smells of lust and perfume, and I can't help myself—I scan the room for a tantalizing glint of copper-colored hair.

Quite a few women have varying shades of red, auburn, or even fuchsia hair, but I can't spot Tamara among the sea of unfamiliar faces.

"Come on." Kiozhi elbows me and presses into the crowd.

I follow, my *Iki'i* thrumming with the anticipation and excitement filling the room. I'm relieved to discover that none of the females seem to affect me as Tamara did, and I pass them by politely. Perhaps what I experienced earlier was a fluke, a residual effect of my excitement to be flying around a new planet. I'd been horny after an exhilarating flight before.

Kiozhi pauses next to a group of females and introduces himself, striking up an easy conversation. I have zero interest in these females, so I nod politely, half-listening as I look around.

A passing tray of *sowain* nuggets catches my attention, and I snag a morsel, popping it in my mouth and chewing slowly. The chefs have outdone themselves, and delicacies from around the galaxy are lavishly displayed on long tables around the room. I grab a tall, thin glass of *Lensoran* bubbly and take a sip.

Red hair near the kitchen doors catches my attention, but it's only a small congregation of Fogarians, their classic russet skin and thick bodies shorter than most of the females. Most of the guests cluster in species-specific groupings. Besides the human females, there are pale Vatosangans, diminutive Hage, and even one Klen, his long green eyestalks drawn close to his skull as if attempting to make his broad-mouthed face look more human. I can't help chuckling when I notice a pair of females gawking at a stone-skinned Khargal who is smugly flexing his admittedly impressive wings. The humans are obviously trying to be subtle, but failing miserably.

Then I spot a flash of copper, and it's as if my shuttle's view screen has suddenly zoomed in on a target. *Tamara.* She stands near the far wall in a sleeveless, emerald-green dress that exposes her pale, freckled shoulders and hugs the delicious curves of her breasts before flaring into ruffled tiers to her knees. She's smiling at a Fogarian with spiked crimson hair and shaggy sideburns.

My insides tense and I clench my jaw. My mind is irrationally demanding, *mine.* I take another sip of my bubbly, trying to calm my senses. What is the Fogarian saying to her? Tamara's smile is cordial, but even with her out of range of my *Iki'i,* I can tell she's feeling uncomfortable. There's a tightness to her eyes, a stiffness to her posture.

A blue hand waves in front of my face. "Hey, you okay?"

I blink at Kiozhi and nod. "Yeah. You're doing great."

"What are you talking about?" My friend's upper lip curls in frustration. "Those females just giggled and walked away. I wonder if I should take off my shirt like those Kirenai over there."

I don't bother looking where Kiozhi's pointing. I can't take my eyes off Tamara. She shifts her large purse to her opposite shoulder, away from the Fogarian, and her smile is now gone. She's shaking her head.

Suddenly, I recall her purse. She had a creature inside—a symbiote, I assume. I meant to ask the steward on the shuttle to document it, but I was so wrapped up in avoiding the females, I forgot. Which means that technically, the creature can be considered vermin and fair game for the Fogarian or any of the other races who enjoy hunting their meals.

Kuzara. If anything happens to her companion, it will be my fault. Before I realize what I'm doing, I push through the crowd toward her. I hear Kiozhi call my name, but don't stop.

"Excuse me?" A female with golden brown hair and enormous silver hoop earrings steps into my path. "You were our shuttle pilot, right?"

I smile politely and try to edge sideways around her. "Yes."

The female puts a hand on my forearm and raises her voice toward a nearby group of her companions. "I told you!" Turning back to face me, she says, "My friends and I are having trouble telling ya'll apart. But I'd recognize those big blue eyes of yours anywhere."

For the first time, I wonder if choosing not to adopt a basic human structure like the other Kirenai crew members might be a mistake. I say, "Many humans look the same to us as well."

"Well, I would love to get to know you better." Hand still gripping my arm, she gestures to a group of human females on the dance floor near the stage, spinning and twirling. "Ever dance with a human before?"

Kiozhi pulls to a stop beside me, radiating frustration. "Where are you going in such a hurry?" Then he seems to notice the female. "Well, hello."

Thank the gods. I move the female's hand from my arm to his. "Kiozhi, this lady would like to dance."

Without waiting to see how that will go over, I resume course.

Except the landmarks have shifted, and she's no longer in the same place.

Concern rising, I pull my matrix into a taller shape, ignoring the gasps of shock from the nearby humans. Scanning the crowd over everyone's head, I spot Tamara and the Fogarian moving toward the dance floor. He's all but dragging her, his meaty hand clamped tightly around her wrist.

Mine. Baring my teeth, I cut through the crowd toward them.

TAMARA

I feel like I've been conned into a timeshare presentation that will last two weeks instead of two hours. Is every mandatory party going to be like this? The rotund alien with crimson hair and sideburns refuses to take no for an answer, and now he's insisting I dance with him. Or *for* him, I'm not sure. All I know is that his clawed grip feels like a vise around my wrist as he drags me forward.

"Thank you, but really, I don't dance," I say. The thought of flailing around in front of all these people makes my heartbeat feel like an earthquake inside my chest.

"I'm going to teach you the Fogarian waltz," the alien shouts over his shoulder as he zig-zags behind a group of gray aliens with wings.

Hoping for an out, I search the crowd for one of my sisters. Suzanne has her back to me and is happily chatting with a group of blue aliens, looking glamorous in her bright red cocktail dress. Jennifer, dressed in a simple black sheath dress, is staring at her phone and ignoring two blue aliens trying to catch her attention. And Bethany is nowhere in sight, probably in the kitchens chatting to someone about the food.

I try jerking my hand free and accidentally elbow a woman in the boob. I cringe-smile at her. "I'm so sorry!"

The woman, wearing a black silk gown slit to expose one shapely leg, levels a haughty glare at me, then sweeps her gaze over the tight bodice of my borrowed dress. With a sniff, she turns away. The dress is Jennifer's, and I wore it because my sisters insisted I looked good in it. Big fat liars. I knew it showed too much cleavage. *This is why I prefer to stay home.*

The last thing I want to do is join the graceful couples twirling around the glossy dance floor as if they've taken dance lessons their entire lives. Everyone at the party tonight is glamorous, all glitter and silk.

"Please, I'm not a dancer," I beg again, hoping he'll listen.

"It isn't difficult, I promise," he shouts without looking back.

Beanie whines softly, conscious of my distress. I cling to my purse strap with my free hand, fighting to keep it up on my shoulder as I'm jostled by the crowd. Suzanne tried to convince me to leave Beanie in my cabin, but a party is exactly the place I need him most. I yearn to go back to my room and hide.

Suddenly, a large blue hand clamps down on the clawed alien's wrist, stopping us in our tracks. "The lady doesn't wish to dance with you."

The deep voice is familiar, and I let my gaze travel from the blue hand up the white uniform sleeve to a broad shoulder. I suck in a breath at the sight of a handsome blue face with large, dark eyes.

Tazhio. I remember hearing this voice over the speaker on the shuttle when our pilot introduced himself. He's even more attractive than I remember. Unlike the other blue aliens who reminded me of Ken dolls with similar short haircuts, tall, muscular bodies, and gleaming smiles, Tazhio is unique. His hair is cut longer, and his square jaw and masculine nose are unmistakable.

Realizing my mouth's hanging open, I snap it closed.

The squat alien releases my hand and shakes himself free from Tazhio's grasp. His hairy face scrunches into a scowl so deep, his eyebrows nearly meet his mustache. "She has not expressed aversion to my invitation."

Tazhio cuts a glance toward me. "Do you wish to accompany this man?"

Cringing at being put on the spot, I shake my head no and quickly shove my newly freed hand inside my bag to touch Beanie's comforting warmth. A warm wet tongue bathes my knuckles, but his kisses can't stop my trembling.

With an indignant huff, the red alien pivots and stalks away.

The relief that floods me feels like a shot of good alcohol, leaving me weak in the knees. I smile at Tazhio. "Thank you."

He puts a hand to the small of my back—an intimate gesture that sends a giddy thrill into my pelvis. It's been a long, long time since I felt anything like that, and without thinking, I take a small step closer. "My name's Tamara."

"Hello, Tamara. I'm Tazhio." He continues gazing at me with an expression that makes my heart flutter. "I suggest you be more assertive about what you want. Would you like an escort back to your cabin?"

I'm not sure how long I'm required to stay to fulfill the requirement for our free tickets, but Tazhio is part of the crew, so if he says I can go, I'll take it. "If that would be all right, yes."

Hand still on my back, he guides me toward the lift platform, joining two other couples. One pair is making out like teenagers and the other is exchanging glances that drip with lust. Embarrassed and slightly aroused, I keep my gaze on the floor as the lift descends. The lust-filled couple exits first, then the kissers. Now alone in the lift with Tazhio, I look up to find him staring at me.

Whoa, Nelly. There can be no mistaking the desire in his eyes.

My heart rises into my throat and my nipples get all prickly feeling inside my too-tight bodice. I hadn't had a partner that didn't require batteries since my last boyfriend left me two years ago, and the idea of Tazhio's hands on me is irresistible. *Should I invite him for a nightcap?* This is a singles cruise, after all, and Suzanne had insisted on stashing a pack of condoms in my room "just in case."

Before I can second-guess myself, I reach over and twine my fingers with his, trying to smile in invitation.

His weight shifts away from me, and a lump fills my throat. My fingers turn icy. *Shit.* I misread him. What was I thinking? I loosen my fingers, ready to pull free, when he pivots to face me. He's close enough for his breath to fan my cheek, and his fingers curl around my hand.

Heat sweeps through my body like I just stepped out of an air-conditioned building into the full force of a sunny day. I tilt my chin to look up into his face. His dark eyes glitter with an intensity that makes me weak in the knees.

Sure he's about to kiss me, I tilt my chin up and close my eyes, trying to be brave and embrace the moment. The softest caress brushes my lips, a whispering touch that sends a jolt straight through my center. I can't breathe. I can't think. It's like I'm floating on air, and every cell in my body feels inexplicably alive.

I'm still processing these feelings when the lift chimes and the door spirals open. Tazhio's low voice hums in my ear. "I believe this is your deck."

I open my eyes and see a familiar, fuchsia-carpeted hallway. Yep, this is my floor. My heart is racing. I just met this guy, and I'm about to take him back to my room. I've never dared have a one-night-stand, and I can't believe this is actually going to happen. *With an alien!* Suzanne will be so proud.

Still holding his hand, I step off the lift.

Tazhio's grip tightens briefly around mine as I tug him after me, but he stops at the threshold and gently extracts his fingers. Keeping his gaze on mine, he bows his head. "Have a good rest of your evening."

I blink, suddenly confused as I watch the lift door spiral closed between us.

For several heartbeats, I stare at my own reflection in the metal, trying to understand what just happened. *But he kissed me...*

Oh, God. Had that been a pity kiss? A hot guy like Tazhio probably has ten women a night hit on him, all more elegant than I am.

Face on fire, I glance up and down the hallway, glad to find it empty. No one had seen my embarrassing moment.

Hurrying toward my cabin, I play the scene in the elevator over and over in my head. He had kissed me, right? My eyes had been closed—he could've brushed my lips with his fingertips for all I know. Worse than a pity kiss. *Why, why, why?*

My door slides open automatically, each cabin somehow programmed to recognize the occupant's bio signature, eliminating the problem of losing your keys. I stumble inside, seeing the king-sized bed has been neatly remade after my nap this afternoon. Some sort of candy sits atop the pristine white pillow.

The cabin is nicer than my bedroom at home, but in an art déco sort of way. The vanity has a countertop that looks like it was sliced from the center of a giant pearl, and the bed's silver headboard rises to a gentle peak, also inlaid with what looks like millions of pearls. The walls are covered in a subtle design with overlapping circles and thick lines in shades of pale pink and dove gray that match the slightly darker pink carpet.

Setting Beanie on a puppy pad in the bathroom, I return to the bedroom and pick up the candy, wishing it was ice cream. What I wouldn't do for a pint of Rocky Road at this moment. *I should've known better than to try and be brave.* What a fool he must think me. Tazhio was just doing his job. And I grabbed his hand without asking… My eyes fly open with horror. *Just like that red alien grabbed mine.*

I groan, plopping heavily onto the edge of the bed. *Way to alienate the only alien you found remotely attractive.*

Snorting at my own silent joke, I unwrap the candy. Popping it into my mouth, I let the sweet, melty caramel flavor flood over my tongue. Not ice cream, but still decadent. Maybe I can order ice cream from room service. *I need room service for the entire rest of the cruise.* I dread the thought of showing my face again. Can I pretend to be sick and stay in my cabin for the rest of the trip? I'll absolutely die if I have to face Tazhio again.

Beanie appears carrying his toy moose and sprawls on the carpet near my feet, gnawing happily on one of its antlers. I sigh and lean back on the plush mattress to watch him. "Good thing we like the room, huh, Beanie?"

His little tail wags in agreement.

"I wonder how long it might take to get ice cream delivered." My gaze shifts to my closed cabin door. A diagram on the back of it shows the layout of the ship—all thirteen decks and hundreds of rooms. I frown. "Wait. How did he know which floor my room is on?"

My stomach does flip-flops that have nothing to do with space travel. He can't possibly have memorized the floor every guest is on. But he could've looked me up. Which meant he felt the same zing I did when we first met on the shuttle. *The elevator kiss was real.*

So why did he break away?

I bite my lip, the foggy memory of the ship orientation meeting returning to me. The cruise director instructed us that the aliens would not engage in intimate contact without express verbal consent. What if Tazhio had been waiting for me to invite him to my room? To actually say the words?

After he rescued me from the red alien at the party, he told me to be more assertive about what I want. Yet on the elevator, I did nothing more than smile and take his hand. So he did the decent thing and stayed back.

I flop backward against the mattress and glare up at the ceiling. "Well, shit."

4

TAZHIO

The entire walk back to my quarters, my body is screaming that Tamara is my mate. But I can't tell her that. The Intergalactic Dating Agency will see to it that I never fly again if I attempt to lure a female away from paying guests. Just stepping in with that Fogarian at the party was probably going to have consequences. Worth it though. If I can't have her, I at least want her to be with someone who respects her wishes.

I reach my private quarters and sit stiffly on my bunk. The mirror on the wall across from me shows a familiar yet altered reflection of my features. My shoulders are a bit broader, and my nose slightly less prominent than usual—my matrix's innate response to Tamara's attraction. When a Kirenai finds his mate, his form will intuitively assume the shape his mate prefers, which becomes permanent once they bond.

She makes my shape want to settle.

I lie back on the mattress, remembering the thrill I felt when Tamara threaded her fingers with mine. The nervous yet certain spark of desire in her ocean-gray eyes. The way her breasts swelled above the neckline of her dress as if aching for me to free them.

I ache, as well. Opening the front of my pants, I reach for my excruciatingly hard shaft. As I stroke myself, I imagine myself sliding my palms beneath Tamara's skirt, up her thighs to her center of liquid heat. I pump faster and faster until my breath comes in ragged gasps. The sweet flavor of the feathered kiss still lingers on my lips, like stardust clinging to the hull of the ship.

Sucking in my bottom lip, I imagine her tight pussy dripping with juices. Imagine lapping them up. Imagine her squirming with pleasure as I penetrate her. Her exquisite heat around my cock.

Tamara. My hips buck upward against my hand, and the cascade of my release shakes me from head to toes.

I let my limbs relax and stare up at the gray ceiling, breathing hard. The pressure in my balls is better, but a hollow yearning still aches in my chest. *She's not for you.* No matter what my body is saying, I can't have her. I head to the lavatory, trying to think about other women I've found attractive in the past, hoping to blot her from my mind. As I shower, I end up thinking of Tamara and masturbating again.

"This is ridiculous," I tell my dick as I step out of the stall.

Going to my resting pod, I force my matrix to relax into my natural, amorphous state. I rarely need to rest this deeply, but perhaps if I'm no longer humanoid, my desire for her will subside. When I wake, I'm humanoid again, and my dick is throbbing with thoughts of Tamara. So much for that idea.

I spend the day in my quarters trying to distract myself with some light reading and more not-so-light stroking of my cock. It's all I can do to stay away from tonight's singles party. Jealousy smolders in the pit of my stomach as I imagine Tamara holding someone else's hand at this very moment. Will she take him back to her cabin? Maybe she's holding more than his hand…

Kuzara. These thoughts are driving me crazy. I dig out my bottle of *hahana* liquor, pour a double shot, and sling it back. Before I know it, the bottle is empty, but at least I get drunk enough to fall asleep.

Hung over and grouchy the next morning, I head to the shuttle bay to run diagnostics for my upcoming shuttle tour of the Singing Planet. I settle into the pilot seat and pull up my flight plan. We won't be landing—reaching the surface safely is nearly impossible, but this will be my first non-simulated trip. The magic of the Singing Planet is in its ionosphere. Navigated correctly, the rivers of charged particles will ignite my shuttle into a symphony of sound and light. It is going to be glorious.

I wonder if Tamara signed up for this excursion.

I stare at my console, trying to make sense of the data on the screen, and it takes me a moment to realize I've opened the passenger list over the top of my diagnostics panel, hoping to see her name. *Idiot!* I close the file with a frustrated jab of my finger. It doesn't matter if she'll be on the excursion or not, because I plan to stay in the cockpit the entire time. There is a minimal margin of error for my calculations, and I can't let myself be distracted.

I'm nearly finished calibrating the sensors when Kiozhi's familiar voice floats toward me from the bay. "Tazhio, you in here?"

I call out, "In the cockpit."

My friend ducks inside and glances around the semi-circular bridge area. He's wearing nothing but a pair of short pants that barely cover his crotch. "Don't you ever stop working?" he asks.

I shrug and frown at his clothing. "Why are you naked?"

Kiozhi glances down at himself. "I'm not. These are called swim trunks. All the males on Earth wear them during cruises." He raises both arms and flexes his biceps. "Human females like to see muscles."

I'm struck by a sudden image of Tamara admiring the muscles of other males. Touching them. *Or being touched by them.* A hard lump fills my stomach. "Do the females wear these swim trunks as well?"

"Only at the pool, and they wear a second piece to cover their breasts." Kiozhi makes an appreciative cupping gesture with both hands. "I believe it's called a bikini." He sinks into the co-pilot seat next to me, shoulders slumping. "But I'm not here to talk about that. I found my mate."

I suck in a sharp breath and swivel my chair to face him. I knew he was on this cruise hoping to find a mate, but to be honest, I never actually thought he would. Kiozhi has been a playboy for as long as I've known him. A slow smile spreads across my face. "Wow. Congratulations."

My friend rubs a hand through his hair. Normally, he's excellent at shielding his *Iki'i*, but his frustration fills the cockpit with a grating sensation. "I'm not sure congratulations are in order. I think I made a mistake."

Alarm spikes through me, and my smile drops. Bonding to a female is nothing to be taken lightly. A bond is permanent, linking the pair together and granting the female an extended life to match her mate's. Considering the fact Kirenai lived for hundreds of cycles, a lifetime bond with an unpleasant female could be worse than a prison sentence. "A mistake? How?"

"We met at the first party, and she invited me to her cabin." A dreamy look fills Kiozhi's eyes. "We had the most outrageous sex, but I didn't use my mating shaft. I read that humans like to be courted before bonding, and I was trying to be respectful." He grimaces. "Let me tell you, that was possibly the most willpower I've ever exerted in my life."

I nod in understanding. I know that if I had let things progress with Tamara, we'd probably be mated right now.

Kiozhi continues his story. "The next morning, I sent her flowers with an invitation to join me for lunch. I even reserved the entire forward pool deck just for us." He stares dejectedly at his clenched fists. "She never showed up."

"This is a big ship. Maybe she just didn't know how to find you?" I offer. On one hand, I understand his distress, but on the other, at least he's allowed to pursue her.

His palpable frustration twists to something more painful. "I wondered that, too, so I had the gift shop send a box of something called chocolates to her room and told her I would pick her up for dinner. She returned the chocolates." He bares his teeth in a snarl. "And the next time I saw her, she was at the karaoke bar with another male, singing her heart out about love."

"Ouch." I cringe. Thank the gods I'd stayed away from the parties and seeing Tamara doing something like that. "I'm sorry. But at least you didn't bond with her. That would make it a hundred times worse."

"You don't understand. She's the one. I know it." Kiozhi's expression is pained. "I know she felt our connection. My *Iki'i* can't lie." He leans forward, gaze intent. "I've been reading about human courting games where mates try to make one another jealous by pretending disinterest. I believe this must be her intention, and I need your help coming up with a plan to win her."

I'd seen my friend with plenty of women, but never obsessed with one like this. *He's as tormented as I am.* There must be something about human females that turns men into idiots. I shake my head. "These humans can be intoxicating, but you need to face reality. If she's spurning your advances, I don't think she's your mate."

"Humans don't recognize their mates right away. If she would just spend some time with me, she'd figure it out."

"You can't force her to spend time with you."

"She's all I can think about," Kiozhi says between clenched teeth.

"I know the feeling." The words are out before I can stop them.

Kiozhi's eyes narrow to slits. "You found a female?"

A painful knot in my chest keeps me from saying it out loud, so I nod. I pat the instrument panel, thinking about how he told me I work too much. "You need to find something else to think about. Like me."

But my friend won't let it go. "Did you meet her at the party?"

"It doesn't matter. The guests are off limits to the crew."

"*Kuzara*, who cares? When you find your true mate, don't let anything stand in your way."

"She's not meant to be mine. The IDA genetically profiled her to match one or more of the guests. She has other males to choose from, just like your female is also investigating other options. Let her go and move on."

"Did you sleep with her?" Kiozhi persists.

"Of course not! I told you, she's off limits." I swivel back toward my console. "The only solution is to find something else to focus on. The excursion to the Singing Planet is today. You should come. It's going to be amazing."

Kiozhi rubs the back of his neck. "This is the trip you've been talking about? The one you just got certified to do?"

"Yes. I've been studying the frequencies the different ionic layers will create—"

"Yes, yes, I know. You're going to play a song with the shuttle. Once-in-a-lifetime experience and all that." Kiozhi taps his chin. "I wonder if Suzanne would agree to view it with me?"

I sigh. "The point is for you to get your mind *off* the female. You should come alone."

"I don't do things alone." Kiozhi scowls.

"You know what I mean. There will be plenty of other female guests there. Or if you prefer, I'll let you sit up here with me in the co-pilot seat."

Kiozhi drums his fingers on his thigh, then stands. "Fine. I'll come along. But I expect this to be the best concert I've ever been to."

"It will be, I promise."

Once Kiozhi is gone, I resume my diagnostic checks. This excursion is going to blow everyone's mind and help us stop brooding over these intoxicating females once and for all.

5

TAMARA

"**I** swear to God it's like you and Suzanne swapped bodies," Jennifer says as we step onto the lift headed to the shuttle bay. "We started this trip with her all gung-ho to party and now she hides in her room half the day, while you swore up and down you planned to be a hermit and now you want to come on an excursion." She loops one arm through mine. "Not that I'm complaining. I think it's great you're coming out of your shell, plus your phone will be really helpful collecting data."

I smile nervously without answering. The moving elevator just made my stomach swoop, and I have to swallow back lunch. How am I going to endure another shuttle ride?

Over the past few days, I've joined every onboard activity that came my way, hoping to bump into Tazhio again. I've strolled along every aisle in the gambling area with its flashing lights and strange gaming tables. I've eaten at every restaurant, much to Bethany's delight. I've even had drinks at the poolside bar with its dizzying view of the stars.

I never once spotted Tazhio among the masses of blue aliens spread across the ship. I was beginning to wonder if he altered his shape just to avoid me until Jennifer pointed out that I've been looking in the wrong places. He's a pilot, so the most likely place to find him is in the shuttle.

Now I just have to get through this excursion without embarrassing myself by besmirching the steward's well-polished shoes.

The lift opens on the shuttle bay, and I hesitate, one hand inside my purse to touch Beanie's comforting warmth. My heart is racing a mile a minute as I take in the familiar purple shuttle resting in the middle of the cavernous bay. Beyond the shuttle, mechanics with tools hanging off their belts move about, glancing up from their work at the arrival of guests. High above, the entire ceiling glows as if it's made of one solid light fixture, and spherical drones flit back and forth.

Just outside the lift, a steward who looks like a classic Area 51 alien with gray-green skin and huge black eyes stands at a podium. He—or she, I'm not certain how to tell the difference or if gender is even binary for these aliens—is speaking with a pair of well-muscled blue aliens in swim trunks.

Jennifer elbows me, and we exchange a smirk. Many of the aliens had taken to wearing the singular item of clothing, and while most women don't seem to mind all the man-candy strutting around, I've felt a little awkward at the more formal evening events.

"Are you here for the Singing Planet excursion?" the steward asks.

Jennifer nods and gives our names.

"More Bloom sisters! How delightful," the steward says with a wide smile. My sisters and I have gained some notoriety among the aliens as siblings traveling together. The small alien points toward a path marked by red velvet ropes leading to the shuttle. "Your other party member is already here. Please have an enjoyable trip!"

Near the shuttle ramp, I spot Suzanne wrapped in a pastel swirl scarf and sunglasses. She's hiding behind a blue-skinned porter in a white crew uniform next to Jennifer's enormous astronomy case. At the first party on board, she hooked up with someone who is now obsessed with her, and she's trying to avoid running into him.

I search the mechanics and other personnel for any sign of Tazhio as we follow the path between the velvet ropes, my flip-flops slapping my heels. Lunch feels like a rock in my stomach. I absolutely knew it was a mistake to eat right before the trip, but Jennifer was hungry and I'm a nervous eater, so I gave in. I keep one hand inside my purse against Beanie's furry shoulders.

What if Tazhio really is avoiding me on purpose? What if he never comes out of the cockpit? *What if I spend the entire flight in the bathroom barfing?*

Seeming to sense my worry, Jennifer again loops her arm through mine. "You'll be fine. You've been on the ship for days now and haven't thrown up. The motion sickness patch is working."

I nod, praying that remains true on a flight that's advertised as a "ride of a lifetime."

"Where have you been?" Suzanne hisses the moment we're within earshot. "Vin Diesel and I have been waiting for at least ten minutes." She gestures toward the big blue porter who's been Jennifer's shadow since we arrived.

I bite back a grin. The guy does look sort of like Vin Diesel, right down to his bald head.

Jennifer scowls, a flush creeping into her cheeks. "Be polite. His name's Nazhin."

The porter's features remain emotionless, but as always, his silvery eyes are locked on Jennifer. "I requested an exclusive spot in the viewing area for you and your equipment," he says.

"Thank you so much." Jennifer smiles and looks around the area expectantly. "Where's Bethany?"

Suzanne rolls her eyes. "She bailed on us. Busy teaching an alien how to bake a birthday cake or something." She lowers her sunglasses just enough to focus directly on me over the dark lenses. "I'm surprised you didn't find an excuse not to come, Tamara. You must really have the hots for this pilot."

"Shh!" I glance toward the open shuttle and duck behind the tall porter, heat rising to my cheeks. My older sister has no shame when it comes to men.

She grins at me and moves toward the ramp. "Let's get inside before I'm spotted."

Jennifer follows, with Nazhin carrying her gear.

I take a few deep breaths to calm myself before joining them. My stomach is tangled up with dread and hope and a whole lot of other feelings that keep rising into my throat. *What the hell am I doing?* Tazhio's way out of my league. He's not only good looking, he's a pilot. Maybe I should forget all about this right now, before it's too late and I ruin the trip for everyone.

A familiar voice booms my name across the shuttle bay. "Tamara! I've been looking for you everywhere!"

I cringe, recognizing the voice of my crimson-haired admirer from the first night on the *Romantasy*. The squat alien is barreling down the path between the velvet ropes, wearing nothing but a Speedo. Apparently, his crimson hair grows other places on his body, as well. *Crap.*

Why is this guy so determined to win me over? I hurry to the ramp. Maybe I can get a seat between my sisters where the alien can't pester me. But Nazhin is blocking the way with Jennifer's load of equipment.

Heavy footfalls pound up the ramp behind me. "I would be honored to have you sit with me," the squat alien booms, slightly out of breath. He comes to a halt with the bare, heated skin of his shoulder brushing my arm, then takes a tiny step back—he's been careful about making physical contact after Tazhio's intervention. But his eyes are nearly level with my breasts, and he seems to have no clue that's not where he should be looking.

I edge sideways. "Thank you, no. I'm with my sisters."

He lifts his gaze to mine, smiling to reveal two rows of pointed teeth. "We can make room for them, too. I've been on this tour before and have reserved a block of the very best seats."

Just then Nazhin clears the doorway, and my heartbeat bursts into a gallop. Tazhio stands at the top of the ramp.

His gaze locks with mine. "Tamara, your VIP seat is ready."

VIP seat? I don't know what he means, but I'm not going to argue. Nodding dumbly, I ignore the spluttering alien beside me and follow Tazhio inside. Suzanne spots me from her seat in the passenger area and grins broadly, giving me a thumbs up.

Heat flushes through my body, and I grin back before turning to follow Tazhio through the circular door into the cockpit. I can't believe this is happening. Not only have I found him, I now know he wasn't ignoring me. Plus, he's offering me a special seat. *Maybe he likes me after all.*

The cockpit is about the size of a small bedroom, with two bucket seats facing what I assume are control panels and a large view screen showing the doors of the shuttle bay. One chair is occupied by another blue alien wearing a cream-colored tunic belted at the waist, green pants, and tall black boots that remind me of a pirate.

He takes me in with raised eyebrows and shoots to his feet. "Aren't you one of the Bloom sisters?"

I nod, too nervous to speak. Sweat has blossomed beneath my arms and I hope it isn't showing through my turquoise blouse.

Tazhio rubs the back of his neck. "Um, would you mind if Tamara took your seat?"

It registers that this guy isn't in a crew uniform. Is Tazhio booting someone for my sake? That seems unfair. I back up a step. "I don't mean to intrude. I can go sit with my sisters."

"No, no, I'm more than happy to exchange seats." The booted alien gestures toward the chair, then squeezes past me with a grin. In the blink of an eye, he's gone, and the door spirals closed. Tazhio stands there a moment, looking at me expectantly.

Nausea rolls through my gut. This is a mistake. The only thing this is going to accomplish is embarrassing me in front of a handsome guy. I turn to look for the door handle. "I'm not sure this is a good idea."

A steward's voice enters the cockpit over the intercom. "Everyone's on board, sir. I'm securing the ramp."

Tazhio puts a hand to my lower back, sending delicious tingles up my spine as he urges me forward. "Too late to change your mind now. Please, sit."

Breathing shallowly, I sink onto the seat, keeping my purse on my lap like a shield. Beanie pokes his head from the top and whines. I stroke between his ears. "It's okay, everything's okay."

Tazhio takes the other chair, and his deft fingers play over the symbols on his console. On the view screen, I watch the shuttle bay doors spiral open. Through the faint glitter of what I assume must be a force-field looms a glowing yellow planet with a band of multi-colored rings.

Oh, shit.

The shuttle rises from the deck and shoots forward into space. My stomach flip-flops, and I grip the arms of the seat. *Oh, God, oh God.*

6

TAZHIO

I guide the shuttle out of the bay toward the glowing, multi-colored rings of the Singing Planet, hyper-conscious of Tamara in the co-pilot seat nearby. The moment I heard her voice on the boarding ramp, Kiozhi sensed my sudden alertness and insisted I at least greet her. When I saw that Fogarian pestering her again, I knew I couldn't leave her on her own in the passenger cabin.

Now she's sitting at my side for this momentous flight. *What if fate threw us together, after all?*

The problem is, her anxiety is getting to me. Sharp and stabbing, it's enough to give me the onset of a headache. If it's this bad for me, it must be excruciating for her.

Her eyes are squeezed shut, and she's frantically petting her quadruped's small head with a trembling hand. The quadruped seems to absorb her anxiety as it looks up at her with huge, liquid eyes, but her tension is overwhelming.

"I'm an excellent pilot and trained extensively for this tour," I reassure her. "You have nothing to worry about. I promise."

She cracks one eye to look at me. "I believe you. I get motion sick is all."

Motion sick. I'd read about the phenomenon as part of the emergency medical training the crew took to prepare for hosting human guests. I recite the diagnosis, "A condition where humans experience a malfunction of the vestibular system resulting in dizziness, nausea, and vomiting."

"Um, yes." She claps one hand over her mouth.

I frown. I need to ease her discomfort or she'll never want to fly with me again.

Since it's a straight shot between the *Romantasy* and the planet, I put the shuttle on temporary autopilot and swivel in my seat to face her. "I believe I can help. Give me your hands."

Her cheeks have a greenish hue, but she pulls her hand from her mouth and hesitantly extends it toward me, keeping the other on her quadruped.

"I'll need both hands if your symbiote will allow."

She blinks in confusion until I gesture toward the small animal in her lap.

"Oh, my dog," she says. "Right." Picking up the creature, she sets it on the floor next to her feet, along with her purse. "Stay, Beanie."

The dog—I will have to remember that word—stands and puts its tiny front paws on her leg. She seems to find comfort in the creature, so I don't interfere.

Taking both of her wrists, I open my *Iki'i*, searching for specific pain receptors beneath her delicate skin. She is so soft and warm, and her perfume reminds me of *malila* flowers opening under the moonlight. I yearn to press my mouth against her palms and feather kisses up her arms, to bury my face in her bright copper hair and pull her lush body against mine.

I shake my head free of those thoughts. She is suffering, and here I am thinking like a rutting *ijin'en*. Locating the correct nerves on her wrists, I press my thumbs into her flesh. "Please tell me if I press too hard."

She shakes her head, her ocean-gray eyes fixed on mine. "I'm okay."

The shorts she wears leave her knees bare, exposing her freckled skin. I can't help but wonder how far up her legs those adorable freckles continue and have to force my attention back to her face. "My medical training said to hold this until the patient finds relief."

A flicker of awe courses through her. "Wow, you're a pilot and a doctor?"

I chuckle. "No. All crew members are trained to treat minor human ailments. We want to be certain everyone has a comfortable and pleasant trip."

She bites her bottom lip and glances away, her cheeks flushing pink. "Of course. That makes sense. It's your job."

A new flavor of anxiety floods my *Iki'i*. Embarrassment? Her capricious flow of emotions is hard to keep up with. "I take no offense," I assure her.

"You're too kind." She lifts her eyes back to mine and squares her shoulders. "I need to apologize for what happened in the elevator. I'm sure I put you in an uncomfortable position."

I suck in a breath. Does she somehow know that I've had my hand down my pants for the last three days? My dick has been half-hard from the moment I heard her voice outside the shuttle, and now it surges to full attention. *She can't know what I've been doing.* Can she? My heart fills my throat, and I wonder if I might've missed some information about humans having telepathy.

Just then, a breathy note of sound passes through the shuttle, and motes of white light dance in the air between us.

"*Kuzara!*" Releasing her arms, I spin back to the console. I nearly forgot we're on approach, and we've already entered the first ionized rings of the Singing Planet.

I disengage the auto-pilot, check the sensors, and level the shuttle's orbit. Timing is crucial for this excursion, and we've entered the planet's ionosphere out of phase. *I can adjust.*

"We're okay," I say, as much for my benefit as Tamara's. But I haven't even engaged the safety restraints yet, let alone prepared the passengers and crew for what's coming. I activate the restraint system, and the seat softens and molds around my body like a harness. I know the same thing is happening to passengers ship-wide.

Tamara gasps. "Oh, God, what's happening?"

The other passengers are likely wondering the same thing, so I open the comm. "This is your captain. I've engaged the safety features of your seats. It's normal to encounter some turbulence during this excursion, so please remain seated until you've been released."

A note like a woman's sigh courses over the hull.

I had an entire script memorized to introduce the tour, but now that we're already immersed, I'll have to cut it short. "Welcome to one of the few known wonders of the galaxy—the Singing Planet. Please sit back and enjoy this symphony of sound and light."

Adjusting our course toward an eddy of ionized particles ahead, I modulate the shielding to complement the frequency. Golden streamers caress the view screen, and a high, sweet chord vibrates through the hull. Pleasure courses through me. This is exactly what I planned for the excursion's first note.

Tamara's posture relaxes, and she whispers, "It's so beautiful."

Her anxiety is gone, consumed by pure wonder.

My *Iki'i* thrums with joy, and I take a breath, letting the mix of sensations wash through me. I've flown countless simulations of the Singing Planet, but the real thing is ten times more astounding, especially when shared with the charming female beside me. I can't help grinning. "It's only going to get better."

I guide the shuttle deeper into the ionosphere, creating a wavering alto that vibrates the deck beneath our feet. Flashing motes of aquamarine join the streamers of golden light, merge, and form rings of emerald green. I glance at Tamara.

Her dog is back on her lap, curled into a furry ball, and she's smiling and holding out one hand as if trying to touch the light. When a wide emerald band seems to slip down her arm like a bracelet, Tamara laughs, the sound as pleasing as the note now gliding along the hull.

Pride fills my chest. I never realized how much I would enjoy seeing someone else's response to the show. *Tamara's response.*

A brassy note creeps into the melody, and I quickly adjust course to avoid a hotspot. The gravitational stabilizers take a second to compensate, and I sense Tamara's nausea rising again. *Pay attention,* I tell myself, though her upset stomach will be the least of our concerns if the shuttle gets mired in heavy ionization. The trick to flying around the Singing Planet is to keep to the shallow currents and take advantage of eddies that will help shed excess ionization on the hull.

The twisting particle-rivers braid themselves into a complicated map, and I merge our trajectory alongside a new current. A wavering chord vibrates through the hull like the fragile wings of a *lonala* moth. Satisfied, I once more chance a look in Tamara's direction.

Sparkling rosy light bathes her pale, freckled skin. "This is the most amazing thing I've ever seen." She grabs her purse and pulls out a small flat device. "I should use Jennifer's new app to record this."

Purple and red light explode like fireworks against the view screen, and I again check our course as the song dips into a low, rumbling moan. Some sort of anomaly has appeared on the sensors. I adjust course, but then my console flickers. The anomaly disappears, only to resurface directly in front of us. *What the* kuzara *is happening?*

Before I can again change direction, the console flickers and goes dark. My hands freeze over the surface for a heartbeat before my training kicks in. I stand up and move over to access the copilot console in front of Tamara.

It's dead too.

"*Kuzara.*" I look over my shoulder at Tamara.

She's gaping back at me. The thing she called a phone is clutched loosely in her hand, human symbols scrolling across its screen. The security team had cleared human technology as non-threatening to our systems, but the device is the only thing I can think of that might interfere with the controls.

"Stop what you're doing." I reach for the phone just as the gravitational stabilizers cut out. The deck lurches out from under me, and I stumble backward, slamming to a stop against the view screen.

Tamara screams, echoed by muted shouting from the passenger cabin. Her fear floods my senses, a drowning wave of panic that momentarily blinds me. I shut down my *Iki'i* to keep from being overwhelmed.

Gravity stabilizes, and I lurch back toward my seat. "Turn off that device!"

The entire shuttle is shaking and rocking, and the music of the Singing Planet has turned into a monstrous roar.

Tapping frantically at the device, Tamara holds up the now dark screen for me to see. "It's off!"

I drop into the captain's seat, glad for the instant grip of the safety restraint as the shuttle jerks sideways. My sensors are rebooting, startup commands flowing across the console. Even without any sensor readings, my instincts tell me we must be caught in one of the heavy ion currents, but I have no way of gauging the shuttle's direction, especially with several huge, pulsing ruptures flashing against the view screen.

Emergency protocols rattle through my mind, and I slam one hand against the emergency beacon while using the other to increase the strength of the safety restraints. The seat cushions soften further, wrapping up and around my legs and torso but leaving my arms free. The restraints in the passenger cabin will encase each passenger completely and act as life pods in the event of a crash.

I check on Tamara, relieved to see she's well secured and clutching both arms around her dog, although her skin looks pale as ice and her features are creased in a grimace of terror.

My console finishes rebooting, and coldness fills my body. The shuttle has entered the planet's stratosphere in an uncontrolled spin. How did we travel so far off course? I engage full thrusters, trying to regain control, but heavy ionization must already have clogged the engines.

The view ahead coalesces into roiling storm clouds. Warnings flash over my console and across the view screen. The shuttle is nearing the atmosphere, and hull temperature is rising. We'll burn up unless I redirect all power to the shields—which means no power for thrusters. No chance of pulling out of this dive.

We are going to crash.

I grit my teeth, boost the shields, and brace for impact. *So much for impressing Tamara with my piloting skills.*

7

TAMARA

I grip Beanie against my chest, watching the view screen in horror. My stomach has been left somewhere behind, but I'm too terrified to be sick. Clouds of shifting color create what would've been a spectacular show if it wasn't for the agonizing screech of sound coursing through the ship. As the shuttle bucks and spins, the seat holds me in place, my own weight crushing the breath from my body.

Tazhio taps at the control panel in front of his seat, teeth bared in a grimace. Blinding sparks cover the view screen, and for a moment, I'm terrified we've caught on fire. Then what appears to be the top of a storm-tossed sea of deep green leaves materializes between the flashes of light.

"Shields are down! Brace for impact!" shouts Tazhio as the shuttle plows into the canopy.

Huge branches slam against the hull, and a tearing sound rips through the cabin. The next thing I know, I'm no longer surrounded by walls, but being buffeted by wind and debris.

Seat still clamped around me like a glove, I hurtle through darkness and trees.

Falling. Spinning.

Leaves as big as serving platters whip by, forcing me to close my eyes and turn my head to keep from being blinded. Pain sears across my knee. I squeeze my eyes tighter and clutch Beanie against my chest. I pray I'm not crushing him to death, but I know if I let go he'll be hurtled like a missile.

Suddenly, my seat slams into something behind me.

And the world goes dark.

8

TAMARA

I'm dreaming about a cozy cabin in the woods with a lumberjack making me pancakes when a strange hooting note brings me awake. I open my eyes to a rainbow of glowing plants and mushrooms, mostly green or purple, with a few clumps of hot-pink and sparkling yellow leaves interspersed among them. The plants seem to be the only light source, creating a sort of murky green haze to see by. I realize I'm no longer in the shuttle seat, but sprawled out on a mattress of leaves with fuzzy undersides as thick and soft as a fleece blanket.

In a rush, the horrific, hurtling fall from the shuttle comes back to me. I sit up, head spinning, and search for my dog. "Beanie?"

Chittering and hooting and other strange jungle noises are all that answer.

Where is everyone? Taking a few calming breaths, I notice that my left shin is wrapped in a leaf, small vines neatly tied around it to keep it in place. Someone has been here with me, then. I peek under the leaf and wince at the sight of a long gash caked with some sort of green goo that smells oddly like maple syrup. *Well, that explains my hunger for pancakes.*

I survey the glowing plants again. "Hello, is anyone here?"

When no one answers, I stand up, body aching with what feels like a million bruises. I've lost my flip-flops, and the cut on my leg throbs. It turns out I'm standing in a pit about as deep as my shoulders, with shrubbery growing up the sides. As far as I can see, gnarled, purple-gray trunks as thick as redwoods rise into the air. The glowing vegetation grows like moss up the trunks, fading into a dark canopy where long, glowing vines dangle from branches like a creepy rendition of a Tarzan cartoon.

"Jennifer! Suzanne!" The thick jungle swallows my voice. "Tazhio? Anyone out there?"

I think I can hear faint barking in the distance. My heart constricts. Who knows what kind of trouble my baby might be in? "Beanie, I'm coming!"

Using the plants as handholds, I pull myself over the edge of the pit onto my belly. The ground dips into another hollow a few feet away, and I realize the entire forest floor is a roiling mass of tangled roots.

Shaking with nerves, I get to my feet. The root is rough under my bare feet, but not unbearable. A surprisingly strong breeze rushes between the trees, making the curtain of vines overhead dance and sway. Butted up against one of the massive trunks nearby, the crumpled remains of our shuttle rests at the end of a swathe of carnage carved into the ground. Pieces of shuttle debris are scattered along the trench. One of the chairs from the shuttle is wedged in a smaller hollow nearby. There's nobody in it, so I think it might be the one I was in.

God, how am I even alive? And what has happened to everyone else?

"Hello?" I call again into the forest.

Beanie yips, a frantic sound that makes my chest tighten.

"I'm coming!" I call back, examining the gouged trench behind the shuttle. The root I'm standing on snakes in a sort of raised trail alongside the debris. It's as good a path as any, so I take a step. I haven't gone too far before I realize my feet aren't as tough as I first thought, but I can't be a wimp, so I find a broken branch to use as a walking stick and keep going.

I follow the trench, climbing over twisted roots and avoiding a patch of slimy looking mushrooms as I make my way toward Beanie's sporadic barking. The forest muffles the sound and makes it impossible to guess how far away he might be. *Please let him be with the others.*

I pause for breath near a giant pool nestled between the roots. The inky depths of the water reflect glowing fairy plants dotting the banks, and if I hadn't been in such dire circumstances, I would've snapped a photo. Then I remember my phone might be what landed us in this mess to begin with— most likely Jennifer's stupid, amped up astronomy app, since that's what was running when the trouble began. *When I find her, I'm going to kill her.* Then I add, *Please, God, let me find her and Suzanne.*

Beanie barks again, and I plant my walking stick, mincing carefully across the rough bark. I'm almost past the pool when an enormous pair of bulbous eyes emerges from the water right next to me.

"Oh, shit!" I take a surprised step back, lose my footing, and topple backwards down into the shuttle trench.

I land on my back; the wind knocked out of me. As I lay stunned at the bottom, it hits home that I'm on an alien planet. There might be creatures here who want to eat me, or toxic plants, or hell, there could be toxic plants that want to eat me. And what about Beanie? He's so tiny and helpless.

Sitting up, I scream, "Beanie, come!"

Something resembling a gargantuan centipede rises over the edge of the embankment where I've fallen, shiny and black and dripping water. Its bulging eyes are definitely focused straight at me.

My pulse goes into overdrive, and I roll to my knees, scrambling toward the opposite side of the trench. I beeline it toward a jagged sheet of purple hull material as wide as a queen-sized bed that's leaning against the wall. I think I might be able to hide underneath it. The jagged edge digs into my shoulder and tears my shirt, but I won't fit.

Spinning, I see the centipede's long body descending over the edge of the trench. My heart hammers against my breastbone. I lost my walking stick when I fell, so I search the ground for another weapon. There's nothing nearby except dirt and leaves.

The thing is coming straight toward me.

"Get away! Shoo!" I pick up a clod of dirt and hurl it as hard as I can. I don't think a shower of dirt will actually be able to stop the creature, but something hard thunks loudly against the beast's body and it shudders. More thuds follow, though I'm no longer throwing anything.

Suddenly, the creature stops moving and coils into a tight ball a mere few feet from where I stand. I gape at it. *What's happening?*

Snarls and grunts erupt behind me, and four-legged creatures that remind me of giant, human-sized ferrets swarm down the bank toward the monster. Rising onto their hind legs, they circle the centipede and begin jabbing it with what appear to be crude knives. Though they arrived on four legs, their front paws seem quite adept as hands, and I now notice they each wear a thick belt strung with what might be more weapons.

One of them turns its beady-eyed attention to me, its muzzle splitting into a grin that reveals blunt gray teeth. Leaving its knife embedded in the centipede's carcass, it holds both hands out to me as it chitters and purrs. *It's trying to communicate.*

I don't know if the sounds it's making are actual words, but I reply anyway. Maybe the universal translator they injected me with when we boarded the *Romantasy* will help. "God, thank you so much."

Then I catch sight of what can only be a glistening pink erection jutting from between the ferret alien's legs. It steps closer purring, "Fffffeeeeem."

Dread clamps my insides as I suddenly get the distinct impression he wants to stab me with something other than his spear. I take an unsteady step backward and raise both hands. "Stop right there."

The other four ferret aliens stop stabbing the centipede and turn to me, all sporting similar bright pink erections. Their muzzles are split in toothy snarls—or perhaps leers? Good God, getting murdered by a giant centipede would be awful, but gang-raped by a bunch of giant ferret aliens will be horrific. I look around frantically, once more in search of a weapon. The trench wall rises sharply behind me, impossible to climb.

"Help!" I scream, hoping someone from the shuttle might hear me as I edge sideways, hoping for a chance to run. "Anyone, please!"

The ferret alien keeps pace while stroking his erection with one six-fingered hand. He reaches toward me with the other.

That's it. If he touches me, I'm done for. I turn to run, but discover one of the others has already flanked me. "Shit."

He thrusts a severed centipede leg under my nose, purring and spouting more syllables. The leg is floppy, more like a tentacle than a bug's leg. Viscous fluid drips from the severed end, flooding the air with a scent like sour milk.

My stomach churns, and bile rises to my throat.

Thankfully, the first alien doesn't like competition. He growls and tries to snatch the leg from his competitor, who jerks his arm back to keep his prize. They fall on each other, snarling and wrestling for possession of the item.

But there's still no hope of escape. The other three aliens are already pressing past the fight, chittering and purring. Their pink penises jut straight at me, and each of them holds a dismembered centipede leg toward me like some sort of obscene offering.

"No, thank you," I choke out. I step backward, my ass against the trench wall. Tazhio's words about being more assertive return to me, so I stand up straighter. "I don't want them. Leave me alone."

The ferret aliens seem undeterred. One sticks the severed end of his centipede leg into his mouth and sucks loudly, then offers it to me again. Another waves his trophy under my nose, spattering my face with centipede ooze. It adheres to my skin with the scent of sour milk and pus.

My stomach heaves. Unable to hold back any longer, I double over, spewing vomit.

The aliens growl and back up.

Eyes watering, I wipe centipede ooze from my cheeks. But I'm relieved to see the ferret aliens seem put off. Their erections have softened and they're now talking and gesturing to each other as if arguing. For once, my sensitive stomach may actually turn out to be beneficial.

I breathe shallowly through my mouth and inch sideways along the trench wall, hoping to slip away.

No such luck. Two of the aliens remove coils of rope from their belts and advance toward me.

"Stay the fuck back!" I clutch my stomach as if I might puke again.

But the surprise has worn off, it seems. In three quick steps, they grab me.

"Stop! Help!" I slap at their hands, but they drive me to the ground. Within moments, they have me strung up like a stuck pig and are carrying me across the trench.

9

TAZHIO

I pause next to an enormous purple-black branch blocking my path. Shattered twigs and crushed leaves lay scattered around the broken limb, and more loose foliage continues to flutter down from the damaged canopy. I've been searching the hollows and swells of the forest floor for hours now, but still can't find any sign of survivors. At this rate, I fear it will take days to find everyone.

At least Tamara is safe. I'd manually ejected the co-pilot seat when we started breaking apart, and I'd located her near the shuttle remains. Aside from a minor cut on one leg, she isn't injured, but she's unconscious. I don't want to leave her, but as the pilot, I'm responsible for all the passengers, not just Tamara.

When the shields failed, the shuttle's passenger seats jettisoned, scattering the life pods across the forested landscape. I'd guided the nose of the shuttle between the massive trunks, trying to minimize the damage. The impact with the ground gouged a wide path through the tangled roots, and the remains of the shuttle now lie crumpled against a tree. I only survived because of my Kirenai abilities.

The lump in my chest rises to my throat again as I think of our future. I'm not looking forward to telling everyone that there's little chance of a rescue. I can count on one hand the number of ships that have made it safely on and off this planet's surface. The ionic storms encasing the atmosphere block communication to or from the ground, which means sensors will be hard-pressed to locate the crash. And even if sensors do manage to find us, finding a pilot willing to brave the storms is another matter.

I watch a miniature tornado spin over the glowing shrubbery nearby, a vortex of rainbow-colored leaves. The brisk wind sweeping in from above is testament to the perpetual storm chewing the upper atmosphere, and I'm worried the debris from our crash will continue to rain down on the area. We'll have to set up camp well away from the shuttle's path to be sure we remain safe.

A familiar bit of cloth hidden beneath the debris catches my attention. Tamara's bag. My heart plummets. What if her dog's still inside? It hadn't been with Tamara when I found her still encased in her seat, and I was too busy piloting the shuttle to pay attention to what happened to the creature during the crash. But I know the dog considers the bag its home.

Hurrying over, I dig the bag free and pull it open. No dog, just some tufts of shed fur. Both relief and disappointment roll through me. I'd hate to have to tell Tamara her dog is dead, but

I also hate to tell her it's still missing. The device Tamara called a phone is inside, along with several other objects I don't recognize, so I loop the bag over one shoulder and continue searching.

I'm attempting to climb over a large root when a faint whine reaches me, barely more than a whimper. The few intrepid explorers who'd successfully visited this planet reported the local wildlife as benign unless antagonized, but it is always best to stay alert. I drop back to the ground and sharpen my *Iki'i*, raking my attention over the bushes.

Huddling beneath a clump of glowing yellow leaves, I spot a familiar, furry quadruped. The poor thing is emanating terror, and I can't see it well enough to tell if it's injured. How it survived the fall so far from where Tamara and her padded seat landed is beyond me.

Right now, all that's important is that the dog is alive, and Tamara will be happy. Smiling, I lower the bag to the ground and hold it open for Beanie to enter. "Come on," I coax. "Let's go see Tamara."

The tiny creature backs deeper into the glowing leaves, still wary.

Using my *Iki'i* to radiate calm, I coax, "It's okay. You're safe with me."

The dog barks and dances away, wariness becoming more playful.

I'm glad it doesn't appear injured, but after several minutes chasing the agile creature, my relief sours to frustration. I sit on a gnarled stump and glare at the dog.

Tiny pink tongue sticking out in a mocking grin, the dog yips once and pants happily.

"You're wilier than an escaped *nezumi*," I grumble, thinking about a rodent-like pet I had as a child. Now I understand why my mother hated that thing. I don't have time for this. I stand. "That's it. I'm done chasing you. There are people out there who need me. Follow me or don't."

I shoulder Tamara's bag and turn away. The faint sound of a familiar female voice reaches me on the wind. "Help, please!"

It's coming from where I left Tamara. *Kuzara, I should've stayed with her!*

I pelt between the trees, leaping over twisted roots and glowing shrubs. It takes several minutes to reach the crash site. How did I manage to wander so far? I burst from the glowing brush next to the shuttle trench. On the far side, a group of furred humanoids are chittering rapidly among themselves. Between them, they carry three horizontal poles strung with what look like dead carcasses.

My stomach twists with dread. *No!*

Then one carcass squirms, and Tamara's hoarse voice shouts, "Untie me!"

Without another thought, I leap down into the trench. "Tamara!"

"Tazhio!" She writhes against her bindings. "Help me!"

The humanoids turn, dropping the poles with their burdens.

I hear Tamara grunt as she hits the ground. I don't know if any of the other poles hold passengers, but that doesn't matter. Tamara is alive, and I intend to keep her that way.

One humanoid brandishes a primitive knife, while several others yank slingshots from their belts. They chitter a string of syllables my universal translator can't understand, but I'm fairly certain they aren't saying anything nice.

I force myself to pull back on my rage. This is a first contact situation, and my job is to be diplomatic. Starting out with bloodshed will only cause ongoing trouble for the survivors, which is the last thing I want if we're forced to stay here long term. But it's all I can do not to rip out their throats and wrest Tamara from captivity.

My universal translator will pick up on the language once it receives enough input—I just need to exercise patience. So I cease my advance and hold up both hands in the universal sign of peace. "I am peaceful," I say slowly. "A friend."

They rally to block Tamara from sight where she lies tied up on the ground. Strong possessive waves strike my open *Iki'i* like physical blows. I know it will hinder my translator's learning process, but I shield my senses. If this keeps up, I'm going to do something I can't take back.

I point slowly toward Tamara. "She's with me. Let her go."

The tallest of the humanoids growls a few syllables, and a bright pink phallus springs upright between his legs. The others' penises also spring to life, and the tall one pumps his hips suggestively, baring blunt gray teeth.

I'm a pilot, not a biologist, but I do like to read, and I know there are many species who use physical posturing to measure status. With a sinking feeling, I realize these beings are probably using the size of their genitals to communicate rank. If I want to speak their language, I have no choice but to respond in kind.

Hardly believing what I'm about to do, I drop Tamara's bag and unzip my flight suit, shrugging it from my shoulders. Standing tall, I will my crotch into a massive erection.

Several of the humanoids grunt, and one strokes his shaft as if trying to coax it into a more competitive size.

Thrusting my hips forward, I say, "The female is mine."

Tamara pauses her wriggling and emits a strangled gasp.

"Ffffeeemal ours." The tall humanoid growls and puffs out his chest. More words follow, too fast for my translator to catch.

A projectile hits me from one of the humanoids's slingshots. The impact isn't painful, but a round yellow object that looks like a burr or a spiny nutshell covered in wicked spines now sticks to my chest. I pluck it free, and it leaves behind a sticky residue. The muscle beneath turns numb, and I realize they must be using some sort of toxin or paralytic.

I harden my matrix just as more spiny projectiles head my way. Though I'm feeling the effects of the first strike, I'm impervious to the rest of them, and the initial numbness doesn't seem to be spreading any farther.

Keeping my gaze steady on the tall one I assume is the leader, I thrust my hips again and say, "You cannot hurt me. Return the female and we'll be on our way."

Instead of handing her over, the leader and one other grab Tamara's pole and dart into the brush.

"Tazhio!" she screams.

"*Kuzara.*" I start forward, but the flight suit is still tangled around my ankles. I kick free, shouting, "Bring her back!"

The three remaining humanoids continue to fire, fanning out to flank me. They've dropped to four legs and move with fluid grace over the rough terrain, quicker and more agile than I am even now that I'm free of my suit. Though they have little chance of hurting me, they can keep me pinned down, and I don't like to think of what might happen to Tamara if I don't catch up quickly.

I need a weapon. On instinct, I reach out and catch one of the missiles, lobbing it back at the nearest humanoid.

My attackers cease firing, and surprise and respect flash against my *Iki'i.* Their attention drops to my erection, which I only now realize is still in place. I widen my stance, keeping my hips thrust forward to show it off. "Let me pass."

A humanoid with a broad chest holds out one of the yellow projectiles, then makes a motion to the surrounding trees. "Va Sheeghr tribe?"

It takes me a moment, but then I realize they're asking if I'm from another tribe. I look nothing like them, but perhaps there are other species roaming this planet. "I'm Kirenai," I say.

The broad-chested humanoid gestures to the forest again. "More?"

It might be helpful if these humanoids know I'm not alone. "Yes. More. Many more."

A smaller Sheeghr purrs, "Fffemales?"

Uh, oh. I don't want these horny locals hunting for female passengers. To be fair, there are no female Kirenai, so I shake my head, grab my cock with one hand, and point down the path. "My female."

A heartbeat passes. Another. Then the broad-chested one points toward the trail. "Come."

The other two growl and shift their weight, as if unsure about this decision, but then return to the trail and retrieve the pole bearing the carcass of something black and segmented suspended by rope mesh. At least it doesn't appear to be another passenger from the shuttle.

As they start off down the trail, I hurry over and pick up my flight suit. I consider putting it back on, then think better of it. If I need to wave my dick around again, it will be better to have it out already. I stuff my suit into Tamara's bag and loop the strap around my neck.

The humanoids are already disappearing into the brush, so with a last glance over the wreckage, I set off after them. I hope the other passengers can find each other on their own and don't run into any more trouble.

10

TAZHIO

The humanoids lead me with unerring confidence over the tangled roots. Little to no sunlight reaches this deep into the forest, but my guides move easily through shadows and glowing vegetation alike. It takes longer than I like to catch up to the pair carrying Tamara, who are obviously unhappy to see me with their friends. The group snarls and chitters, cocks raised like masts among them. I originally thought the word Sheeghr meant cock, but it turns out it's the name these people call themselves.

"Tazhio, what's going on?" Tamara asks hoarsely, swinging from her bound hands and feet on the pole as the Sheeghr gesture wildly and chatter over one another in excitement. "Can you understand them?"

"A little. My translator is still learning." They're obviously in dispute about whether to take me with them, but I don't have a context for much of their reasoning.

Suddenly, the leader hands his end of Tamara's pole to another and shoves his muzzle close to my face. His breath smells like river water as he growls, "Toozeer gary."

The two Sheeghr carrying Tamara move a few steps into the brush, as if preparing to run off again.

"Wait!" I don't know what a toozeer gary is, but I doubt Tamara will enjoy whatever it is. I can't stop them from taking her, but hell if I'll let her go face this alone. Willing my cock to grow larger, I broaden my chest and shoulders for good measure. "I will come, too. Untie the female and let me carry her."

The leader stares at me a moment, then heaves a sigh and pulls a crude knife from his belt. In a couple of swift strokes, he's severed Tamara's bindings. She lands on the ground with a thud, rolling onto her side and rubbing her wrists. The leaf I bound over the scratch in her leg is askew, and a crimson trail of blood marks her pale ankle.

The tall Sheeghr nudges me from behind. "You gary. Go."

Ah, gary means carry. That makes more sense. Perhaps Toozeer is their leader. "They want me to carry you. Okay?"

She nods and I slide my arms under her knees and shoulders, cradling her to my chest. My erection tingles with awareness of her nearness as we walk.

"Do you know where they're taking us?" Her voice sounds choked, and she's trembling violently.

I hold her tighter. "No. But wherever we end up, I won't let them hurt you."

Her arms tighten around my neck. "Thank you."

As I follow the Sheeghr deeper into the forest, I pray I can keep my promise.

11

TAMARA

I'm nearly numb from anxiety overload as I cling to Tazhio's neck and focus on simply breathing for a few minutes. Every time I think my panic has reached a new threshold, something else happens. I need my dog. I want to go home. Hell, even some salve for the rope burns on my wrists and ankles would be nice. It takes everything I have to keep myself present in the here and now instead of turning into a catatonic zombie.

You're alive, I keep repeating to myself until the words have no meaning, so I switch to focusing on the warmth of Tazhio's powerful arms and chest as we follow the ferret aliens deeper into the trees. I'm not certain if they intended to rape me or have me for dinner—or both, but at least Tazhio has stopped them for now.

My mind is still spinning over the accident, though, and I need answers. I touch the strap of my bag hanging from Tazhio's shoulder. "Did you find Beanie? I thought I heard him barking."

He nods. "He's alive, but refused to come to me."

A small sob of relief fills my chest. "And my sisters? The other passengers? What happened to them?"

"I didn't have a chance to find them, but the safety restraints should've protected everyone." He grimaces. "The problem is that they're scattered all over the forest."

My heart constricts, and I look at the ferret alien walking in front of us. He's carrying one end of the centipede carcass and rocks back and forth as he walks, as if he's unaccustomed to using only two legs. But I still remember how fast they moved on four legs, and how easily they took down that centipede monster. Then there was the way they responded to me...

I gulp, imagining my sisters encountering these creatures. "What if these ferret aliens find them?"

Tazhio's lips are a hard line, and he keeps his attention on the aliens ahead. "One thing at a time, *kikajiru*. Let's figure out what they want first."

One alien growls something, and several others make a chittering sound that might be laughter. I'm once again filled with dread about where we might be going and why.

"Are they taking us to their village?"

Tazhio tilts his head, listening to them chitter and purr. "That would make sense. They likely have a settlement somewhere nearby."

"Why are they insisting we go with them?"

"I think they want us to meet their leader."

"That makes sense, I suppose." I rest my cheek against his bare shoulder, breathing in his masculine scent layered with a hint of what I can only define as tropical. "Thank you for coming to my rescue." My voice thickens as I recall those terrifying moments when the ferret aliens came toward me. "I dread thinking of what they wanted to do to me."

"Don't worry." His arms squeeze me gently. "I won't let them touch you."

He steps over a bump in the path, and the head of his cock nudges my ass. I try to ignore it because I'm pretty sure he just competed in some sort of dick-measuring contest on my behalf, and he probably needs time to let his hard-on wear off. But my panties grow damp, and I can't help squeezing my thighs together at the memory of his impressive size. Are all the blue aliens that big? Seems there should've been a warning in the dating brochure. *Or a selling point.*

I push back those thoughts. I should be coming up with a plan to get away from these ferret creatures, not thinking about riding a big blue dick. But it's hard to focus on anything else when I'm skin-to-skin with a powerful, naked man.

Seeming to sense my discomfort, Tazhio clears his throat. "I hope my earlier display did not offend you. The Sheeghr determine rank by the size of one's phallus." As if to reinforce his point, his cock brushes my ass again. *How long can he stay hard?* "I must compete for respect."

Heat floods my cheeks as I imagine uses other than competition for status. I swallow thickly. "Well, keep up the good work."

A smile twitches the corners of his lips. "I'll keep it up as long as it takes."

The heat in my cheeks intensifies, and I choke back a giggle. *Good Lord, how can we be flirting at a time like this?* But it feels good to get my mind off our current situation.

Ahead, the ferret aliens stop without warning, and Tazhio's smile twists back to a frown. The tallest one chitters quietly, and I think I hear the word danger repeated. Is it possible I'm learning their language? Maybe my universal translator thing will come in handy after all.

"What is it?" I ask.

Gaze scanning the area, Tazhio answers, "I believe they detect a predator ahead."

One ferret turns and hisses at us.

"He's asking for silence," Tazhio whispers.

My arms tighten around his neck as we continue forward, slogging off the trail to tiptoe around something that looks like a Venus flytrap with alligator heads. Several enormous mouths are open to expose gleaming, leaf-like teeth, and one closed mouth holds something the size of a large dog that twitches and jerks. *God, I hope Beanie's okay.* He wouldn't stand a chance against monsters like that. I need to get back and find him.

My heartbeat doesn't stop racing until we're well past the spot and the ferrets resume their purring chatter. I can swear I'm now catching words here and there. Home. Food. Danger.

Still keeping to a whisper, I ask, "Will my translator learn their language eventually, too?"

"Yes, but mine will learn faster because of my *Iki'i*," Tazhio replies, his voice also still soft.

I'm about to ask what an *Iki'i* is when I spot another group of ferret aliens approaching on all fours through the murky green light. There are at least a dozen, scurrying, chittering, purring, tussling. Several of our escorts call out, and I hold my breath as the newcomers near. Am I about to witness another dick jousting contest? But although the new ferrets circle us curiously, they make no sexual display and don't appear to be aggressive.

"They are young ones, I believe," says Tazhio, never breaking stride as the new ferret aliens keep pace by leap-frogging over each other beside the trail. Some run ahead, while some fall to wrestling and drop behind.

Soon we reach a small creek trickling between the roots and turn to follow it. Ahead, the trees open onto a clearing where the ground terraces up in a long slope to the base of a gargantuan tree trunk, the largest I've ever seen. A hollow in its broad side forms a cavern with golden yellow light radiating from inside. Emerging from the mouth is a horde of ferret aliens.

And it looks as if every one of them has his dick out.

12

TAZHIO

My steps slow at the sight of the oncoming group of Sheeghr. There are too many to count, and unlike the young ones who followed along with us earlier, it seems as if every one of these Sheeghr sports a bright pink erection.

"Oh, God," Tamara gasps, body rigid in my arms.

The horde races to surround us, pushing and wriggling to get a glimpse of the newcomers as we follow the burbling stream up toward the cavern. We climb terraces filled with cultivated rows of plants, and several of the Sheeghr standing between the rows hold what I assume are agricultural tools. I'm worried they'll be turned into weapons if the situation goes bad, and clutch Tamara firmly against my chest, lifting her higher to allow my cock to show prominently. How far can my display get me among so many competitors? The Sheeghr traveling with us from the crash site hadn't hesitated to start violence with their slingshots. I can't let this escalate into a bloodbath—especially with Tamara as the prize.

"Fffertile." The word is repeated among the crowd, and my *Iki'i* is drowning in a single emotion—*lust*. I'm forced to shut down my senses before I'm overwhelmed by the bombardment of prurience.

"The female is mine." I bare my teeth at any Sheeghr who comes too close.

"Why are they so interested in me?" Tamara's voice shakes. "Don't they have any women of their own?"

I've been wondering the same thing; so far I haven't seen a single adult individual without a phallus on display. "I don't know." I stare down a Sheeghr with bushy black eyebrows who is hovering too close for comfort. "But I won't let them touch you."

Tamara cringes away from a particularly energetic member of the crowd who is stroking himself with lewd abandon. "There are so many. How can you stop them?"

"Let me worry about that," I say, keeping my voice calmer than I feel.

Ahead, the roiling crowd parts in a wave, revealing an overly large Sheeghr with dark purple fur and huge glittering eyes. In one six-fingered hand it clutches a gnarled staff inset with pink crystals, and its stomach is distended and heavy. *Pregnant.*

In the cave's mouth behind her, more Sheeghr stand waiting, not a dick in sight, and I realize we've just discovered where they keep their females.

"Look. They do have women." I smile reassuringly.

Tamara sighs. "Oh, thank God."

The males escorting us drop the segmented carcass they're carrying at the female's feet. The tallest of their captors points toward Tamara. "This fertile one is offended. We brought her here to be soothed so she might evolve."

My translator struggles with the nuances of the words while the crowd boils with excitement, hips gyrating and phalluses throbbing. A spurt of what might be ejaculate carves an arc through the air and lands at my feet. I bare my teeth and search the nearby crowd for the culprit.

"Take her, take her," a few in the crowd begin to chant.

"My female," I roar.

The crowd backs up, but their chittering grows higher pitched, anger beating against my shuttered *Iki'i*.

The pregnant female thumps the base of her staff against the ground, and the crowd quiets. "Females choose." She stands almost a head higher than any of the other Sheeghr and emanates a sense of command. "Not males."

This might be good news for Tamara, but I need to be sure I understand correctly. Focusing on the leader, I open my *Iki'i* a crack, wincing at the heightened emotions that immediately zing across my senses. I grit my teeth and endure. I need every advantage if we hope to establish an understanding with these people.

"What's she saying?" Tamara asks.

"She says females choose, not males."

"Really?" Tamara pats my chest with one hand, a steely resolve emerging from her nebula of fear. "Then let me stand."

Surprised, I lower her gently to her feet but keep one arm around her waist for support if she needs it.

Facing the female with the staff, Tamara points at me with her free hand and speaks slowly, "I choose him."

The pregnant female turns a critical eye toward me. Her gaze drops to my crotch, and I push my hips forward as I've seen so many of her males do. But I sense only disdain as she returns her gaze to Tamara. "I am called Zeer from the Dovlu matrilineal line. What are you called, female?"

Tamara grimaces and glances at me. "My translator didn't catch any of that. What did she say?"

"She says her name is Zeer and asks for yours." I'm not used to being dismissed, but I'm wary about what is culturally acceptable here. The knots on the leader's staff resemble female labias, each crystal embedded in the swollen slits made to look like a pink bud of pleasure, and I'm beginning to think that the females rule. It's good Tamara is stepping up to speak for herself, and I hope my need to translate won't count against her.

Straightening her shoulders, Tamara stares down the Sheeghr leader, outwardly confident, even though her anxiety rails against my senses. "My name's Tamara. This male I've chosen is Tazhio. I insist you let us go now."

Zeer stares pointedly at my dick. "I have not seen a mating rod this color. Is that why it is defective?"

The crowd chortles.

Tamara flushes and looks sideways at my crotch.

Just her glance makes me grow painfully hard, and I push more of my matrix into the shaft, swelling it further. What is the Sheeghr female trying to accomplish by belittling me? I obviously dwarf every one of these other males in size. Thrusting my hips forward, I say, "I am more than adequate."

The surrounding Sheeghr erupt into a chittering discussion peppered by both admiration and doubt. "Impregnate."

"Fertile."

"Insufficient."

That steely sensation coming from Tamara grows more solid, and to my utter surprise, she reaches over and grips my engorged shaft.

Kuzara! Excruciating bliss makes my eyes flutter briefly as all my earlier fantasies about her crowd my mind. I'm filled with a single thought. *Mine.* My arm at her waist flexes, pulling her tightly against my side. This is not the time or place to lose control. Yet all it will take is one firm stroke of her palm and I'll spill my seed all over the ground.

"My male is strong," Tamara says, baring her teeth toward the Sheeghr female, her small hand still firmly around my girth. Her translator might not be picking up the language yet, but she obviously has the gist of the situation.

I breathe shallowly, unable to think straight, let alone speak.

Zeer blinks, radiating confusion. "Then why are you not with child?"

Gathering what I can of my wits, I shift my attention to the females assembled at the mouth of the cave. Most are visibly pregnant, and I have a feeling the rest probably are also, just not yet showing.

"What did she say?" asks Tamara from the corner of her mouth.

"She asks why you're not pregnant." My voice is thick in my throat. Does she have any idea what her touch is doing to me?

Tamara sucks in a breath, and her hand leaves my dick. "Are you kidding me?"

Losing the pressure of her hand around my shaft is almost painful, and I take a steadying breath. I'm not sure there's enough blood in my head right now to interpret anything correctly. "Look at how many of them are pregnant."

She turns her head to scan the females assembled at the cave mouth. Just then, the tall male who captured us pipes up, "They said there are more males in the forest, plenty to fill this female, yet she remains empty."

Zeer's six-fingered hand slides down her staff, bumping over the knots along its length almost suggestively. "Perhaps she requires an Orgy of Alignment."

I take a beat to let my translator sift through the words. But the reignited lust pounding against my *Iki'i* forces a single word from between my teeth as I glare at the crowd. "Mine."

They chitter louder, and Zeer scowls. "Let the female speak."

We need to stop things before they go any further, but Tamara doesn't yet have an adequate grasp of their language. I hold up both hands in a sign of peace. "She doesn't understand your language. We are visitors from far away, only here by accident. Our females often go a long time without breeding. Please allow us to be on our way."

The crowd rustles, filling the air with disbelief and no small amount of worry.

"Impossible." Zeer points the top of her staff toward Tamara. "Females who do not breed are dangerous."

"No. Our females are not like Sheeghr. We are different." I point to my erection, which Zeer had already commented on as unusual.

Zeer pounds her staff. "Unmated females attract Gloor. If this female can't or won't take a male's seed, she must be removed."

The crowd shifts like a tide, murmuring, "Menace."

"Blood."

"Slaughter."

Tamara is trembling against my side, head moving from side to side frantically as she looks at the Sheeghr. "What are they saying?"

I don't want to frighten her more than she already is, but I can't deny that my own panic is rising by the second. "They fear something called a Gloor. They think you're going to attract it." Taking a deep breath, I address Zeer. "What is this creature you speak of?"

Zeer shakes her head. "Not a creature. Gloor is the Twisted God. He comes at night seeking unmated females to carry his eggs. His progeny are ravenous and will consume everyone in the village."

The crowd grows more agitated as Zeer explains, and several now raise blades as well as voices.

"Just let us go," I say. "We'll go far from the village and trouble you no more."

"No." Zeer raises her voice over the roiling crowd. "She will take a male's seed this night, or tomorrow she must die."

"Jesus!" Tamara makes a choking sound. "Did she just say I have to fuck them or die?"

My mind is only half on my answer as I search the area for anything to help us escape. "I don't think it's a matter of sex so much as pregnancy."

"Hell no!" Balling her hands into fists, Tamara plants her back against me as if ready to face them all down. "I'm not getting pregnant with some alien ferret baby."

The crowd is too close, and there is nowhere for us to go, nothing to serve as a distraction. I could envelop her in my matrix to keep them from touching her, but that won't last more than a few minutes if the Sheeghr use their toxin on me. I don't know what to do. All I can think is that I've failed her.

"Prepare her for the Orgy of Alignment!" shouts Zeer.

Several Sheeghr move toward us with ropes. I slug the nearest in the muzzle, knocking him back. Another grabs my arm, while a third throws a net over my head. Tamara screams as a second net pulls her to the ground. I break free of one Sheeghr's grip, but more hands pin me down. Within moments, we're both bound, and Tamara is being hauled inside the cave.

"Tamara!" I shout. I've lost sight of her, though I can still hear her screams, and it's killing me.

Zeer comes to stand over me. After a moment of watching my useless struggles, she lowers the tip of her staff and presses it against my chest. "You are not of our ways, but she chose you. If you agree to abide, I will offer you the honor of first penetration."

I stop struggling against the ropes. From the moment we met, I dreamed of being with her. I know she wants me, too. I've sensed it many times, even as recently as our trek through the forest. But I know if I try to impregnate her, it will turn into more. I want to make her my mate. To form a permanent bond. I won't be able to stop myself. My desire for her is too strong.

I feel sick to my stomach. She shouldn't be forced to choose between me and the Sheeghr, but there are no other options.

With a sigh, I tell Zeer, "There will be no need for an orgy. I accept your offer."

Zeer raises her wispy purple eyebrows. "Good." She gestures to the Sheeghr who are restraining me. "Present him to the female. But if she refuses, we will prepare the Orgy."

13

TAMARA

This is not happening. They've tossed me into a circular enclosure in the back of the enormous tree cavern, and dozens of ferret-like Sheeghr now leer at me through the wooden bars, penises still grotesquely engorged. I'm having a nightmare, right? Any moment I'll wake up in my own bed, soaked in sweat and shaking, but Beanie will be licking my face and telling me it will all be okay. *Beanie, where are you?*

After a minute of lying there trying to calm my racing heart, I have to accept I'm not dreaming. This is all too real. From the prickle of the dead leaves I'm lying on to the strange, half-intelligible mutterings from the ferret aliens on the other side of the bars. I feel like a hamster in a cage, and all I want to do is burrow down into the litter and hide.

Instead, I force myself to inhale a shivering breath. Freezing with panic won't help. I need to remain calm and think. I stare at the high ceiling. It's plastered with bright yellow and fuchsia plants. My therapist suggested focusing on the positive when I feel stressed, but I can't come up with many positive thoughts right now, so instead I imagine the pattern of plants overhead is a cross-stitch project. I count the stitches until I'm no longer gasping for air.

Slowly, I sit up. The horrid aliens are still packed around my cage, but beyond them I see that the cavern floor is terraced like the ground was outside. A cascade of water gushes from a crack in the cavern's wood wall and flows in a steady stream past my prison toward the exit. The burbling stream can't block out the muttering crowd, and my translator keeps picking up on key words like fuck and death. A tiny crack opens in my numbness, and I realize I'm angry. Not angry - *furious*. These creeps want to turn me into a sex slave.

Balling my hands into fists until my nails bite into my palms, I glare through the bars at a nearby ferret who has big dark eyes that make him look a bit less feral than the others. Then he grins, showing blunt gray teeth and waggles his erection at me. Okay, maybe I was wrong about him seeming less feral. He dips a cup into the stream and thrusts it between the bars. "Choose me."

I bat the cup away with a hiss, spilling water across the leaves. "I don't want you and I don't want water. I want out. Where's Tazhio?" They didn't bring him to the cage with me, so where is he? Is he hurt? My throat tightens. *What if they killed him?*

Another alien shoves a bowl of gray mush that smells like dirty feet into the cage. "Good. Pleasure."

Bile rises into my throat, and I scoot backward until my spine hits the cavern wall. Last time I threw up, they hog-tied me and carried me away, and I don't want to find out what they'll do to me if I vomit again.

A ferret alien with brilliant, almost magenta-colored stripes smooths a six-fingered hand over the fur on his chest and purrs, "Me. Protect. Gloor."

"If you're so worried I'm going to attract this Gloor thing, then why did you bring me to your village? Let me go and I'll lure it away." I stand up, realizing this might be exactly the argument they need to hear.

But my admirers turn away as a mummy-looking figure appears over the heads of the crowd. It's being passed along from hand to hand, and when it reaches the bars, the crowd surges forward and dumps it over the top into my enclosure. The mummy plops to the floor, looking like it's been flattened by a mac truck. Between the thick rope bindings, I see patches of familiar blue skin.

"Tazhio!" Terrified they've killed him, I rush over to check, falling to my knees beside him.

He sits up and shakes off the ropes, his limbs rippling and reforming like liquid. I halt with my hand outstretched. This is the first time I've seen a Kirenai alter his shape, and it's incredible. Outside the bars, the ferret aliens are also chittering exclamations of awe.

I sit back on my knees, feeling like my eyes are going to bug out of my head. "Are you okay?"

"I'm fine. There's little they can do to hurt me." He looks me over as though checking for injuries. Then he lifts the leaf bandage on my leg, revealing a long scab. "What about you?"

I'd almost forgotten about the scratch, but moving the bandage still makes me wince. "I'm okay, but—"

A loud banging sound cuts me off. I turn to see the pregnant female called Zeer knocking her staff against the bars. "If fertility later exists," the Sheeghr leader announces over the noise of the chortling crowd, "Orgy of Alignment begins."

Shit. It sounds like the gang rape is moving forward. I lift my chin defiantly. "I won't go down without a fight. Rape is a crime among my people."

"Rape?" Zeer cocks her head. "Word not known."

"Force me to have sex."

Zeer stiffens as if offended. "Force not! Female to choose."

"I already chose Tazhio! Why did you lock us up?"

The Sheeghr leader responds with a rap of her staff against the bars. "Safe space for you to ensure fertility."

The pit of my stomach flip-flops as I realize they're expecting me to have sex with Tazhio right here, right now. While they watch. Still, I turn to him for verification. "What's she saying?"

Tazhio folds the leaf bandage and tosses it aside before meeting my gaze. "You chose me, and…" He swallows, and his eyes dart to the onlooking crowd before he continues. "And they've agreed to allow you to have sex with me first."

"First?" I choke out, staring out the bars toward the glistening pink palisade of ferret alien erections.

"Don't panic," he says, reaching toward me, then pausing as if unsure. "If you get pregnant right away, none of them will touch you."

I can't help the hysterical laugh that escapes my throat. "Getting pregnant can take months! Besides, I don't want to have a baby. Not yet, at least."

His lips press into a hard line. "It may actually be a blessing they found us. If I understand them correctly, there's a creature or a parasite on this planet that they believe is a god. It lays its eggs in fertile women, and when the eggs hatch, the brood eats the woman and apparently everyone else nearby. The Sheeghr keep their females continually pregnant to prevent that from happening."

"Oh, God." I gasp in horror, wrapping my arms around my chest. "Is that what this Gloor thing is?" I've seen a few nature shows where wasps lay eggs in other insects, followed by horrifying sped-up images of the babies eating the host alive. My insides squirm at the idea, and I feel like I can't breathe. To think I just offered to lure it away from the village… "You mean they're trying to protect me?"

"I guess so, yes."

Then I go back to the other issue. Sex. Tazhio is offering to have sex with me. I recall his massive erection, and heat floods my entire body as my attention shifts to his lap. I can tell he's still hard even though leaves and rope cover his lap. Swallowing thickly, I say, "I'm not on birth control, but most people don't get pregnant the first time."

He puts his fingertips gently on my knee. "Humans have proven to be highly receptive to Kirenai mating. I have no worry about your ability to carry my child."

A zing of arousal races through me, and the flutters in my stomach move downward to my pelvis, settling with low heat between my legs. I lift my gaze to his face. The same desire I remember seeing in the elevator is there, and I bite my lip, recalling the way his mouth had felt on mine.

I quickly drop my attention back to the contrast of his blue skin against my pale knee. My mouth has gone completely dry, and my lungs feel like they're being squeezed by a giant hand. I'm super conscious of the ferret aliens still watching us outside the cage, and I don't think my introverted heart can feature in a porno show for them without exploding. "Are they planning to watch… everything we do?"

Tazhio sighs. "Yes." He takes my hand, squeezing my fingers gently. "But there's something else I need you to understand. I can't make love to you without forming a bond."

I frown. Why is he warning me about something like that? A man who forms an attachment during sex is more than I could ever hope for, especially in a situation like this. Perhaps aliens think that's weird. His expression is so serious, I feel I have to ask, "Is that… bad?"

His dark eyes are like bottomless pools as he gazes into my face. I have his total attention as he says, "Kirenai mate for life."

My heart is beating so fast, I think he must be able to hear it pounding against my ribs. *A mate for life.* No worries about being ditched for someone else. No deadbeat dad. No concern about growing old alone. And Tazhio is not only sexy as hell, he's proven to be a caring, protective man.

But then I realize Tazhio is actually saying this isn't about me. It's about *him.* I'm not the only one who'll be locked into the bond. He's offering to give up all hope of future relationships just to save my life. *Well, fuck.* I can't ask him to do that, no matter how much I want to avoid those disgusting ferret things.

I firmly remove my fingers from his grip. "I can't."

TAZHIO

Tamara's sudden rejection takes me off guard. She'd prefer to lie with one of the Sheeghr over bonding with me? I'd been using my *Iki'i* to gauge Tamara's emotions, and I never once detected her attraction to one of these males. I lean forward, frowning as I try to understand. "Am I so terrible a fate?"

"It's not you!" A pretty pink flush blooms over her freckled cheeks, but she refuses to meet my gaze. "I just don't expect you to ruin your life to save mine."

"Ruin my…?" Then I understand what she's implying. She thinks I'm offering this out of pity. I take her hand again, caressing the back of her knuckles with my thumb. "You have the wrong idea. I've dreamed of bonding with you since the moment we met."

"You're just saying that to make me feel better." She attempts to pull her hand free, but I hold it firmly.

"Even if I am, that doesn't mean it's not true."

Her gray eyes are stormy. "Then why didn't you come with me after the party? You led me on with a kiss, then abandoned me when the elevator reached my floor."

Now I understand. She thought I rejected her. That I hadn't wanted to be with her, even though the opposite was true. "I'm sorry. I certainly didn't mean to hurt your feelings. It's just that they forbid the crew from socializing with the female guests." Her doubt feels like a wall of thorns against my *Iki'i*, and her lips are pressed into a tight line, but I continue anyway. "But those rules no longer apply now that we're stuck down here."

She finally raises her gaze to mine, her eyebrows furrowed with confusion. "But we're not talking about having a fling. We're talking about bonding or mating or whatever and having a child. We hardly even know each other."

"I never wanted to have a fling, Tamara. You will make an excellent mate and mother. I'll be honored to claim you as mine."

"You think I will, huh? Tell me, then." She lifts her chin in challenge. "What, exactly, do you like about me?"

She thinks I can't come up with anything, when the real problem is that I'm attracted to everything about her. I don't know where to start. "The first moment I saw you, I was drawn to your hair." I reach out with my free hand and push a copper curl behind her ear. "It's a bit like a Fogarian's, but much prettier."

"Pfft." She remains stiff, doubt still stinging my *Iki'i*. "There were at least a dozen women on that ship with reddish hair, my sisters included, and every one of them is way more attractive than I am. Plus, the color of my hair says nothing about me as a person."

I frown. I don't like to hear her talk that way about herself. "You are amazing. I can tell you are nurturing because of the way you care for your dog. I love how brave you are—"

"Ha!" she interrupts. "Brave? I've been quaking in my boots since the moment I spotted the shuttle on the tarmac."

"Yet you got on board anyway. That's brave."

She stares at me as if stunned, a flush rising up her throat and spreading across her cheeks. "No one's ever called me that before."

I drop my voice, leaning forward to speak more intimately with her. "It's true. And I think you're the sexiest woman on the *Romantasy*. I had to pleasure myself every time I thought about you." Her eyes widen in shock, but her arousal floods my *Iki'i*. I grin. "Which happened a *lot*."

"Oh." The pinkness in her cheeks deepens to red.

I can no longer resist. I press my mouth against hers. For a single heartbeat, she remains rigid, then softens, opening to me.

I sweep my tongue past her teeth into her sweet mouth. She's as exquisite as I imagined, hot and breathy and willing. Her arms wrap around my neck, her tongue dancing with mine. I thread my fingers into the hair at the nape of her neck, deepening the kiss. She hasn't said yes, but she hasn't outright told me no, either.

She moans softly into my mouth. *Kuzara*, she's enough to drive a man crazy.

I palm one of her breasts. Through the fabric of her blouse, her nipple hardens to a peak. I'm dying to touch her skin, to explore every inch of her with my hands and my mouth. I push her gently back against the leafy ground, my lips still locked on hers. The Sheeghr are muttering approval, and I'm worried it will become a distraction, so I hum a low growl to drown them out.

As I hoped, she seems to find the sound attractive, and her fingers creep around my shoulders, fingers threading my hair. I can sense she's nervous, but her desire for me is primary, and I love it.

I slide my palm down to her waist and up under her shirt, skimming her softness. She wears another layer over her breasts, something with a wire and what feels like lace. I growl low in my throat at the barrier and tease her hardened nipple through the fabric.

She gasps and arches up to meet me.

I nudge one knee between her legs, pressing my thigh up to her apex. My dick is a rod of agony, waiting to be quenched.

Feathering my mouth along her jaw to her ear, I murmur, "I don't know how to remove your clothes."

She nods mutely, panting as I push my knee against her center in a pulsing rhythm, my hand alternately kneading her breast and circling her nipple. Twisting one arm around behind her, she releases a clasp, and the underclothing pops loose around her ribs.

I nip her earlobe as I slide my fingers under the wire. Her full softness fills my palm, and I groan with pleasure. Her skin is warm and velvety soft, the nipple puckered to a tight bud, and I no longer have patience for mere teasing. I thrust her blouse up to expose her to me and lower my mouth to her flesh. I suck the nipple in, hard, then release it and roll my tongue around the point, nipping and sucking until she's mewling like a newborn *nezumi*.

"Delectable," I murmur, lips still against her skin.

Her hips are rocking against my leg, and my cock is harder than it's ever been, surging with desire every time her hip rubs against my balls. "Your pants," I growl, and begin kissing my way down her belly.

She doesn't hesitate. With one hand, she yanks the drawstring loose and pushes the waistband down to expose the lacy top of her panties.

I have no patience for any further barriers and yank the garment off her legs, grudging that I have to break away from her heat to do it. Through the lace of her panties, I spy the dark copper curls covering her sex. My dick throbs at the sight. I want to rip the fragile cloth aside and bury my face between her legs, but I know this may be the only clothing she has for a very long time, so I slowly hook a finger beneath the band and ease it away from her mound. The scent of her arousal reaches me, warm and musky. None of my self-pleasuring imagination can compare with the real thing.

Lowering myself once more to her belly, I kiss the tender skin just above her pubic bone as I pull the panties down her hips. When the thin fabric reaches her knees, she lifts one leg and pulls her foot free. The parting of her thighs calls to me, and I put my palms against her soft skin, holding them open. I lower my mouth to her slit, sliding my tongue along it over the swollen nub barely poking from between her lower lips.

She cries out, legs going stiff in surprise. But I also feel the zing of her delight, the cresting desire inside her.

I lick her again, flattening my tongue and applying more pressure until she parts like a flower, releasing the delicacy of her arousal. She's slick and hot, and I plunge my tongue deeply into her channel while my hands hold her thighs apart.

Her inner walls flutter, and she moans loudly. I block out the chittering sounds of the Sheeghr watching us, glad Tamara seems blissfully lost to her own pleasure as I continue stroking, rubbing my tongue over a ridged spot that seems to please her. I push deeper while my dick throbs with the need to feel her around me. *Patience.* I will bring her to ecstasy over and over before we are through.

I move up again to circle my tongue over her clit. It's engorged and pulsing. She's breathing hard, both hands clutched loosely in my hair. My cock is throbbing with anticipation as I crawl back up her body and position it at her entrance. I rub the swollen head between her wet folds, and she flexes up to meet me, legs widening and breath speeding up. "Take me," she pants.

I thrust forward, burying myself to the hilt in her pulsing heat.

She inhales sharply and stiffens.

I pause, suddenly worried. "Did I hurt you?"

Eyes squeezed shut, she shakes her head. "You're big."

My *Iki'i* senses that she doesn't mind the slight pain—enjoys it, even—nevertheless, I offer, "I can make myself smaller."

Her eyes fly open, a small crease between her eyebrows. "No!"

A triumphant growl rises in my throat. I pull back and thrust deep into her slippery heat. My eyes roll back at the rapturous sensation of her tightness. If I'm not careful, I'll spill myself inside her before she orgasms again, and I want more than ever to feel her come around me. *"Kuzara,"* I grit out, grasping at every ounce of control as I repeat the pull and push, pausing deep inside her each time so the organ at the top of my shaft can stimulate her clit.

She gasps, arching up to meet my strokes, her skin glistening with a slight sheen of perspiration that slicks between us as I increase my pace. Each stroke is pure madness, and coupled with the lustful emotions pounding the edges of my *Iki'i* from the surrounding Sheeghr, I don't know how I'm going to keep myself from exploding before she reaches her climax.

My secondary mating shaft is throbbing with the need to penetrate her backside, to insert the genetic marker that will claim her as my mate, and it takes every ounce of my willpower to hold back. I can impregnate her without claiming her, but I don't want to. I want my life bound to hers in every way possible.

Her body begins to shake with a rising orgasm, and I pound her harder, faster, driving her over the edge until she cries out in pleasure.

No longer able to restrain myself, I extrude my mating shaft. It probes her ass, sliding through the juices flowing between us and easing into her puckered hole before her orgasm has completed. The double sensation makes me groan, and I open my eyes to see her gaping at me, mouth open in surprise even as her body continues to spasm.

"Tazhio," she chokes out, pupils wells of dark desire. Her hands claw into my back as though she's holding on for dear life. "Oh, God!"

"I will cherish you for the rest of my life, Tamara," I growl. Then I slam myself home once, twice, three times before ejaculating my seed deep inside her womb. Never did I imagine the pleasure of sex could be so consuming. So spiritually life altering. I see stars. Planets. Entire solar systems spread out before me.

I bury my face against the side of her throat, panting. "You are mine."

15

TAMARA

The heat of Tazhio's cum pumping into me draws my orgasm to incredible heights; I think I must be having an out-of-body experience from the pleasure. By the time I feel like I can breathe again, my arms and legs feel like jelly and my entire body tingles with a warm glow of satisfaction. He's collapsed on top of me, panting against my neck. I take a moment to recognize that the chittering I'm hearing is from the ferret aliens still watching us outside the cage. I resist the urge to look at them, not ready to lose the sliver of intimacy I'm feeling at the moment.

Tazhio lifts his head to look into my eyes. "Did you find pleasure in our bonding?"

I'm still spent from our activities, or I'm sure I would laugh at his question. Instead, I say, "Are you kidding? That was amazing."

He gives me a lazy smile that makes me feel all fuzzy. "We're mated now."

I swallow. "Are you sure? I don't feel any different."

"Of course you don't feel different." He gives me a self-satisfied wink. "You've loved me from the moment we met."

"Cocky bastard." But I can't help grinning. He's right, of course.

Then my throat tightens as I think about the second part of our coupling. *Am I pregnant now?* How would the ferret aliens even know? I let myself glance at the Sheeghr milling around outside the bars. It looks as if they're having an orgy of their own now. Couples rut gleefully on the floor, and solitary males watch while stroking themselves. At least they appear to have lost interest in us. "When do you think they'll let us go?"

Tazhio rolls aside, pulling me with him to lie on his chest. He kisses my forehead. "Once they can verify you're pregnant. I'm guessing their senses can detect it very early since it's so important to their survival."

A tight ball of worry remains in my stomach, a dichotomy of emotions at the thought of having a baby versus the concern that I can't. I have several friends who had trouble conceiving, and one who gave up. I try not to think about what will happen if Tazhio doesn't get me pregnant. My sister, Suzanne, got knocked up with twins at seventeen, so I hope fertility runs in our family.

I fall asleep in Tazhio's arms, and when I wake, the light in the cavern hasn't changed. As I stretch, I idly wonder if the plants ever go dark. My shirt and shorts are draped over me along with my bag, which immediately makes me long for Beanie. I pray he's alive and well and reunited with my sisters and the other passengers. Sitting up, I feel like a homeless person sleeping under a bunch of newspapers, but I'm grateful my nakedness isn't on full display.

Then I realize Tazhio's nowhere in sight. My heart kicks into overdrive and I look around frantically. Four ferret aliens guard the enclosure, each holding a spear and looking outward, as if protecting me from someone coming in rather than me getting out.

I quickly pull my clothing back on, watching the activity on the terraces outside the cage. The community seems to have returned to daily life, cooking and weaving and whatever other mundane tasks need tending. It's as if having someone locked in a cage in their midst is an everyday occurrence. I think longingly of the water I batted away when I first arrived. My throat is parched, and the stream is just out of reach of the cage. But I hesitate to engage with the guards for fear they'll try to molest me again. I much prefer they continue facing away from me.

Then I see a familiar blue figure striding between the groups of Sheeghr toward the cage. My heart swells with relief. Tazhio's carrying a netted bag in one hand and a tall, thin jug in the other. When he reaches the bars, his body thins, and he slips between the slats, easily resuming his normal shape once inside. I shake my head, still in awe of this ability.

He holds out the bag. "I gathered some food and water."

Remembering the bowl of porridge one of the Sheeghr offered me earlier, I wrinkle my nose. The bag holds what looks like golf ball-sized purple fruits, long white sticks, and some wrinkled brown items that might be nuts. "What are those?"

"Food. The Sheeghr shared with me. I've sampled these items, but you should start by trying just one and see if it agrees with you. I suggest the *urru*." He sits cross-legged on the ground and removes one of the golf balls. With a twist, it comes apart to reveal a juicy, nearly black interior. He holds half out to me. "Here."

I can't deny the pinch of hunger in my stomach, so I take it. The fruit smells sort of like cantaloupe, so I tentatively lick the surface. The juice is sweet. I watch Tazhio scrape the inside out using his teeth, so I do the same. I've never been a fan of melon, but I'm hungry enough to eat a second and a third of these strange fruits when Tazhio shares with me.

"Let's wait to be sure your stomach is okay," he says, setting the basket aside.

I'm really glad he's here, because I would probably starve to death if I was stranded alone. I drink greedily from the jug of water, then lie back in the nest of leaves. "I bet my sisters are hungry," I say. "They don't know anything about surviving in the wilderness, let alone on an alien planet."

He stretches out next to me, pulling me close again. "There were a handful of crew on the shuttle. They'll try to gather the survivors and take care of them."

I remember the porter carrying Jennifer's case and pray he's with Jennifer and Suzanne now. He looked like he could protect them against giant centipedes and whatever else might be out there. I settle my cheek on Tazhio's chest so I can hear his heartbeat. "How long do you think it will take for a rescue team to find us?"

His body goes rigid for a moment, then he sighs. "I won't lie to you. We may never be rescued."

My breath catches and my fingers claw against his ribs. I've just had sex intending to get pregnant, and now I learn I probably have to give birth without a hospital, too? I try not to hyperventilate as I ask, "Why not?"

He explains that the planet's ionosphere not only blocks most scans; it creates a perpetual storm around the planet that's nearly impossible to navigate safely. "Even if they were to locate us and find a pilot willing to attempt a landing, there's no guarantee a rescue shuttle would make it down safely, let alone be able to take off again."

I feel numb. *I can never go home?* It's inconceivable. There has to be a way to get off this planet. I'm not ready to give up yet.

Tazhio sighs. "I'm sorry I let you down."

I frown. "What do you mean?"

"This was my first flight around the Singing Planet, and I knew it was dangerous. I shouldn't have allowed anyone to distract me."

I bite my lip. He'd been distracted, all right. Distracted by me. Then I tried to use Jennifer's app on my phone and everything went to shit. This is all my fault—well, mine and hers. "Don't blame yourself. I'm pretty sure my phone interfered with your controls."

He drums his fingers against my hip as if in thought. "I know it seemed to coincide, but the IDA vetted all human devices for safety compatibility."

"Maybe they didn't know about the changes my sister made to boost our signals."

"Well, whatever the cause, what's done is done. We have to make the most of our current circumstances. Once we're out of this, um, situation, we'll find the others and establish a camp. What I've learned from the Sheeghr might actually be helpful."

I swallow. "Like the Gloor."

He nods. "Yes. And they can help us find food. The Sheeghr are friendly as long as they don't think a female is in danger."

"You think they really were trying to protect me?"

"Yes. But they may have trouble acknowledging our mating bond. In case you hadn't noticed, they're inherently promiscuous."

My back is still facing the main cavern, but I can vividly recall the sight of the frenetic orgy that accompanied our lovemaking. "But once I'm pregnant, they won't bother me, right?"

"I hope so, but I saw pregnant females in the orgy."

I shudder. "Thank you again for coming to my rescue."

He takes my face in both hands, looking deep into my eyes. "I'd die for you, Tamara."

"I hope it never comes to that." I try to laugh, but his words are too sincere to actually be funny.

16

TAMARA

e sleep again, and I wake to Tazhio nuzzling my neck. "I think we need to make sure there's a baby inside you."

I won't lie, his words sort of turn me on. I glance toward the cage bars, worried we might still have an audience, but this time not a single Sheeghr is even looking our way.

Tazhio's kisses turn to sucking and nipping, sending small jolts of pleasure through me. I lift a sleepy hand and run my fingers along the shell of his ear and down to his muscular shoulder, loving the solid heat of his body lying against me.

He lifts his face to mine, tongue caressing the seam of my lips, probing until I open to let him inside. Little shivers of delight enter my bloodstream, and I let my fingers slide lower over his ribs. His heated skin is hard and smooth, and his weight on top of me is significant, but not crushing. It feels like a protective shield, and I tilt my chin up to kiss him back.

As his lips devour mine, I marvel at how gentle yet hungry he is. He tastes like sweet oranges on a hot summer day. Braced on one elbow, he cups the back of my head with one hand while the other slides beneath the hem of my blouse, leaving a trail of need across my skin.

His heated palm stops just below my breast, once more encountering my bra, but this time the clasp at the back comes undone as if by magic. I don't have time to ponder as his fingers slide underneath, massaging their way to my aching nipple. He rolls over the hardened tip with a thumb. I whimper, arching my chest up to meet him.

Using one knee, he nudges my legs apart, and heat floods my pussy. The hand at my breast travels downward to the waistband of my shorts. He pulls the drawstring slowly, making my breath hitch with every inch until the knot finally pops loose. Then his hand dips inside, the pads of his fingers sliding across my hipbone and toward my sex. He reaches the top hem of my panties—I'm so glad I wore my nice, lacy ones for this trip—and dips beneath the fabric with ease.

He finds the top of my slit and makes a deep, sexy sound into my mouth. Then his fingers glide over my mound, cupping my lower lips. One finger dips into my aching slickness, and it's as if a dam bursts. Heated moisture floods from me. I spread my legs and flex to meet him as he circles shallowly around my opening, pushing my lips aside and moving in wider and wider arcs until he's gliding over my clit, the sensation making me tense with anticipation and pleasure each time he rolls over it.

Slowly he focuses on the swollen bud, stroking up and down, dipping between my folds again and again. The pressure builds inside me, and my breaths match his pace, increasing in tempo until I'm panting with need.

As he strokes, he kisses behind my ear, nibbles my throat, his tongue hard, then soft, his teeth sometimes grazing my flesh as if about to bite. I grip his sides, bringing one knee up so I can pump against him in time to his rhythm on my clit. A frenzy is building inside me, a tightness that feels like it's borne of years of deprivation.

I begin to shake, my climax just out of reach. I need more. I need to be filled. Panting, I buck harder, encouraging his stroking to delve deeper, to penetrate me. But when he does, it's still not enough. I grab his wrist, panting. "I want you. Please."

Breathing hard, he pushes up onto his knees, exposing his cock to my view. Up close, it's bigger than I remember, shaped somewhat like a club with a pronounced head. A net of thick veins scrolls down its considerable length, visibly pulsing all the way to the base, where a small, sucker-like appendage sits right over his pubic bone. I vaguely realize that's what must've stimulated my clit while he fucked me senseless last time.

He grabs my shorts and panties and yanks them from my legs in one sure move. Planting himself between my thighs, he lowers his body on top of me. I feel his heat probe my entrance.

I keep my gaze on him, and his dark eyes meet mine with a look of satisfaction as he slowly pushes his girth inside me, millimeters at a time, stretching me with an exquisite pressure that makes my eyelids flutter. Wrapping my legs around his firm backside, I draw him against me until he's fully seated. My clit throbs as the bud above his shaft makes contact, and I swear it's sucking me gently, bringing me to the brink of orgasm. I let out a shuddering moan.

He lets out a breath, as if trying to maintain control. "You're so tight… so wet."

"Keep going." The pressure inside me is delightful, but I want him to move, to heat my channel with friction until I can't take anymore.

He pulls back, pausing. Just as I think he's about to pull all the way out, he slams forward again, burying himself until his hips crush against mine.

I gasp, mini-rockets of pleasure shooting down my legs to my toes. I thrust up to meet him. He takes up a steady rhythm, pumping in and out; huge, hot, throbbing. Every thick, hot slide feels amazing, nearly magical, as if he's melding with me, body and soul.

"So close," I pant. I'm right at the edge, but my body refuses to let go. My pending orgasm has built to such excruciating heights, I feel like it's going to kill me when it arrives.

I'm struck by the urge—the *need*—to take control. I want to ride him harder, faster. I want dirty and rough. I want to make us both come undone. "Let me," I beg, my words barely coherent.

But he understands. He rolls onto his back, taking me with him. Still locked together, I straddle him and sit up, pressing my palms against his gloriously muscled chest. He looks magnificent lying against the bed of leaves, his muscular arms reaching forward to grip my hips, his gaze intent on my face. "You're the most beautiful woman I've ever seen."

I don't feel beautiful so much as I feel fierce. Strong and unashamed. Fuck these aliens and their egg-laying monster. I've wanted Tazhio from the moment I saw him, and I'm going to enjoy having him, no matter the circumstances.

Tilting my hips, I rock down onto his hard cock. I've never felt so satisfied yet starving at the same time. I growl between my teeth, keeping my gaze locked with his.

He thrusts upward, gripping my hips almost hard enough to hurt, impaling me on his length. I shudder and clench, leaning back slightly for more friction and heat. His attention dances over my breasts, down my belly to our center of connection. I look down as well, watching him slide in and out of me as I ride him. The tiny appendage on his pubic bone can't reach my clit at this angle, but he circles my slick nub with his thumb. "Come for me, Tamara."

I'm so close, I can barely see straight, but I can't find the crest. I need more. "Please, Tazhio."

Something probes my ass again, entering me and adding to the fullness. My orgasm breaks into a monumental vortex of ecstasy. I cry out, my entire body quaking with release.

Tazhio's hands are like vises on my hips, and he groans, his voice matching my own. Heat fills me, geysering upward until I can feel it in my heart.

I whimper and collapse forward onto his chest, choking on my own labored breath. His chest is heaving, too, his heartbeat strong and fast under my cheek. Sweat slicks his skin and mine, while the musky scent of our union fills the air. I can barely keep my eyes open.

A gentle hand cups the back of my head, stroking my hair. "I love you, Tamara."

I sigh, feeling more content than I ever have before. "I love you, too, Tazhio."

17

TAMARA

The clatter of wood rouses me from my dreams. Tazhio's on his feet in an instant, and the sudden departure of his heat jars me to full wakefulness. I have no idea how long we slept, but my mouth feels cottony, and my nether regions are a bit sore. I suddenly realize I'm still naked from the waist down and search the leaves for my discarded shorts and panties.

Zeer is standing outside the cage, and one of the guards is removing slats from the enclosure. "Praise Gloor," says Zeer. "Fertility is complete."

I pull my clothes on, no longer caring if I'm discreet. The ferret aliens seem to have no concept of nakedness, anyway. "You mean we can go?" I ask, relief blossoming in my chest.

"Danger has been averted. No need to protect you any longer."

They really believed they were protecting me. I grab my bag and put it over my shoulder. Then another realization settles over me. "So, I'm pregnant? How do you know?"

Zeer raises her muzzle and inhales. "Obvious."

Tazhio takes my hand, a proud look on his face. My heart swells as I realize once again that he's mine for life and we're going to raise a family together. I just hope we won't be stuck on this planet, especially if I'll have to stay pregnant for the rest of my life.

"We thank you for your protection," Tazhio says to Zeer. "I hope this means our people can have beneficial ties with the Sheeghr in the future."

The Sheeghr leader nods briefly at him, but keeps most of her attention on me. "We are open to discussion."

I swallow, realizing that as a female-led community, they probably expect me to speak up. "Thank you for allowing me to choose my mate. Our ways are different, but I hope you can continue to respect that."

Zeer bares her teeth in what might be a smile and nods, fondling her erotically carved staff. "Respect is appreciated."

I'm not sure she really understood me, but right now I just want to get out of here and find my sisters and Beanie. As Tazhio and I walk down the terraces toward the cavern exit, the Sheeghr go about their business with hardly a second glance in our direction. Apparently, now that I'm pregnant, they have little to no interest in us.

When we reach the first terrace, Tazhio pauses to look out over the massive trunks and roiling roots beyond the cavern. Then he turns to me and grimaces. "I'm not thrilled with the idea of exposing the rest of the passengers to the Sheeghr, but I'm not entirely sure how to get back to the shuttle."

"Crap." I hadn't paid attention to our route, either. Plus, there was that carnivorous plant along the way, and who knew how many giant centipedes or other creatures? I swallow and glance around, relieved there are no pink penises in sight. "I wonder if they can draw us a map or something."

Just then, a three note ping comes from my bag. I jump. My phone? I thought I turned it off before we crashed. I dig in my bag and pull it out. A small red light is blinking in one corner. "What the heck?"

Tazhio looks over my shoulder. "What?"

"I don't know what this means." Other than the red light, the phone seems to be off. I turn it on. After a minute, the screen is active, and my mouth drops open. The app is still engaged, and there's a message from Jennifer. *Follow the arrow. Hurry.*

There's not a map, but a small green arrow points out toward the forest. When I turn the phone to show Tazhio, the arrow moves like a compass, always pointing in the same direction. "I think we can find my sister with this. Or at least her phone."

He takes my hand. "Then I guess you'd better lead the way."

NAZHIN

I HAVE ONE CHANCE TO COMPLETE MY ASTRONOMY THESIS ON TIME - BUT ONLY IF I CAN KEEP MY EYES ON THE STARS INSTEAD OF THE HOT, BLUE-SKINNED PORTER HANDLING MY LUGGAGE...

NAZHIN

$\mathcal{I}$ take another sip of *Lensoran* bubbly, letting the sour fizz linger on my tongue as I watch the blue-green planet called Earth grow larger in the viewport. Two cabin stewards—blue Kirenai like myself who are also in human form —bustle between the shuttle's empty rows of plush red seats, readying everything for the first human passengers. Earth is the most exotic destination in the galaxy at the moment, off limits to unauthorized surface traffic, and I'm the only "guest" currently on board. I pulled a lot of strings to get on this flight.

I'm curious to meet my first human, but that's not why I'm here. My marketing team needs images and data to promote a new line of sensors from my family's company, Demod Industries. This is an incredible opportunity to get rare footage of the strange new planet.

One of the stewards pauses next to my seat. "We're almost ready to land, sir. Can I get you anything else?"

I hand him my glass. "No, thank you."

We'll only be on the ground long enough to pick up our human guests—all female—for the IDA cruise, and I need to double check the atmospheric sensor mounted on the outside of the shuttle before we take off again. The Intergalactic Dating Agency charged me nearly as much for the permits to install my equipment as I had to pay in bribes to get a seat on the shuttle, and the trip will be a waste if the sensor isn't working.

The moment we touch down, I stride toward the hatch and wait patiently while the boarding ramp unfurls. Hot, humid air sweeps in, making me nostalgic for my home on Kirenai Prime, though here it smells of bitter petrochemicals rather than sweet happa fronds. I pause at the bottom of the ramp to take in my surroundings.

Our shuttle is the only vessel on a pad made of some sort of hard-packed aggregate painted with white and yellow lines. A strip of shorn green foliage runs down one side of the landing pad, and crude buildings sit in rows in the distance. I can barely make out tiny figures moving around near the structures, but none approach us.

While the stewards position themselves next to the ramp to await guests, I move to the nose of the shuttle and double check the settings on my company's sensor. Everything is within expected parameters, so I upload the data already gathered before stepping away to take a few look around while I have the chance. The view near the vessel is less than spectacular, but I didn't coordinate any extra time for exploration. I activate the Integrated Circuit Chip embedded in my arm to capture images of a few of the buildings, then bend down to examine an interesting green plant growing from a crack in the aggregate.

The plants on Kirenai Prime are blue or red, so the green fascinates me, as does the fuzzy yellow flower in the center of the toothed leaves. A flying creature with a striped thorax lands on the flower, and more excitement fills me. This will be an excellent piece of marketing material. As the owner of Demod Industries, I have all the latest sensor upgrades for my ICC, so I quickly scan the creature's vitals.

Before I have time to review the results, a grating rumble reaches me from the other side of the shuttle. I move around to see a low, boxy vehicle coming to a stop. A female with red-gold hair climbs out, and I start recording as she engages a steward to take her luggage. He leads her up the ramp, and I swivel my recorder back toward the vehicle.

Three other females are getting out, and a human male is removing luggage from the rear of the vehicle. A female with dark hair struggles to remove an enormous case from the rear passenger door. Her sleeveless blouse and shorts expose pale skin that intrigues me, and I wonder if it's as soft as it looks. My current human form is based solely on holo images provided by the IDA to help Kirenai guests assume a form that will appeal to the human females.

After a moment of recording, I realize she can't budge the box on her own and rush forward to help. "Please allow me to assist."

My *Iki'i* immediately registers warm tendrils of gratitude as she turns to me. "Oh, God, thank you. I almost dropped it."

Her hazel eyes connect with mine, and I suck in a breath. She's the loveliest being I've ever encountered. Her brown hair glints with auburn highlights and is held away from her face by a silver clasp decorated with pointed stars. An intoxicating smell surrounds her, like the petals of a *malila* flower. I stand there holding one end of the box until she raises her eyebrows. "Do you need another porter to help you?"

Porter? I flush with embarrassment, realizing the other end of the case still rests on the seat inside the vehicle. I pull the case easily from the vehicle, determined to prove I can lift anything she needs, even though I'm not part of the crew.

"Please be very careful," she says. "This is expensive equipment."

The case is more awkward than heavy as I hold it against my front and follow her toward the shuttle. I can't help letting my gaze slide down her back to her pert ass and bare legs. "What sort of equipment, may I ask?"

"Astronomy. I'm writing a thesis on the atmospheric properties of an exoplanet we'll be passing during the cruise."

Beautiful and smart. I'd been on matchmaking cruises before and never found a mate—finding a genuine match is rare for Kirenai. But I'm drawn this female, despite having known her a matter of moments.

We reach the top of the ramp and I wave off the steward who tries to take over. "I've got this."

Inside the shuttle, she turns toward me. "Where can I stow this?"

I blink, then cut a gaze across the cabin. "I'm not sure."

The steward gestures toward the back. "If you would follow me, sir, I can show you."

Her mouth drops open. "I'm so sorry. Are you not part of the crew?"

I should tell her I'm not, but I want to keep helping her. So instead, I smile and say, "I'm here to serve. My name's Nazhin."

"Jennifer," she says, following close behind as I carry the case to where the steward points.

My mind is spinning with all the questions I want to ask her, and my crotch is aching with other needs. I haven't felt so strongly attracted to anyone in ages. After stowing the case, I turn around to find her holding out what looks like a slip of colored paper.

"What is this?" I ask, taking it between two fingers.

"A tip." She frowns. "But I guess Earth money probably doesn't do you much good, huh?"

I chuckle and hand it back. "A tip isn't necessary. Though I'd love it if you'd sit with me for the flight up to the *Romantasy.*"

Wariness pings my *Iki'i* as she takes a half-step backward. "Sorry, no. I realize this is a singles cruise, but I'm only here for my research. Thank you, though." Without even a glance back, she turns and sits next to the woman with copper-bright hair.

My *Iki'i* reels as if it just collided with a wall. I don't think anyone has ever dismissed me like that, and my chest aches with an uncontrollable desire to be near her. Should I tell her that my company specializes in high-end sensor design? Certainly she'd be interested in that. Then again, she was very clear that she's not interested in being social.

I settle into a seat a few rows behind her as I ponder my options. She's not even open to getting to know me. How can I pursue her if she won't let me near her? And the longer I look at her, the more the need to be near her grows.

She's here to do research. I glance toward where her case is stowed. I bet she'll need to lug her equipment around and will ask for a porter. All I need to do is to be present whenever she needs a hand. And if she thinks I'm part of the crew, well…

The difficulty will be in keeping the secret long enough for her to get to know me without ever actually lying. And the more I ponder it, the more I like the idea. Smiling to myself, I lean back in my seat. I've always enjoyed a challenge.

JENNIFER

My sister, Tamara, and I step off the elevator to discover a maze of fancy velvet ropes winding across the shuttle bay floor between us and the purple rosebud shaped shuttle. For the past three days, I've dodged alien advances and endured tedious soirees. Now, finally, my long-awaited opportunity has arrived. We are about to embark upon an excursion through the ionosphere of exoplanet RAx-P-7—known as the Singing Planet to the rest of the galaxy. I've seen hazy images of it through NASA satellite images, and I'm giddy with excitement over the opportunity to document the atmospheric spectrography up close.

Traveling into space has been my dream since Dad gave me a junior telescope for my eighth birthday. The first moment I viewed the night sky through the eyepiece, I knew I wanted to be an astronomer. But after my lab partner ex-boyfriend stole a year's worth of research and published it as his own, I thought my dream might be lost for good.

Then my twin sister, Tamara, won tickets for this alien space cruise, giving me one last chance at a Hail Mary to complete my college thesis on time. So, while most of the other women on board are here for the hot aliens, I'm only interested in viewing the stars and testing my new app. Nobody on Earth has ever captured telemetry like this before, and I know I'm going to blow my professors away with this thesis.

Ahead of us on the shuttle deck stands a small gray alien in a white crew uniform who looks like he came straight from Area 51. He's talking to a pair of tall, broad-shouldered Kirenai wearing Speedos.

Tamara nudges me with her elbow and points with her chin toward the Speedo-wearing guys as they thank him and enter the empty maze. "Jennifer, look."

I chuckle. "Nice."

Somehow, the aliens have it into their heads that human males wear swimming trunks on cruise ships. Now almost every alien guest we encounter wears them—even when there's no pool in sight. Not that I'm complaining—I never imagined aliens could be so good looking, from the blue Kirenai shapeshifters to the gargoyle-like Khargals. Even the short red aliens called Fogarians aren't terrible to look at if you can get past their abundant red body hair and beards.

"More Bloom sisters! How delightful," the gray alien says. The crew members are fantastic about remembering names and have bent over backward trying to make us comfortable.

The alien at the podium points a thin finger toward the shuttle. "Your other party member is already here. Please have an enjoyable trip!"

"Thank you." I lift the nearest rope and duck underneath it. I want to get to the shuttle and set up my equipment before the good seats are all taken.

Tamara grabs my arm and hisses, "They've set those up for a reason, you know."

I scowl at her. Sometimes I wonder how she and I can be twins when she's such a scaredy-cat, but I adore her anyway. I gesture to the empty maze. "It's not like I'm cutting in front of people."

She clutches her big purse closer, one hand inside it to pet her emotional support dog, Beanie. Our other sisters complained about her bringing the animal, but I know Beanie is the only way Tamara can face stress, so I don't mind.

After a moment of hesitation, she grimaces and ducks under the rope with me.

I give her a proud wink and hurry forward, ducking and winding until I spot our sister, Suzanne, skulking near the shuttle ramp. She has wrapped a pastel swirl scarf around her head and neck, and sunglasses hide the rest of her face. She's been trying to avoid a Kirenai admirer she hooked up with on the first night of the cruise.

But my sister and her shenanigans aren't what draw my attention. Next to her towers Nazhin, the brawny blue porter I met the first day of the cruise. Each time he carries my equipment, he looks a little different. He's completely ditched the Ken-doll haircut so many other Kirenai have and is now completely bald. His eyes have acquired a slight silvery sheen, and he's also developed huge muscles—I assume he's shifting to increase them because he's been hauling stuff all over the ship. Even here, from across the shuttle bay, I can see his biceps straining the short sleeves of his uniform. *I wonder what he looks like in a Speedo...*

Shoving the thought aside, I refocus. This might be a singles cruise, but I'm not here to hook up or even flirt. I've already turned down at least half a dozen aliens, the latest being a jerk at the party last night who tried to tell me women shouldn't have careers.

Suzanne spots us and steps out from behind the porter's broad frame with her hands on her hips. "Where have you been?" She gestures toward Nazhin. "Vin Diesel and I have been waiting for at least ten minutes."

I clench my teeth. She's probably been hitting on Nazhin since she got here. Since her divorce, my older sister is determined to do whatever it takes to have a good time.I try to remind myself it doesn't matter as long as she doesn't interfere with him carrying my equipment, but I don't enjoy seeing her flirt with him, especially when she's so flippant about it. "Be polite," I snap, turning an embarrassed smile toward him. "Hi, Nazhin."

"Greetings." Nazhin picks up my equipment case, arm muscles bulging deliciously. "I reserved an exclusive spot in the viewing area for you and your sisters."

When I asked about reserving seats earlier, I was told it was first come, first served. He must've pulled some strings with his buddies on the crew. I drag my attention away from his gorgeous biceps, prepared to thank him, and find his dark eyes locked on me. My heart flutters into my throat. I never get nervous around men, but he's giving me butterflies. Maybe it's because he's bald—I've always had a bit of a kink for bald men. *Once I finish my research, I should find a way to "thank" him for his help...*

My cheeks heat at the thought, and I scramble for an excuse to turn away. Our youngest sister still hasn't arrived, so I look over my shoulder toward the ropes. All I see are two short red Fogarians and a ghostly pale alien with blue hair moving through the maze. "Where's Bethany?"

Suzanne shakes her head. "She bailed on us. Busy teaching an alien how to bake a birthday cake or something." She lowers her sunglasses and stares at Tamara. "I'm surprised you didn't find an excuse not to come, too. You must really have the hots for this pilot."

"Shh!" Tamara cringes and moves to put us between her and the open shuttle door. "He might hear you."

"I thought you *wanted* to get his attention. Speaking of attention, let's get inside before Kiozhi shows up looking for me." Suzanne spins and hurries toward the ramp.

I hurry after her with Nazhin carrying my gear.

A three-foot-tall gray alien with a big head greets me in the hatchway. "Hello, Miss Bloom. Welcome to the Singing Planet excursion—" He spots Nazhin and my equipment, and his small mouth puckers. "I'm terribly sorry, but you'll have to leave your luggage behind."

"This isn't luggage," I say. "It's my astronomy equipment."

"Well, regardless of the contents, you'll have to leave it here. This flight is for passengers only."

I look over the short alien's head toward the double row of seats near the back of the shuttle. "There's plenty of room for my equipment in front of our seats. It won't take up any extra room, I promise."

"I'm sorry, but I must insist." He turns toward Nazhin. "Please return Miss Bloom's items to her cabin."

My chest tightens. My entire thesis rests on the photometry from this excursion. "I was told I could use my equipment anywhere I liked during this cruise."

The small alien's mouth turns up in what I think is a conciliatory smile, and he raises his thin, bony arm to bring up a holographic image with glowing alien symbols. "I see. Do you have a permit number?"

Permit? Shit. I'd let the aliens put my equipment through a crap-ton of scans to be sure none of it would interfere with their systems, and they cleared me for using the telescope on board the *Romantasy.* But I never thought to ask about using it on the shuttle.

Nazhin nudges me to one side, still carrying my case. The muscles in his forearms are nearly as big around as my thighs, and his shoulders take up the entire width of the aisle. He looks down his nose at the smaller alien with a scowl that could crush rocks. "Were you not instructed to accommodate the human guests in every way possible?"

The smaller alien blinks his huge black eyes and takes a step backward. "There is no room—"

A third crew member appears in the aisle, a Kirenai this time. He hurries toward us and puts a hand on the smaller alien's shoulder, keeping his gaze locked with Nazhin's. "What's the problem here?"

An emblem is emblazoned on the breast pocket of his uniform, so I assume he must be a supervisor. "I'm cleared to use my telescope on board the *Romantasy.* I didn't know I needed a separate permit for the shuttle. Can I get one now? Please, my entire career rests on gathering data from this excursion."

The two put their heads together and mutter too low for me to hear. Based on the way they glance at me, though, I know they're about to deny my request.

Nazhin, however, doesn't appear to care what they decide. He bulldozes past them into the cabin, heading straight to the seats in the back.

My heart is slamming against my ribs, but I scurry after him. *He's going to get me kicked off the excursion altogether.* I can't afford to lose this opportunity.

When I reach the seats, he's already set the case down near a floor-to-ceiling viewport looking out over the mechanics on the shuttle bay floor. There are four seats here set up like train seating; two pairs facing each other with a small table for beverages between them. Suzanne sits in one of the window seats, watching Nazhin with an appreciative gaze that makes me heat with jealousy. *What on Earth is wrong with me?*

I shake off the feeling and glance over my shoulder toward the approaching crewmen who wear fresh looks of determination.

"Shit," I mutter and squat down to retrieve my spectrometer from the case, shoving it into my cross-body messenger bag. If they make me leave my telescope behind, I might be able to record enough data with the smaller instrument and the app I installed on my sisters' phones to produce a passable thesis.

"What's going on?" asks Suzanne.

I keep my attention on the supervisor, raising both palms to face him in a placating manner. "Can I talk to the captain or pilot or something?"

"I have already taken this as high as I can go." He turns to address Nazhin. "Do you want us to call another porter to return the luggage to Miss Bloom's cabin?"

Nazhin crosses his arms over his expansive chest. "That won't be necessary. Please check your log again for a permit."

"We're scheduled to depart momentarily and—"

Leaning forward slightly, Nazhin repeats, "Check. Your. Log."

I'm startled that he speaks to his supervisor this way, but the other alien gulps and calls up a holograph over his forearm. A second later, he licks his lips and turns toward me. "My apologies, Miss Bloom. You are cleared for your study. Please keep all your equipment out of the aisle."

I can hardly process what he's saying, but heck if I'm going to argue. "I will, thank you."

The previously reticent crew members leave, and I set my messenger bag into the chair facing my sister.

"Well, that was tense," says Suzanne.

I blow out a breath and nod, turning a smile of relief toward Nazhin. "Thanks for backing me up."

The look he gives me ignites the butterflies in my stomach again. "It's my pleasure, Miss Bloom. I'll remain on board in case you need further assistance."

"Please, call me Jennifer," I manage to stammer out. "Can you sit with us?"

Nazhin's silvery eyes are bright as he looks at me. "As you wish, Jennifer."

The way he says my name makes me light-headed, and I put a hand on the headrest of the nearby seat to keep my balance. He sits down in the aisle seat next to mine, and I realize I'm still staring at him.

Turning quickly, I open my case and begin setting up my telescope. It's difficult to concentrate with Nazhin at my back, and for the first time in my life, I think I might prefer looking at a man to looking at the stars.

3

NAZHIN

I watch Jennifer arrange equipment in her case and then aim her primitive telescope toward the viewport with a self-satisfied smile. I've enjoyed helping her with her project, and with the aid of a small bribe to the cruise director, I've been present the few times she's called for a porter. Moments ago, I was even able to secure a last-minute permit to bring her equipment on this trip without her knowing I intervened, though I'm worried her sister may suspect something is up after she saw me use my ICC interface to contact my liaison.

I glance toward Suzanne sitting across from me near the window. I know I'll need to reveal my true identity soon. She needs to hear it from me. If anyone else tells her, I don't think Jennifer will take it well.

Luckily, Suzanne's attention shifts to something in the aisle behind me. "Oh, no. You've got to be kidding."

"What?" asks Jennifer, following her sister's gaze.

I twist in my seat to look as well, worry thudding in my chest. Did something go wrong with the permit?

A Kirenai in a cream-colored tunic and dark-green pants tucked into high boots is striding down the aisle toward us. As shapeshifters, Kirenai are often not recognizable by how we look, so I focus my *Iki'i* senses to identify him. I recognize him as a billionaire playboy named Kiozhi; I've met him a handful of times at parties. He's currently in a human form, as are ninety-five percent of the Kirenai on board, with perfectly even features and thick hair. A wide grin splits his mouth, and it's obvious he's heading straight for Suzanne.

Kuzara, he's likely to recognize me. I try to make eye contact and hush him before he says anything, but he doesn't even seem to notice I'm here. He plops into the seat next to Suzanne. "I hope you don't mind, but your sister traded seats with me."

Suzanne turns her shoulder away from him and crosses her arms. "I absolutely do—"

The intercom interrupts the rest of her words. "We've closed the hatch and are preparing to take off. Please remain seated until we clear the docking bay doors."

Jennifer perches on the edge of her seat, one hand holding tight to a leg of the tripod. "Shit, I didn't think about turbulence," she says, leaning down to look around the floor. "Is there a way to secure this to the deck?"

I wrap my fingers around the tripod so my hand brushes hers. Her skin is slightly chilly, and I long to take her fingers in mine and share my warmth. Instead, I say, "It's unlikely we'll experience turbulence, but I'm happy to hold this in place for you."

She frowns, her hand stuck like glue to the tripod. Yet her pupils are dilated as she looks at me, and my *Iki'i* can sense her attraction. She's been looking at me with increasing interest, and my form has been subtly shifting into this strong, hairless build to please her. "Oh, no, I'll hang onto it," she says. "You've done so much for me already."

"It's nothing, really." I want so badly to close the distance and kiss her plump lips, but I keep myself in check. Once I've helped her complete her research, I'll reveal myself. By then, she'll understand that I only want the best for her. "You need to be free to take notes."

She inhales slowly, her eyes dark pools of appreciation. "Are you sure?"

"Absolutely."

"Thank you, Nazhin." She releases her grip, but instead of simply withdrawing, she rests her fingertips briefly on my forearm.

A thrill races through me at her touch, and I stare at her pale fingers against my blue skin. I want to lift them to my mouth and suck each digit gently. To kiss her palm and slide my lips up the gentle curve of her arm to her collarbone.

I'm jarred from my daydream by Kiozhi's voice. "Hey, I know you, right? Nazhin?" He leans forward to stare at me, though I know his *Iki'i* doesn't require it. "You own Demod Industries."

Kuzara. This is not how I want Jennifer to learn the truth. I'm proud that I haven't outright lied to her, only allowed her to believe what she sees. But if I deny Kiozhi, it will be a lie, and I never want that to be something she can hold against me.

I clear my throat, deciding the best course of action is to answer his question with another. "Why would the owner of a corporation need to work as a porter?"

I let my eyes flick meaningfully toward Jennifer, hoping she doesn't notice, but Suzanne is staring straight at me, mouth open.

Kiozhi seems to take the hint and reclines back into his seat, affecting a disdainful expression, though I can sense his admiration through my *Iki'i*. "My mistake. Back to your portering." He leans one elbow on the armrest and edges closer to Suzanne. "Do humans have something against rich guys? Is that why you keep rejecting me?"

"Could you be more full of yourself?" She scowls at him, though the sexual attraction is thick between them. I don't know what their deal is, and I don't care. I'm only grateful that her attention has been drawn away from me.

"What's Demod Industries?" Jennifer asks.

"A company that designs high-end sensor equipment." I keep my voice even. "I believe they're currently the largest manufacturer in the galaxy." It was probably a mistake to add the last bit, but I'm proud of my company, and it's hard not to boast.

Interest sparks in her eyes. "Like astronomy equipment?"

"Certainly," I say. "But I'm afraid humans are not permitted to acquire advanced technology until your planet is no longer on probation."

Kiozhi butts in. "I could probably smuggle you a few things."

"Really?" Jennifer leans forward, eyes full of excitement.

Jealousy rises like a storm inside me. She should be looking at me that way, not him. How dare he offer her gifts from my own company?

Suzanne rolls her eyes. "Don't encourage him, Jennifer."

"Can you get me a sensor that can calculate the Roche limit of a planetary body?" Jennifer asks.

"I'll ask my contact once we get back to the *Romantasy*," Kiozhi says, gaze fixed on Suzanne. "Is there anything I can get you?"

He's obviously doing this to impress Suzanne, not Jennifer, but I still want to punch him in the face. He doesn't even have a clue what piece of equipment Jennifer's talking about.

Just then, multi-colored light dances across the window, and everyone gasps. We turn to the viewport where the outer ring of the Singing Planet has come into view. A braided tangle of brilliant pink, green, and yellow light flows against a backdrop of velvet black space.

Jennifer pats my wrist. "You can let go now, I think. I need to start recording."

I realize I'm still gripping the tripod leg hard enough to make my fingers ache. I let go, and she rises to look into the eyepiece of her telescope. Her luscious backside is aimed at my face.

I glance toward Kiozhi, who's leaning halfway across Suzanne's lap to look out the viewport beside her. I'm still seething about his offer. He shouldn't be the one giving Jennifer gifts.

Nobody's paying attention to me, so I bring up my ICC interface and access my corporate account. I know I'm breaking galactic law, but I quickly arrange to have my company's most comprehensive astronomy kit waiting for Jennifer the moment we get back from this excursion. She'll initially think it's from him, but I'll clear that up after I tell her who I really am.

I just hope the right opportunity presents itself soon, or I might end up ruining everything.

4

JENNIFER

I make one last adjustment to my telescope as we enter the outer ring of the Singing Planet, check that it's synced with the laptop CCD array in my case, then settle back into my seat. Outside the viewport, a storm of white lights streak by, reminding me of a snowstorm in the headlights of a car. Everything's moving too fast for me to see, but after we get back to the *Romantasy,* I can slow down the recording for analysis. Every nerve in my body thrums with excitement, and I feel like my entire life has built up to this moment in time.

I pull my phone from my pocket and verify that it's connected to my other equipment. The app I designed will tether our phones and boost my digital processing power.

"Turn on your app," I remind Suzanne, then look around and realize Tamara isn't with us. Feeling guilty that I didn't notice until now, I ask, "What happened to Tamara? Did she chicken out after all?"

"She got a front-row seat with her lover boy." Suzanne holds up her phone to show me her app is running, then returns her gaze to the viewport, giving Kiozhi a blatantly cold shoulder.

This is the first time I've met the guy she's been trying to avoid, and to be honest, I'm not sure how she can tell him apart from the hundred other Kirenai on board. Then again, I've never been great with faces. Show me a star cluster, and I can probably tell you its name along with seven key attributes, but people? Not so much. I slide my attention toward Nazhin, appreciating that he looks unique. *Unique and hot...*

My thoughts are drawn from my musings as a soft, drawn-out note fills the air and golden streamers of light float through the cabin like fireflies. I gasp, and the other guests exclaim in wonder. I understand the ionosphere is only reacting with the hull to create sound and light, but here in the moment, it feels like magic.

The seat cushion softens beneath me and molds up around my body, pulling me firmly against the backrest. "What the—?"

The pilot's voice comes over the speakers. "This is your captain. I've engaged your chair's safety features. It's normal to encounter some turbulence during this excursion, so please sit back and enjoy this galactic symphony."

Turbulence? I struggle to free my upper body, but the seat has me locked down. A spark of panic jolts through me. I need to secure my equipment. The telescope is on loan from the university, and if anything happens to it, I'll be out twenty grand.

As though reading my mind, Nazhin leans over my legs and grabs the tripod again. "Don't worry. I'll hold on. You enjoy the show."

Gratitude warms my chest. I don't know if the other porters on board are this attentive, but Nazhin's anticipation of my needs impresses me. His elbow brushes my bare knee, the feathery contact sending flickers of heat straight to my core. I can't help imagining his hand leaving the tripod to splay over my inner thigh. Without conscious thought, I widen my knees.

Then I realize Nazhin is looking right at me, a slight smile tugging the corners of his mouth. *Oh, God.* He must've noticed what I just did. My entire body feels like it might burst into flames.

Suddenly, the music against the hull shifts, turning into what sounds like a woman moaning in pleasure. I almost groan along with it.

Still, I'm unable to break my gaze from Nazhin's and I'm aware of a pooling heat in my center and a dampness in my panties. I haven't felt this flustered over a guy since my crush on Toby Harrington during my sophomore year in high school. *And I bet Nazhin's a way better kisser.*

Motes of aquamarine have now joined the gold streamers floating between us, merging into glowing emerald rings. I dig into every reserve of willpower I have and tear my gaze away from Nazhin's sultry, silvery eyes to look at my phone. My app seems to catch and freeze before resuming its scroll of code. Something's slowing it down. Then I realize that Tamara's app isn't connected. Without her phone synced in, I won't be able to capture all the data.

She's probably busy making goo-goo eyes at the hot pilot. But she also knows how important this is to me. I don't want to interrupt her, but I have little choice. I text, *Turn on your app please.*

Just as I hit send, purple and red lights explode against the view screen, coating us in a lurid glow. The music dips into a low, mumbling groan, and the ship jolts as the deck starts to shudder. My stomach lurches, and I glance at Nazhin, who's still holding tight to my telescope. "What's happening?" I ask.

His mouth is a grim line, and he shakes his head. "I'm not sure."

Across from us, Kiozhi has one arm flung protectively across Suzanne's middle. Her knuckles are white on the arm rests. "The pilot wasn't kidding about turbulence," she says, her voice higher than normal.

I still can't sit forward in my seat to help hold my telescope and am more grateful than ever for Nazhin's help. Shoving my phone into my pocket, I grip my armrests as the ship's groaning swells into a monstrous roar.

5

NAZHIN

I clutch Jennifer's telescope as the vibration on the hull crescendoes into a shrieking whine. Something is definitely wrong. The scent of broken foliage and ozone fills my nose, and a storm blasts through the cabin, ripping the telescope from my grip. I automatically harden my matrix as wind and debris pepper my skin, then suddenly remember Jennifer doesn't have that ability. *I must protect her.* Twisting, I reach for her just as the seat locks us down, completely encasing us in a mold of safety foam.

My heart races. The only reason the safety pods would engage is if we're going to crash. I can't see. I can't move. Even turning amorphous would be useless because the pod is designed to withstand the vacuum of space. At least I'm in the adjoined seat, so whatever happens, Jennifer and I will be together.

The foam presses around me, filling every nook and cranny. It holds me completely immobile, but I can tell we are spinning, tumbling toward the planet.

And there's nothing I can do except ride it out.

It feels like we bounce several times before we jolt to a stop with teeth-clacking force. Frustrated and helpless, I wait for the foam to deflate and release its hold. *At least it feels like we're right side up.*

The instant warm, humid air hits my body, I tear myself free and stand to make sure Jennifer is unhurt. "Are you all right?"

"What happened?" Her voice is raspy, as if she's been screaming. Her hazel eyes are huge, and her hair has come free of its silver clip, but she looks undamaged. She sags forward, and I reach down to support her so she can stand.

"We crashed." Clasping her against my chest with one arm, I tilt her chin up so I can see her face. "Please tell me you're all right."

"I think so." Nodding, she stands a little straighter, but loops her arms around my waist, as if needing the support while she gets her bearings. I'm more than glad to give it. I haven't had the opportunity to be this close. Her hair smells like warm rain on *happa* fronds, and her body pressed against mine is thrilling, even if the circumstances are dire.

She inhales softly, leaning closer, and her breasts press deliciously against my chest. "God, I can't believe we're still alive."

Before I realize what's happening, her mouth is against mine. Or is mine against hers? All I know is that her lips are as soft as clouds, and when she flicks her tongue against my mouth, she tastes like sugary *kazhitu*. For a flickering moment, I lose myself in the sensation and sweep my tongue against hers, deepening the kiss. My cock throbs with need.

Then I pause. I've dreamed of holding her against me, but not like this, when she feels like a fragile, frightened bird. She's not in her right state of mind, and neither am I.

I gently pull back and press my lips to her forehead instead. My body is at war with itself, demanding I move forward and claim her. But now isn't the time or place. "We should find the others."

She blinks and looks around. "Oh, yes. Where's Suzanne?"

I also glance around the area. Now that my eyes have adjusted, I realize we're standing in a forest of enormous tree trunks. The ground is a tangled mess of roots peppered with bioluminescent plants. Bits of leaves and small branches damaged during the crash flutter down around us like rain. I turn my attention upward. Beyond the faint loops of vines high in the canopy, everything is dark. "The pods must've jettisoned before the shuttle hit the ground and scattered along the flight path. We'll have to search."

A small sob wracks her body. "Do you think they're okay?"

"I'm sure the safety pods protected them." I squeeze her gently. "Can you walk, or do you want me to carry you?"

She sniffles, but says, "I can walk."

Yet her hands remain locked around my waist. Terror, panic, and shock all war for dominance against my *Iki'i*. She needs to focus on something normal so she can reestablish her bearings. Something comforting. I reach up and gently remove her silver hair clip. She's worn the jewelry every day of the cruise, so I know it must mean something to her. I smooth her soft, dark locks away from her face and re-affix the clip. "This jewelry suits you."

As I hoped, the distraction brings her back to herself. She puts a hand to the clip, nostalgia edging into her emotions like a calming tonic. "Thank you. My mom gave it to me. I'm glad it didn't get lost."

On instinct, my fingers glide through her hair down the back of her neck. "I'm glad, too."

Jennifer nods and takes a shuddering breath, her eyes locked on mine. "Thank you for sticking with me, Nazhin. You always seem to know just what to do."

I smile, pleased I've made her happy. But my satisfaction quickly wanes as I realize her equipment is gone, probably destroyed in the crash. "I'm sorry I couldn't save your telescope."

She looks at me with furrowed eyebrows. "Don't be sorry. None of that matters right now. The most important thing is that we find my sisters and the others. Oh, wait!" Pulling her phone from her pocket, she raises it into the air and spins in a slow circle. "I still have my phone."

"You've spoken of this phone before. What does it do?" I wanted to ask when she first brought it up, but the question seemed awkward considering she thought I was just a porter.

"Lots of things. But right now, I'm hoping it will guide me to the other phones." After two rotations, she drops her arm. "I think I need to get out of this hollow."

The forest floor is rough and uneven, and our safety pod rests in a wide depression filled with tangled roots. She pulls her bag from where it's still wedged against the armrest of her chair, then checks around the immediate area for anything we want to salvage. Finding nothing, she leads the way toward the highest spot we can see.

Jennifer stands on top of a tall root and spins with her phone in the air once more. "It's not working."

I nod. "I'm not surprised. The planet's ionosphere is probably causing interference."

Her shoulders slump. "Crap. I guess we search the hard way, then." Raising both hands to her mouth, she yells, "Hello! Suzanne? Tamara? Anyone!"

We listen, but the only sounds are hoots and crackles, which I assume are normal for this planet's flora and fauna. I help her slide back down the root, and we move through the forest, continuing to call out. The uneven ground is slow going, and we can't keep a straight line. We pause by a pool of inky black water and Jennifer licks her lips. "I'm really thirsty. Do you think it's safe to drink?"

"I can check for known toxins and parasites." I drop to one knee next to the pool and activate the Integrated Circuit Chip on my arm.

For most people, the ICC is little more than a comm device with some data connectivity to the galactic web; mine has several prototype sensors, including one we developed to detect for contaminants after the emperor was poisoned. I've had few opportunities to field test it, and I have to admit I'm excited to see if it's useful.

I lower my arm into the water up to my elbow. A few moments later, I bring it out and read the interface. "Water, some microorganisms which are to be expected, no known toxins." I look at her in triumph. "If we boil it, it should be safe."

One of Jennifer's dark brows arcs in surprise. "Do all the porters have technology like that?"

I hesitate. My ICC is several steps more advanced than what a porter should have. *Kuzara,* with all the sensor upgrades I have installed, it's several steps more advanced than what almost anyone should have. "I need to tell you something." Standing, I shake water from my arm. "I'm… not a porter. I'm the owner of Demod Industries."

She stands there a moment, both eyebrows now raised and her mouth hanging open. I can see the gears turning inside her head. "The company Kiozhi asked you about?" she asks.

I nod.

She crosses her arms, and indignation jabs my *Iki'i*. "The company you very blatantly said you didn't own."

I shrug. "I never denied it. Only asked why such a person would need to work as a porter."

"Yes, that is an excellent question. Why would the owner of a huge galactic tech firm carry around a stranger's luggage for days?"

I rub my lips and move to a nearby root to sit. "When you and I first met on Earth, you made it very clear you had no interest in dating. So…" I swallow, knowing what I have to say but also realizing how bad it's going to sound. "I had to find another way to get to know you."

"That's shady as fuck, you know that?" She spins in a circle as if looking for somewhere else to go. Then she rounds on me. "Why do men always have to lie? I can't believe I actually kissed you!"

Each word blasts my *Iki'i* like a laser to the chest. This is going worse than I expected. Much worse. "I didn't mean to deceive you. Really. You're just so fascinating, intelligent, determined, but also completely walled off—"

"Because I'm not interested in a relationship! What part of that did you not understand back on Earth?"

I clamp my mouth shut. I'm in the wrong here and I know it. Dropping my gaze from hers, I say, "I'm sorry."

She stands there for a few minutes, seething. Then she turns to the water. "I suppose we're stuck with each other until we find the others. So I sure hope you have a gadget for starting fires on that arm of yours, because I sure as hell don't have a way to boil water."

"No. But I will find a way to start one for you." Despite her anger, an ember of hope flickers inside my chest. We are here, together, with nowhere else to go. I can still prove to her that I'm worthy.

6

JENNIFER

*N*azhin's apology blurs my focus on my anger as surely as fingerprints on an aperture lens. I can't recall ever having a man admit he's wrong before, let alone mean it. Yet from the slump of his shoulders to the way his eyes hold mine, I'm certain Nazhin is sincere.

I cross my arms, trying to cling to my anger as I watch him break a thick branch over one knee and tuck the pieces under a well-muscled arm. *Dammit, why does he have to be so hot?*

I have zero interest in another horrible, lying boyfriend. But I also appreciate the way Nazhin has taken care of me. He's been nothing but helpful from the moment we met, caring for my equipment, standing up for me with the crew, and even keeping away suitors who might interfere with my research. I swallow, realizing that last bit of help probably had ulterior motives. *Arthur started out nice, too, and look where that got me.*

Well, Nazhin and I might have to work together until we get off this planet, but I won't let him keep taking care of me. I don't need a knight in shining armor. Or big blue muscles. All right, maybe his big blue muscles will come in handy, but that's it. No more letting him coddle me, and definitely no more kissing.

I tromp through the glowing bushes, looking for branches to build a fire, grateful this planet doesn't appear to have any alien spiders or other creepy bugs. The leaves remind me of nebulas I've studied through my telescope—glowing clusters of magenta, gold, emerald, and azure—and I pause to snap a couple of photos with my phone. Might as well have souvenirs of being stranded on an alien planet. Then I bring up my app and turn in a slow circle, hoping I might see the little arrow pointing toward one of my sisters. Nothing. With a deflated sigh, I gather a few sticks and return to the pool.

Nazhin has already accumulated a decent pile of wood, so I kneel and start arranging kindling for a fire. Arthur and I used to go camping to escape the city lights. He would build the fire and set up the tent while I looked at the night sky with my telescope. I assumed he was just being nice and letting me pick what we'd be viewing that evening. Now I know he was simply biding his time and letting me do all the actual work so he could steal it.

"Are you okay?" asks Nazhin, setting down more wood. "You seem… angry."

I look down to see I've snapped the kindling into tiny pieces; the pads of my fingers now prickle with tiny splinters. A surge of self-pity rocks me, and I blurt, "No. My sisters are missing.

I've lost tens of thousands of dollars in equipment. And I know this sounds petty, but my thesis is trashed, and I've lost any chance of earning my degree."

Nazhin sits on the ground across from me. "Is the Singing Planet the one you wanted to research?"

I laugh, a bitter, humorless sound. "Yeah, just not quite this up close and personal."

He chuckles, too, and soon we are both laughing hysterically. Tears leak from my eyes, and I lay back on the uneven ground, belly aching.

"Hello?" A male voice calls through the trees.

My laughter chokes off and I scramble to my feet. "Hey! We're over here!"

A Fogarian—one of the dwarf-like aliens from the cruise— emerges from among the glowing bushes, his shock of crimson hair tangled with twigs and glowing leaves. A Ken-doll Kirenai emerges right behind him. They're both wearing Speedos.

I choke back more laughter. *Can this get any weirder?*

The Kirenai looks around. "Are there more of you?"

"No." Nazhin rises. "You're the first passengers we've encountered."

The Fogarian says, "My name is Erud, and this is Handsy."

"I told you not to call me that." The Kirenai looks at me and puts a palm against his bare chest. "My name is Hanzhu."

Erud gives me a sharp-toothed grin that reminds me of a claymation abominable snowman. "You are one of Tamara's siblings, are you not?"

"Yes, I'm Jennifer, and this is Nazhin."

"Very nice to meet you. I'm eager to find your sister. I believe she may be my mate." His eyes burn with hope beneath his bushy brows. This must be the Fogarian Tamara complained about on the cruise.

I give him a sympathetic look. "I think she already has her sights set on someone else, unfortunately."

Erud sighs. "Unfortunate indeed. I direly need a mate." His attention drops to my chest. "Are you available, perhaps?"

Oh, no. The last thing I want is him transferring his attention to me. But before I can form a reply, Nazhin puts an arm around my shoulders. "She is not."

My heart leaps to my throat. I'm not available because I'm working, but Nazhin's arm around my shoulder portrays a different reason. However, I doubt my desire for scientific research will deter Erud's advances. *Nazhin's unspoken hint that we're already together is the easiest way to guarantee Erud leaves me alone.*

Feeling like a complete hypocrite for the deceit, I nod, standing stiffly under the weight of Nazhin's arm.

The Fogarian scowls and crosses his arms. "The IDA should've been more clear about the female to male ratio on this cruise."

Hanzhu points toward the pool behind us. "We should move away from the water. We saw an enormous creature with hundreds of legs come out of a pond like that not too long ago."

Nazhin drops his arm from my shoulder and turns. "I believe this pool is unoccupied. We've been here for some time and detected nothing. Besides, we're going to need a source of water to survive."

Hanzhu reluctantly agrees, and I finish preparing wood for the fire. But without a lighter or matches, I'm at a loss how to start it.

"Please, allow me," Erud says. He scrapes one long claw over a nearby rock, sending sparks onto the tinder, and soon a merry blaze licks up the wood. I have to confess, I'm pretty awed by the ability.

Nazhin rubs the back of his neck. "We don't have a pan to boil water."

I pick up an enormous fallen leaf the size of a dinner plate and begin folding it into a cup. "When I was a kid, we used paper cups to boil water on the campfire. Let's see if a leaf works."

I fill the folded leaf with water and set it right into the fire. My throat is parched, and if this doesn't work, I might have to drink straight from the pond. I'm relieved when the water steams and boils. As expected, the top edges of the leaf char and fall away, and getting the cup out of the fire is a challenge, but I lever it out with a pair of sticks. It smells a little like wintergreen and the previously clear water has darkened.

My heart sinks. I never thought about the fact that boiling water in an alien leaf would create potentially toxic tea. "Can you test this again before we drink it?" I ask Nazhin. "In case the leaf is poisonous."

"Of course." He dribbles some of the boiled water over his arm. After a minute, he shakes his head. "There are compounds here that aren't in my chip's database." Then, without even batting an eye, he downs it in one long gulp.

I grab his wrist. "What are you doing?"

"The only way to test it is for one of us to drink it. If I have no adverse reactions, then it should be safe for you, too."

"I understand the concept, but we should've drawn straws to see who gets to be the guinea pig!"

He tilts his head and frowns. "I don't understand. The cup you fashioned works perfectly well without the use of a straw. And what is a guinea pig?"

I press my fingertips to my temples and take a calming breath. These cultural misunderstandings would be funny if he hadn't just put himself in danger. "A guinea pig is a test subject. The term draw straws means to select someone at random." I gesture to Hanzhu and Erud. "There are four of us now, and we need to be fair about taking risks."

Nazhin doesn't even look at the others. "I'm afraid I can't do that."

"Nor I," says Erud.

Hanzhu shrugs and shakes his head in agreement. "You're female. I'll protect you at all costs."

"Absolutely not," I insist, crossing my arms. I've read enough reverse harem romances to suspect where this might be going, and I have no interest in hooking up with an alien dwarf or a Ken doll. "We're in this together, so we share the risks."

"I agree with what you say," responds Nazhin. "But my physiology is far more resilient than a human's. The risk-reward ratio is greater if I am the kin-ay-peeg."

"Guinea," I correct his pronunciation as I glare at him. Although I want to argue, he has a point. I can't imagine a situation where I might be more resilient than an alien shapeshifter, but it could happen, so I say, "Using that logic, if the risk is lower for me in other circumstances, you let me be the one to take it, right?"

He presses his lips into a thin line and bobs his head once. "After we've considered all other options, yes."

I bite my cheeks and regard him for a moment. He obviously wants to say no, and I have to admit it feels nice to have someone who wants to protect me, but it also feels good to be a productive member of the group rather than a female to be protected. I turn to the other two. "Agreed?"

They glance toward Nazhin before nodding in acceptance.

Nazhin passes more leaves around. "We should boil more water so it's ready for you once we determine I'm okay."

We boil several cups, and after an hour, Nazhin says he feels fine. But now, I'm so thirsty I might consider drinking straight out of the pool. Instead, I sip cautiously at the boiled water. It's a little astringent, but not unpleasant, and hits the bottom of my empty stomach with an aching thud.

"We're going to need a lot more than water to keep us alive if we're stuck here much longer," I say. "How long do you think it'll take for rescue teams to find us?"

Nazhin looks away uncomfortably.

A ball of worry settles in my gut, and I glance at Hanzhu and Erud, who also avert their eyes. "What are you not telling me?"

Nazhin returns his attention to my face, dark eyes somber. "The ionosphere around this planet is nearly impenetrable to sensors. It's unlikely we'll ever be found."

I gape at him, using every spark of brain power to comprehend what he's telling me. I knew the ionosphere was thick, but I assumed alien technology would easily be able to see through it. Dread fills my stomach. *I'm never getting off this planet.* And here I thought my biggest problem was that I'd never finish my thesis.

7

NAZHIN

Jennifer's voice is soft, nearly lost below the crackle of the flames. "Are you telling me we could be stranded here forever?"

"I'm afraid so." I want to pull her to me, but she hasn't forgiven me yet, and the last thing I want to do is make her draw farther away.

"No." She stands up. "I refuse to accept that." She removes her phone from her pocket and holds it up, doing her little circle again. "We're going to find my sisters, then we're going to find a way off this planet."

I can't help smiling. I love her determination, hopeless as it might be. "We'll do everything we can."

Hanzhu rises. "I'm going to rest a bit, then head out to find more survivors." He moves to a thick pile of leaves at the base of a nearby tree and stretches out.

"Same," says Erud. He finds a spot several yards away and uses his clawed hands to dig a shallow depression between the roots. Within a few minutes, he's completely hidden from view.

"That's impressive," says Jennifer, eyeing the hole.

"Yes, Fogarians are skilled excavators." I prefer not to trap myself in a hole in the ground, but I ask, "Would you also like to sleep in a hole like that? I can dig one for you."

"Oh, God, no. I need open air." Jennifer settles down next to me near the fire and looks around. "Should one of us keep watch?"

"Sleep. I'll keep an eye out."

She shakes her head. "You're tired, too. Let's play-rock-paper-scissors for it. Winner keeps watch."

I frown, uncertain. "What is this rock game you speak of?"

Her eyes are rimmed pink, and I can feel exhaustion rolling off her with every breath, but she chuckles. "Right, you wouldn't know what that is." She makes a fist. "This is rock. And this is paper and scissors." She holds her hand out flat, then curls her fingers so only two are extended. "Paper covers rock, rock crushes scissors, scissors cut paper."

I mimic her movements. "All right."

"On three." She counts, moving her hand in time to the beat, and on three holds out paper.

I stare at it, and she laughs again. I grin back. I want to make her laugh all the time. "Now what?"

"You have to do it, too."

"Oh." My grin turns sheepish, and I lift my hand, once more mimicking her.

On three, I hold out a fist. She chooses paper again, and slides her hand over my fist to cover it with her warm palm. "Paper covers rock. I win."

The physical contact, innocent as it is, still sends a thrill through my bloodstream. "Paper can cover rock any time she likes."

Jennifer's cheeks flush pink and her eyes darken. Her hand lingers over mine before she slowly pulls back. "Uh, so, that means you sleep, and I'll rest after you wake up."

I know I won't be able to sleep, but I lie down anyway and close my eyes. I hear her rustle in her messenger bag and crack open one eye to see her pull out a few gadgets. Her mood is pensive as she looks at one item after the other. I recognize her spectrometer and a compact with a small mirror, but the other items are a mystery to me.

She yawns before stuffing everything back in the bag. Standing up, she stretches and inhales deeply while looking at the surrounding brush. I can tell she's struggling to stay awake, but I doubt I've feigned sleep long enough to claim it's my turn to watch. She paces around the fire, checking on Hanzhu and peeking in the hole Erud dug. Her circles widen as she moves to the perimeter. Her patrol takes her behind the massive trunk opposite to where Hanzhu sleeps. Several heartbeats later, there's no sign of her.

I sit up. During our trek here, she wanted privacy when she relieved herself. Perhaps that's what she's doing now. Except I hear her moving farther away from camp, and she doesn't appear to be slowing down. *Where is she going?*

I get to my feet. We know next to nothing about the Singing Planet's inhabitants, and Hanzhu's mention of a monster has me concerned. She shouldn't venture too far on her own.

"Jennifer," I call.

She doesn't answer.

I move past the tree and call louder. When she still doesn't answer, I lengthen my stride and shove my way through the glowing brush. "Jennifer, where are you?"

"I'm coming!" Jennifer replies, but her voice sounds strangely muted.

I frown and stretch my matrix taller to get a better view over the bushes. She's nowhere in sight.

"We're down here!" an unfamiliar voice reaches me, female and very faint.

Alarm spikes through me, and I move toward it until I reach a shallow crevasse between the roots. The hole deepens at one end, disappearing into a dark cave. I hear movement inside. "Jennifer!" I shout.

"Down here," she calls back. "I think I found someone."

"Wait for me," I call and leap down into the crevasse, moving forward into the darkness. The space is narrow, barely wider than my shoulders, and continues to descend into pitch black. Within a few steps, the passage twists to the right and narrows, forcing me to walk sideways to maintain my human form. I continue on until I see a beam of light. Jennifer stands next to a floor-to-ceiling crack in the wall no wider than my palm. Her cell phone emits a bright incandescence.

"What are you doing?" I ask. "You mustn't wander off alone."

"I heard someone calling for help." She turns to look at me with a puzzled look. "It sounds like they're inside this fissure."

I exhale roughly and grasp Jennifer's arm. "Don't run off like that again."

Jennifer scowls at me and jerks away. "I didn't run off. I was on patrol."

"Can you hear me?" a woman's voice comes from the fissure.

"We hear you," says Jennifer. "Where are you?"

"I don't know. Something was chasing us and we ran and then fell down this hole."

I ask, "How many of you are there?"

"Just me and one of the crew. He's unconscious."

"All right. Don't worry, we're coming." I look at Jennifer. "I'm going to take you back to camp, then I'll come back and find them."

"But I want to help dig them out."

"We don't know what things look like on the other side. Digging might cause a cave in. But I can reach them without disturbing anything." I back up, pulling her along after me. "The best way for you to help is to wait in camp. Boil more water and get ready in case they're hurt."

"Fine. But I can get to camp myself. You need to hurry."

I scowl. "Something chased them into that hole. I'm not letting you go back alone."

Jennifer huffs but follows me. "It's not your job to take care of me, Nazhin. I need you to understand that."

"And I need you to understand that I'll always put you first. I know you're capable, but I couldn't bear it if something happened to you."

Her expression tightens, but she lifts her chin and follows me out. We hurry back to camp where we find Hanzhu and Erud awake.

"What's going on?" asks Hanzhu.

"We found more passengers," Jennifer says. "But we can't get to them."

"I can," I say, giving Hanzhu a meaningful look. He understands immediately that I mean to devolve into my amorphous form.

"Do you want my help?" he asks.

"No," I say. "There's only room for one of us. It also sounds like one may be injured. Get the fire going again and boil more water. I'll be back soon."

I return to the cave where we heard the voice. Releasing my matrix, I squeeze through the small opening. The fissure makes several twists and turns until the space opens up again.

A woman sits on her knees next to a small Hage in a white uniform. Dirt covers her skin, and bits of glowing leaves are stuck in her dark hair. A long tear in her sleeve exposes a plump arm, and the bodice of her red dress is covered in dark spots. Blood? The Hage is on his back, large eyes closed and spindly limbs unmoving. Overhead, I can see the outline of the crevasse they must've fallen through, and crushed, glowing plants and clods of dirt lay scattered on the floor.

I solidify into my human shape. "Are you injured?"

The woman gasps. "N-no." She rises, slightly unsteady. "I'm fine."

"I'm Nazhin. What's your name?"

"Sophia." She points to the unconscious crew member. "He hit his head when we fell."

The Hage's eyelids flicker, and he has a nasty bump on his bald gray-skinned skull, but his pulse is strong, so I think he'll be all right.

"I'm so glad you found us." Sophia clutches her middle, face creasing as if in pain. "First that creature attacked us, then we fell down here. I'm afraid to try to climb out in case it comes back."

I smile reassuringly. "I'll get you out of here, don't worry. We have a camp set up nearby. Tell me about the thing that was chasing you."

Sophia gestures toward the her companion. "Ubi and I were looking for other passengers and sat down to rest. I fell asleep and woke up to something breathing in my face. When I opened my eyes, this… *thing* was on top of me." She cringes, her whole body tightening. "It had pincers instead of a mouth, and wings and scary barbed legs that were wrapped around me like it was trying to carry me off." She runs her hands over the blood spots on her middle, then looks at the crewman, features pinched with worry. "Ubi beat it away with a stick. That's when we ran and fell into this hole. The monster buzzed around outside for a while, but I think it must've been too big to fit through the opening."

She buries her face in her hands.

I pat her shoulder. "It's okay. I don't hear anything now, so I bet it moved on." I look at the opening above my head. "Let me look around up top to be sure."

Sophia clutches my arm. "Don't leave me alone here!"

"We can't stay here indefinitely. I'll be right back, I promise." I gently disengage my arm from her grip. I much prefer Jennifer's obstinate attempts to be bold over the terror consuming this poor female.

Stretching to my full height, I jump and grab the edge of the opening. I just hope Sophia's fears are unfounded.

8

JENNIFER

*S*pace at the edge of the firelight, waiting for Nazhin to return. I never wanted him to be my knight in shining armor, but now that he's out there facing down monsters and rescuing some other damsel in distress, I'm jealous. Not gonna lie.

The moment I hear voices, I bolt in their direction. Above the brush, I see Nazhin with a small, gray Area 51 alien in his arms. Behind him limps a dark-haired woman in a torn red dress. Dirt and blood smudge her perfectly tanned skin and clothes, and she's got one hand hooked into the back waistband of Nazhin's pants.

White-hot jealousy blurs my vision, and I grit my teeth. He's not mine. I shouldn't want him. Yet I can't help the relief flooding my chest. I rush forward.

"You made it! I was getting worried." I force a smile at the woman. "Hi, I'm Jennifer."

"Sophia," she says, coming to a stop so close to Nazhin, her breasts smash against his back.

I loop an arm through hers. "Come meet the others," I say, tugging her away from Nazhin. "We have a nice fire and drinking water."

She looks over her shoulder as we move away. "Thank you so much for coming to my rescue, Nazhin. I don't know how I can ever thank you."

Geez. Can she be more obvious?

"Thank Jennifer," he says, his silvery eyes locked on me. "I wouldn't have discovered you without her."

Sophia returns her attention to me. "Oh, uh, yes. Thank you, too, Jennifer." She leans close to whisper in my ear, "Are you two together?"

My stomach churns. I know I should say no, but I don't want her to think he's up for grabs. "He sort of latched onto me from the moment I boarded the *Romantasy.*"

"Ahhh." She nods and sighs wistfully. "I've heard the Kirenai can be like that when they find a mate."

I squirm with discomfort at the thought. Nazhin isn't my mate. I mean, the kiss we shared was electrifying, but I need more than chemistry in a relationship. I need trust, and he lied to me. Except that regardless of how we got to know each other,

Nazhin has proven to be a damned nice guy. Furtively, I glance over my shoulder and find his gaze locked on me like the Hubble telescope on a starry nebula. Warming shivers ripple through me, settling in places I shouldn't even be thinking about right now. I quickly face front again but can't keep my lips from twisting into a satisfied smile.

We reach the camp, and Erud and Hanzhu hurry over to offer Sophia help—which she accepts with over exuberant gratitude. *Has she no shame?* I swallow back my distaste. For all I know, she could be the last human I ever see, so I need to be gentler with my judgements.

After a round of introductions, we all settle in next to the fire. Nazhin sits next to me, close but not touching, and I'm glad Sophia seems to have decided to focus her attention on Hanzhu for the moment. The unconscious crewman rouses enough to sip water from a leaf cup Hanzhu holds against his lips. Even with the Kirenai propping him up with one arm, the crewman's head wobbles like a POP figurine, and I worry he might topple over at any moment. I prop a piece of firewood behind him to help him stay upright, then stifle a yawn. I don't know how long we've been stranded here, but it feels like days.

But I'm not ready to sleep yet, not when my sisters are still missing. I glance around at our motley group. "How many people were on the shuttle?"

"I counted five females," says Erud.

"What about males?" I ask.

The bushy-haired alien blinks at me. The guy has a one-track mind.

The wobbly crewman, whose name is Ubi, speaks softly. "Counting crew, there were fifteen people on board."

"So that means more than a third of us are already here," I say, trying to sound cheerful. "The pods must not have dropped us too far from each other."

"This is a good place for a camp," says Erud, glancing around the flattened area at the edge of the pool. "I'll start digging shelters."

Sophia shudders. "I prefer not to be stuck in a hole again."

Erud's whiskers droop, and he glances toward the rest of us, as though begging for support.

Hanzhu pipes in, "We can construct shelters out of wood, too."

"I can help with that," Erud says. "My claws are good for many things."

Sophia gives both men an appreciative smile, which makes Erud grin and edge closer to her. Luckily, she doesn't seem to mind.

"What about food?" I ask. Besides how tired I am, my stomach is an empty, gnawing pit.

Ubi pulls a purple orb about the size of an egg from his uniform pocket and holds it out. "I discovered these growing in the forest. Sophia and I have been eating them."

I glance with alarm toward the other woman. "Are you sure they're safe?"

Sophia shrugs. "He says his species can tell if food is nutritious or not. I've eaten several since we crashed, and I'm not dead yet."

Nazhin smirks. "You're lucky he shared. Hage are known for their addiction to food." His smile fades, and he examines Sophia with a critical eye. "But didn't you say your stomach hurts?"

She half shrugs and nods. "Yes, but I think it's just stress. Ubi, your stomach is fine, right?"

"I have no discomfort," the crewman answers. He twists the orb until it splits open, revealing a juicy interior, and offers half to me. "Would you care to try it?"

I reach for it, my mouth already watering, and sniff the fruit's sweet, musky odor. It smells a bit like cantaloupe. I glance at Sophia. She's dirty, scratched, and her eyes look tired, but she's not doubled over or running off to retch in a bush.

"It's probably fine," I say as much to myself as to everyone else and touch my tongue to the juice. It's sugary and mellow, far better than the water I've been drinking, and I quickly slurp out the pulpy inside. My stomach cramps a little, but I think it's because I'm beyond hungry, not because the fruit is poisonous. Just to be safe, though, I shake my head when Ubi offers me the other half. "I better wait to see how my stomach reacts. Let someone else have some."

Erud accepts the challenge and gobbles it up. "I think I saw more of these on the trail here," he says, licking his dirty claws. "Hanzhu and I will go get them."

They leave, and Nazhin stands. "You all should rest. I'll keep watch."

I want to argue that it's still my watch, but my eyes droop and my head spins with exhaustion. *Maybe the food is poisonous after all.* I feel like I'm on a psychedelic camping trip. Or it's just the stress from the day catching up with me. I yawn, my jaw audibly cracking, and lie down. Within moments, sleep overtakes me.

I dream of sitting in my computer chair, lines of code circling around me like the rings of a planet. But each time I try to focus my telescope on a single command, light blinds me like I just tried to point it at the sun. I blink and try again, bouncing from one line of code to the next. With each bounce, the signal gets stronger. My focus gets clearer. Soon I can see... *I can see—*

I wake with a start. *I know how to reach my sisters.* Why didn't I think of that before? I scramble for my phone before I lose the idea in my head. I'll probably have to delete my astronomy data to make this work, but right now, finding my sisters is more important.

"What are you doing?" Nazhin asks from behind me.

"I know how to get a message to my sisters." I get into the backend of my app and start scrolling through its programming. "If I adjust the frequency of my app settings to send radio signals, I can give my phone a longer broadcasting range."

My hip and shoulder ache from where I was laying against the ground, and the fire has died down to coals, so I know I've been asleep awhile even though the ambient light hasn't changed. Worse, my phone battery is down to ten percent, which means my sister's phones are probably just as depleted. I can recharge mine with my power pack, but that won't matter if their phones die before getting my signal. I'm running out of time. "If I can bounce the signal off the ionosphere, it will travel farther."

"But what if they turned off their devices?"

"I used an override code when I installed the app to give me access, and there's always a tiny bit of power feeding the firmware. I can force a notification to pop up even if their phones are turned off. It's similar to how the NSA tracks spies."

Nazhin raises his eyebrows and nods. "You seem well versed in your technology. I run a tech company, and I usually can't keep up with what my development team is doing."

"I studied computer science for a few years," I say without looking up, though my cheeks warm under the compliment. "There isn't much money in astronomy, and I needed a backup to pay the bills."

"Wise. And it seems you're able to combine the two in a unique way. Your employer is lucky to have you."

"It would be nice if I could find a job that let me do that, but it's hard to be taken seriously in this field when you have breasts."

Nazhin raises an eyebrow. "I think your breasts make you even more desirable."

My cheeks feel hot as sun flares right now, and I can't stop from grinning, but I keep working. "Shh. I need to focus right now."

"Of course." Nazhin sits beside me, his muscular shoulder pressed against mine as he watches me work.

I'm a bit self-conscious, feeling clumsy as I try to to program using my thumbs to input the text. Normally, I do this on my computer before transferring it over. But I enjoy having him close, so I don't complain.

I find the lines of code I'm looking for. To implement my plan, I have to delete everything that might require processing power. Once I make the changes, the phone will no longer be able to receive, only broadcast. *Or it won't work at all.*

Hoping I don't royally screw everything up, I edit the commands and reboot my phone.

When I open the new interface, I gulp. All my beautiful astronomy data is gone, replaced by a dark screen with a blinking cursor. My heartbeat feels fragile and fast. If there's a glitch, there's no way for me to know. But, hopefully, my sisters' phones are now displaying a prominent arrow pointing toward my phone.

Mouth dry, I type, *Follow the arrow. Hurry.*

9

NAZHIN

Jennifer lowers her phone to her lap with a sigh. Worry and uncertainty sour her emotions. "I hope I didn't just destroy my app for nothing. I don't even know if they got my message. Being separated from them is killing me."

Concern flares in my chest. "Do human siblings require proximity to remain healthy?"

She gives me a confused look, then laughs. "Killing me is just a saying. I'm not really dying." Then her mirth fades. "But seriously, I really need to do something to take my mind off my sisters."

I can think of several things I'd like to do with her that would help her get her mind off of them, but I don't think she'd appreciate such a suggestion. I'm just glad we seem to be on good terms again. "We can go gather firewood and forage for food together, if you like?"

"That's a good idea." She stands up and brushes dirt off her clothes.

We let the others know we're heading into the forest, then set out. Worried about stumbling into a hole like Sophia and Ubi, Jennifer uses a long branch to prod the matted vegetation ahead of her. I let her lead the way, scratching marks into tree bark to keep track of our route and enjoying the sway of her ass as she walks.

At a patch of brown shelf-like fungi, she pauses and snaps off one the size of her hand. "Can your sensor tell if things are edible?"

"It's designed to detect known toxins and contaminants, but it won't tell us if it's digestible or nutritious. We'll need Ubi for that." I activate my ICC and purse my lips. There's an unfamiliar alert blinking on my screen. "Hold on. I'm receiving a signal."

Jennifer presses against my side to stare at the interface. "You are? From who?"

Then I recognize the text. It's the same string of human symbols Jennifer sent to her sisters. "It's your phone."

"Oh." Her shoulders slump.

I'm not sure if I should, but I put an arm around her and give her a quick squeeze. "No, that's good. It verifies that you're transmitting. Plus, if my unit is receiving it, other passengers with ICC implants might be, too. You might've just found a way to draw everyone here."

She brightens. "I hope you're right."

I grin at her. "I hope so, too."

Looking at the fungus in her hand, she sniffs it, grimaces, and tosses it aside. "Ugh. Don't bother testing that one. It smells like melted tires."

I'm uncertain what melted tires are, but if they smell anything like that specimen, I don't want to eat them, either. We move on, using my ICC to test a dainty yellow mushroom that Jennifer says smells like waffles, some tender stalks and leaves that look promising, and a few things that resemble nuts. My sensor readings say they're not harmful, but that doesn't mean they won't cause gastric distress. We store them in Jennifer's messenger bag to take back to Ubi.

High on a vine circling a nearby tree, I spot more of the purple fruits like Ubi found. I point. "Look."

Jennifer scrunches one eye half shut and follows my gaze. "Do you think you can lift me high enough to get them?"

I could easily stretch myself up and harvest them on my own, but I prefer her suggestion. It means getting to touch her. I kneel on the ground. "Of course. Sit on my shoulders."

Her eyebrows shoot up. "Are you sure? I'm not exactly a waif."

"Nonsense. You can't possibly weigh more than your equipment."

A flush infuses her cheeks. "I'm not so sure about that."

"I am." I bow down. "Get on."

"Fine. But don't say I didn't warn you." Settling her messenger bag's strap across her chest, she climbs onto my shoulders, positioning herself with my head between her legs.

Kuzara. I feel as if I've been drugged as her sweet scent surrounds me. All I can think about is spinning her around and burying my face between her thighs. Tasting her sweet center. Making her moan with pleasure…

I tamp down on my impulsive desires as I slide both hands up the front of her thighs and rise. I can sense she's focused on our task, and I don't think she'd welcome my overtures just now. The back of my neck tingles as her center settles against my skin. She's warm, even through her shorts, and the skin on her legs is softer than I imagined. My cock rises to full attention inside my pants—luckily, she's not in a position to notice.

When I'm fully upright, Jennifer sways, both hands gripping my forehead. "Oh, God." She laughs, the sound both nervous and joyful. "Don't drop me."

"Of course not." I grin and move close to the vine, hands still on her knees. "Can you reach them now?"

"Yes. Hold still." She stretches up and plucks the purple orbs from the vine, adding them to the collection in her bag. Her breasts are soft against the back of my head, and I wrap my hands more firmly over the tops of her legs. My fingers slide higher on her legs, almost of their own accord, until my fingertips are beneath the cuffs of her shorts near the apex of her thighs.

She flexes slightly and stops moving. I reach my fingers higher, and the heat on the back of my neck increases. She still grips my forehead with one hand, and I can sense her breathing becoming more shallow. My *Iki'i* feels slightly drunk on her surge of desire.

"I think…" Her voice is husky, and she clears her throat before continuing. "I think you can let me down now."

My nostrils flare. I don't want to let her go, yet I can't keep her on my shoulders forever. Lowering myself to one knee, I set her feet o the ground and duck out from under her. But when I rise again, I can't force myself to back away. I'm so close, my chest brushes against her shoulder blades.

She remains frozen in place, her breathing still shallow as she clutches the strap of her bag. A small shudder ripples through her, but she doesn't turn around or move away. Encouraged, I lower my face to inhale the fragrance of her hair. "You smell amazing."

She slowly removes the bag's strap from around her neck, then turns to face me, close enough for our breaths to mingle as she looks up into my face. Her attention drifts down my chest to the obvious swelling in my pants. A soft sigh escapes her, and she licks her lips, staring at my crotch.

Kuzara, I want her to touch me.

She takes a step backward, and my heart constricts, certain she's withdrawing. Her back hits the tree trunk, and she looks into my eyes. Her face is flushed, and she licks her lips. Then, ever so slowly, she reaches out and curls her fingers into the waistband of my pants, tugging me forward.

I need no more encouragement. In a single stride, I'm pressed against her body, drawing her against me for a kiss.

10

JENNIFER

I want Nazhin. I want him like I've never wanted a man before. Perhaps it's the stress of our situation. Of not knowing if we'll live or die on this alien planet. But from the moment we first met, he's been fun and supportive, and every time we touch, I can barely think past the hormones flooding my system. If the bulge in his pants is any indication, he feels the same way.

In a single step, he's pressed against me, one hand behind my head, the other around my waist, pulling me against him. His arms are like a fortress around me, protecting me from this scary alien world.

I tilt my head back and open my mouth to his probing tongue, wrapping both hands around his ribs as he plunders my mouth. Every stroke between my lips and teeth sends jolts of growing lust through me and I moan. He's Kirenai, a species rumored to be the best lovers in the galaxy, and this kiss is so much more potent than I ever imagined a kiss could be.

In the back of my mind, a little voice is telling me I'm crazy. I shouldn't be doing this. Shouldn't be letting another man get close to me. But I can't stop. Nazhin feels right, despite our rocky introduction. And I'm sick of always over-thinking every decision. It's time we act on our mutual attraction.

He tastes like ambrosia, and I can't seem to get enough. I run my hands over the solid muscles of his back and ribs, losing myself to the headiness of the kiss. The handful of guys I've been with tended to be thin, more brain than brawn. Nazhin is a bodice-ripper's dream—not only clever, but tall and strong. A guy any woman would swoon over.

My head is swimming as his tongue leaves my mouth to lick down my neck and settle against the hollow of my throat. He swirls it there, pressing me back against the solid trunk of the tree while his cock throbs against my belly. The hand around my waist slides up my ribs, lifting my shirt. With one big thumb, he snags the bottom of my bra, pulling upward until my breasts are free. I lift my arms over my head as he strips off my clothing. The heat of his palm cups my breast, sending shivers of pleasure through my chest and abdomen. Falling to his knees as if in worship, he latches onto an exposed nipple, sucking and teasing until my back arches. I'm on the edge of coming already, and we've barely begun.

"Nazhin!" I gasp as I grip his shoulders, holding myself up while sparks course through me from his touch. The bark of the tree is rough against my shoulder blades as I writhe, and he moves to my other nipple, sucking it into a hard point to match the first.

His hand slides down my belly and flicks open the waistband of my shorts. As his fingers delve into the top of my panties, I tilt my hips toward him, eager for more. He cups my pussy, and I can feel my arousal slicking his fingers. With a final tease of my nipple, he drops to his knees, tugging my shorts down to my ankles. The fingers cupping my pussy slip between my folds, pressing against my innermost folds, and I gasp. Leaning forward to press his face between my legs, he slides a long finger deep inside me while his tongue flicks against my clit.

I'm not usually into oral sex, but this is mind-blowing. My legs tremble, and I grip the back of his bald head for support while his tongue laps my clit, finger working in and out of my wet center. My blood is on fire, my skin hot as he works me toward the edge of release with a talented, twisting motion I can't even begin to describe.

A tidal wave of pleasure fills my center, and I open my mouth on a silent wail, thrusting my hips against him. Pleasure rolls through me in a cascade that leaves me panting.

He continues stroking me until my legs threaten to give out completely, then he rises and sweeps me onto my back among the fallen leaves at the base of the tree. I think he's going to mount me and take his own pleasure, and I'm ready for it. Ready to feel his weight on me and the driving force of his hips against mine. Instead, he lifts my calves to his shoulders and puts his head between my legs again. His breath cools my hot, wet pussy, and I squirm.

"Nazhin, I want you," I whisper.

"Not yet." He crawls up my body and lies beside me, sliding one arm under my neck as a pillow.

I'm aching for more, but he simply gazes at me with his silvery eyes, a smile on his lips. He's making no move to finish what he started.

What's going on? Does he need me to do something? I reach over and try to pull him on top of me. "You can have me, too. I'm ready."

He shakes his head and cups my cheek. "You're too tempting. I'm afraid I'd claim you."

I know what he means—I've read all the literature about Kirenai mate bonds. But at this moment, I'm so drunk on sex, I'm not sure I care if he claims me. And the fact that he respects me enough to stop himself makes me want him even more.

Not this time, I tell myself. I'm not ready to be bound to him. Not yet. Still, I'm dying to see what his pants are hiding. I also don't want to leave him hanging and frustrated. Rolling toward him, I reach for his fly.

His eyes widen, and he remains perfectly still as I open it and reach inside. He doesn't appear to be wearing underwear, and I look down, my eyes going wide at the sight of his shaft. It's heavy in my hand, long and thick and slightly curved with ridges from base to crown, and the tip is slick with pre-cum.

I wrap my fingers around him and press my thumb over the slit at the top, circling the slippery head. He lets out a shuddering breath, and I glance up to see his eyes closed. He's so sexy, all pent-up sexual energy. I watch his face as I stroke him, sliding along his shaft, increasing my speed as his hips thrust in time to my rhythm.

He flings out a hand and grips my hip, back arching, and I squeeze harder, pumping up and down until he grunts and jerks against me. A stream of milky fluid jets out of him, coating my stomach and thighs. When he stops jerking, he pulls me close, pressing his forehead to mine. "Thank you, my *bareshi.*"

"It's the least I could do." I softly brush his lips with mine. "What's a bareshi?"

"It means brilliant one." He pulls me close, so I'm lying on his chest, his arms a warm cage around me. I've never been given a pet name before, and it gives me a warm glow. I'm not sure I've ever felt more content, despite being stranded in the wilds of an alien planet.

I have the feeling if we're stranded here much longer, I may just let Nazhin claim me after all.

11

NAZHIN

My body is sated, but my mating urge remains strong as I cradle Jennifer against me. Her scent lingers around me, and I can still taste her on my tongue. Before too long, my cock hardens again, and though I'm reluctant to break away, I know I must. My mating shaft burns with the need to claim her, and I'm not sure how restrained I can be if we stay naked together.

We get dressed and trace our way back to camp. Sophia is napping while Erud and Hanzhu are out gathering more wood. Ubi is carefully folding more leaves into cups near the fire. "I'll have to try them one at a time," he says, sniffing the leaves and setting them aside. "Just to be certain there aren't delayed complications during the digestion process."

"Of course."

"Try this one first," says Jennifer, holding out the yellow mushroom. "It smells good."

He nods, sniffs it, then takes a minuscule nibble, his mouth puckered into a frown as he chews. "This needs to be cooked to make it edible."

We build up the fire, and Ubi skewers the mushroom on a stick, holding it over the flames.

I twist open a purple fruit and hand it to Jennifer, then open one for myself.

"Thanks." She sucks out the juice and makes a face. "Oh, I think this one isn't ripe or something. It's bitter."

I taste mine. It's sweet with a lingering, almost sap-like flavor, but I'm fairly certain it's ripe. I hand her the other half. "Here, this one's okay."

We eat several as the mushroom sizzles. As it cooks, a rich, savory scent fills the air. Jennifer groans. "Damn, that smells amazing."

I set another unripe purple fruit aside and eye our dwindling pile. "I hope it's worth gathering. At this rate, I don't think these will last as long as we hoped."

Ubi pulls the mushroom off the fire and nibbles one edge. "Mmm." He gulps down the whole thing, chewing with relish. "That's good."

Jennifer stares at him enviously. "So it's edible?"

The Hage smacks his lips. "I need time to digest before I know if it'll cause gastric issues."

Her impatience beats against my *Iki'i* like a drum. "How long will that take?"

"I can't say for sure."

She sighs and nods, then flops onto her back to stare upward. "I wish I could see the sky. I don't think there's been a shift between day and night since we arrived."

I lay on my back on the carpet of fallen leaves next to her, close but not touching. Both my cocks are throbbing with need, and I'm wondering if it was a mistake to let myself go as far as we did earlier. All I can think about is her smell and her softness, and it's taking everything I have to keep myself from rolling over on top of her.

Instead, I focus on science and facts. Things Jennifer will be interested in. "The trees on this planet are well over sixteen-hundred of your Earth meters tall. I don't believe sunlight ever reaches the surface."

"Seriously? Mile-high trees?" She sits up and stares at me. "So there's more than just the ionosphere interfering with sensors. There's a bio-mat between us and any rescue crew searching for us?"

I nod, and she lays down again.

"Well, shit," she says softly, hopelessness falling like rain against my *Iki'i*. I don't like her feeling this way, but it's probably best she accepts our fate. I just hope our earlier intimacy is a sign she'll eventually accept me as part of her future.

Hanzhu and Sophia join us at the fire. They sort through the remaining purple fruits, while Ubi retires to a pile of leaves to rest. I let my eyes drift closed.

When I wake, Jennifer's back is against me. From her even breathing, I can tell she's asleep, but she's shivering slightly. I roll over and spoon my body against hers, draping an arm over her hip. Her shivering eases and she sighs. But her nearness makes my groin ache, and soon my cock feels like a fiery rod pressed against the softness of her backside.

She stretches, wiggling her ass slightly, and I can't restrain the groan that rolls from my throat.

Ubi clears his throat from across the fire, and Jennifer sits bolt upright, scooting away with an adorable pink flush staining her cheeks.

"The mushroom appears to be an excellent source of protein," Ubi says, rubbing his belly.

"Oh, good. I don't think those purple fruits agree with me," says Sophia from where she's lounging against a sizeable piece of firewood. Hanzhu and Erud are busy lashing together long poles to form a shelter. Sophia bats her eyes at me. "Can you bring me back some?"

Jennifer rolls her eyes, and I can sense her distaste for the woman against my *Iki'i*. "We'll bring back some, then everyone will know what to look for when they're out gathering food."

She puts a subtle emphasis on *everyone.* "Why don't you fold more leaves and boil water while we're gone, Sophia?"

"The leaves make the water taste funny." Sophia sighs and sits up, reaching for the stack of leaves we gathered to fold into cups.

"Well, you're welcome to drink straight from the pond if you prefer," says Jennifer flippantly. She picks up her messenger bag and heads back into the forest.

I follow along behind, glad I marked the trees along the way. Over time, our trails will probably become more apparent, but right now, the brush is still high and it would be easy to get lost. When we reach the mushroom patch, I bend down to pluck the largest one I see.

Jennifer shakes her head and presses the top of the cap. "Not that one. It's gone soft." The indent of her finger remains in the golden brown cap. "See?"

Tossing it aside, I pluck a smaller one. It feels nice and firm. "How about this?"

"Perfect." She puts it into her bag. "We need to be selective in our harvest, though. If these are like Earth mushrooms, we need to leave about half of them to reproduce." She touches several caps before selecting a few and placing them into her messenger bag.

Thinking it might be best if I let her do the picking, I stand and survey the surrounding forest. After all, the creature that attacked Sophia may still be around, and I don't want to be caught unaware. "How do you know so much about fungus?" I ask. "I thought you were only interested in the stars."

One side of her lip curls in distaste. "Arthur liked to hunt for edible fungi. He was always looking at the ground." She huffs, and I feel a jab of her self-recrimination against my *Iki'i* as she mutters. "I was so stupid not to see it then."

"What do you mean?" I ask, not liking this turn in her emotions.

She shrugs. "He was an astronomy major who never looked at the stars. I should've guessed he was after my research all along."

My hands curl into fists at my sides. *How dare someone steal from her?* "Who is this *Arthur*?"

"Ex-boyfriend. Ex-lab partner. Ex-everything." She shoves a cap into her bag with more force than necessary. "He's the reason I have to gather data on this trip." Her self-loathing is like a noxious cloud against my *Iki'i*.

Although I'm glad to hear he's out of her life, I want to pound the guy into the dirt. I'm snapped from my thoughts of retribution, however, by the sound of rustling brush.

"Something's coming." I signal Jennifer to remain still. Her eyes widen, and she picks up a long stick before pressing her back against the tree. She's frightened, but not in a panicky way, which I appreciate. I lengthen my matrix to peer over the brush toward the sound.

A group of furry beings on four legs lope in our direction. And they all appear to be armed with knives.

JENNIFER

I grip my stick and prepare to swing as a pack of furry creatures bursts from the brush, chittering and purring. They quickly surround us, staying just out of range. Nazhin stands in front of me, muscles bunched for action, but there's no way he can fend off this many adversaries, even if I help. At first I think we're being attacked by a pack of human-sized weasels with beady eyes and sleek purplish fur. But then they rise to their hind legs, and I see they're wearing belts or harnesses. Their paws appear to have six digits instead of five, and some of them hold crude knives. *Sentient, then.* And aggressive. Even more disturbing, each of the creatures has an erect pink phallus jutting from between his bandy legs.

I shrink back against the rough tree bark. What the hell do they want? I feel like I'm in an episode of Alice in Wonderland on roofies.

Then a familiar voice calls, "Jennifer!"

My heart almost leaps from my chest. I know that voice. "Tamara?" I lean around Nazhin's broad frame to search for her.

My twin sister pushes between the weasel-men, her copper-colored hair tousled and her freckled face flushed. Her clothes are dirty but undamaged, and a few steps behind her is the large-eyed Kirenai pilot from the shuttle. Tears blur my vision as Tamara yanks me into a tight hug.

I squeeze my eyes shut and clutch my sister tightly. The relief singing through my veins makes me tremble. "I'm so glad you found us," I choke out through a sob.

"I got your message." One arm still around me, she draws her phone from her pocket. The screen is dark except for a small green X in the center that signifies she's reached her target: me.

I release my hold on her and take the device in both hands, zooming out and searching for any sign of an arrow pointing toward Suzanne. All I see is my own green marker. "Have you seen Suzanne? She should've gotten the notice, too."

"No. You're the first people from the shuttle Tazhio and I have found." Tamara pushes the phone down, forcing me to look at her. "Listen. I have to tell you something."

"What?" I ask, recognizing the sincerity in her gray eyes. She tends to be over-anxious, but I sense in this case her worry might be valid.

"There's a parasite on this planet that lays eggs in fertile females," Tamara says. "When the eggs hatch, the spawn eats the host from the inside out. You and all the women from the shuttle are in danger."

Alarm spikes through me. "How do you know this?"

She waves a hand toward the weasel beings still surrounding us. "These, uh, people—they call themselves Sheeghr—"

The word sends a buzzing purr through the group, and the Sheeghr wiggle their hips, their pink boners wagging like flagpoles in a parade. I'd be more alarmed if they seemed interested in me, but all their attention seems focused on Nazhin, who's stripped out of his shirt and is sliding his pants down his perfectly rounded ass. And now that I can see Tamara's pilot friend from the waist down, I realize he's also naked as a jay bird.

"Nazhin, what are you doing?" I gape at the two Kirenai.

Tamara shakes me, trying to draw my attention back to her. "It's a status thing. Now listen!"

But I can't stop looking at Nazhin as he puts his hands on his hips and widens his stance, mimicking the postures of the weasel men. His back looks solid as a marble statue, every naked angle and plane of muscle in full definition. The Sheeghr all have hard-ons—does that mean Nazhin's hard, too? From my angle, I can't tell. I gulp, recalling his massive erection in my hand, and force my gaze to swing back to my sister.

"The Sheeghr say the only way to protect yourself is to get pregnant," Tamara continues, completely blasé about the naked aliens all around us.

I blink, trying to decide if I heard her correctly. "I'm sorry, what?"

"Yeah, I know. Crazy. But you need to get pregnant as soon as possible." She cuts a glance toward Nazhin and then leans next to my ear. "Tazhio and I are mated now, so he's off the menu, but maybe your porter can help?"

"He's not a porter," I grumble. Then my attention drops to where she holds a hand flat against her belly. "Wait, did you say mated?"

"And pregnant, yes." She nods and then shrugs.

I frown, concern forming a lump in my stomach. My twin has always been a nurturer, and I knew she was bound to have kids someday, but not like this. And how the hell does she know she's pregnant? It's not like she ran to the store to buy a pregnancy test.

"Tamara, you can't possibly be pregnant that fast. You just met him." My sister isn't dumb, but I've seen how determined these aliens can be when seeking a mate. And I've never seen her crush on anyone as hard as she did the pilot. But we've only been on this planet, what, a day? Two? She knows better than to jump into something as permanent as a mate bond after such a brief interval. Frustration swells inside me, and I glare at the pilot's bare backside. "Are you sure he didn't trick you into this?"

"Of course he didn't! I was the one pursuing him, remember? And I am pregnant. I know it seems unbelievable, but the Sheeghr can sense it. It's part of their survival instincts to ward off the parasite." She grimaces. "If you don't get pregnant, too, the Sheeghr will try to, um, help you out. They offered to have an orgy with me before Tazhio and I were mated."

I look around at the jutting pink penises, my doubts suddenly turning to fear. We're on an alien planet, and I have to accept that the rules are probably different from what I'm used to. "Is that what they're doing now?" I nearly choke on the words as a nearby Sheeghr grins at me, baring a mouthful of blunt purple teeth as he chitters. "Are they offering to fuck me?"

Tamara rubs the back of her neck. "Sort of, yes. But they allow you to choose your partner. They're matriarchal and respect females."

"They don't look like they respect me. They look like they want to jump my bones."

Nazhin turns around, and my insides do a flip-flop. The head of his upright shaft touches the second row of his eight-pack. *Oh, God.* My legs feel wobbly, and a fresh flood of warmth rushes between my thighs. This is possibly the worst moment in history to feel turned on, but I can't look away.

"It seems you don't need to worry," he says, his expression unreadable. "The Sheeghr say you're already pregnant."

I stumble back a step—literally stumble. *What's he talking about?* "Impossible. I haven't had sex with anyone in months." I also have a dermal implant that should be good for another year. My focus is on my thesis and my career, not popping out babies; I'm very careful when it comes to sex.

But then I remember the copious amount of cum Nazhin jetted over my belly not too long ago. I'd read that Kirenai and humans were extremely compatible for reproduction, but…

My mouth falls open and I stare at him, worry flooding through me. "Just jizzing on me couldn't have gotten me pregnant, could it?"

His eyes narrow. "Of course not. But you said you had a boyfriend on Earth."

I frown and shake my head. "I know for certain Arthur didn't get me pregnant."

Tamara clamps my arm in a death grip. Her eyes are filled with terror like I've never seen before. "Have you encountered a flying creature while on this planet?"

"No, I—"

Tazhio wraps a protective arm around Tamara and attempts to pull her away from me. "If there's a chance she's infected," he mutters, "we have to leave her."

My sister shrugs him off, scowling. "I'm not leaving her. Besides, she said she hasn't met a flying creature."

Nazhin comes to my side, arms akimbo, as if he's ready for trouble. Tazhio stares at me, keeping his arm around Tamara. For the first time, I realize she doesn't have her emotional support dog, Beanie, with her. Concern fills my heart, and I glance around just to be sure, but there's no sign of the tiny chihuahua.

She shrugs off Tazhio's arm and glowers at him. I have to admit, I'm impressed—my once-timid sister seems to have grown some balls since we landed on this planet.

"Are you taking birth control?"

"I still have my implant, yes."

Tamara nods thoughtfully. "I wonder if that makes you immune to the parasite."

I almost sag with relief. "That makes sense."

Tazhio is eyeing me warily. "What is this implant?"

"I have an implant that suppresses ovulation, basically making me infertile."

"I bet it keeps the parasite from being attracted to her," adds Tamara.

I nod, hoping my sister is right.

"Is birth control common among humans?" Nazhin asks.

I half shrug. "Considering we were on a singles cruise and nobody wants to get knocked up on a first date, I'd say it's highly likely most of the women are on some form of birth control."

"That's good news." Tazhio's shoulders relax. "It gives us time to locate the others."

I pick up my messenger bag, hoping the mushrooms inside are still in decent shape. "We've set up a camp not too far from here. There are four other passengers already there."

"Wait." Nazhin takes my arm, stopping me from walking away. He looks at Tazhio. "Describe this parasite."

"I haven't seen one, but the Sheeghr say it's big, at least the same size they are. It lives in the canopy and flies down in search of females when it's ready to lay its eggs."

My heart stops beating for a moment. Nazhin's grip on my arm tightens. I can barely force the words out of my constricted throat. "That sounds like the thing that attacked Sophia."

13

NAZHIN

"How can we purge someone of the parasite eggs?" I ask, glancing at the pack of Sheeghr surrounding us. There are too many to count, and it doesn't help that they seem to be in constant motion. I'm relieved Jennifer won't attract the parasite, at least for the time being. Much as I yearn for her to bear my child, her career is important to her, and if we ever get off this planet, I want her to be able to pursue her dreams.

Tazhio shakes his head slowly, his wariness reflecting off my *Iki'i*. "I don't know. The Sheeghr were ready to kill Tamara if she didn't get pregnant."

Jennifer grimaces and grabs my arm. "We can't lead them to Sophia."

I nod and look toward camp. "But if she's going to explode with hungry parasite spawn, the others in camp are in danger.

Someone needs to warn them."

"The problem is, we can't seem to lose our friends here," Tamara says, gesturing toward the milling Sheeghr. "Tazhio and I tried when we left their cave, but they insist on tagging along. I think they're curious about us."

Just then, a feral howl echoes through the woods. Everyone startles, and Jennifer steps closer to me. I'm pleased she unconsciously thinks of me as her protector. "What was that?" she asks.

The Sheeghr's chatter turns to low growls. My universal translator has been identifying a few words, but now there are too many voices at once, and I can't catch any of it. A mix of protective anxiety rakes across my *Iki'i* just before every Sheeghr around us takes off on all fours.

My gut churns. They're headed toward our camp.

A woman screams in the distance.

"Shit! They must've found Sophia." Jennifer takes off through the bushes toward camp.

I'd rather she was moving in the opposite direction if there are parasites around, but she's obviously determined to protect Sophia, so I race after her. My longer strides quickly catch up, and we burst into the clearing around the pool together. Sheeghr seem to be everywhere I look, and the morass of emotions filling the area nearly blinds me. I quickly shield my *Iki'i*.

Next to the fire, Hanzhu slumps sideways to the ground as if in a dead faint. Erud and Ubi are already sprawled motionless. Sophia screams and struggles while several Sheeghr bind her to a long pole.

"Stop!" Jennifer shouts, dodging through the crowd toward the other woman.

My heart thunders against my ribs, and I plow forward, ready to kill anyone who tries to harm her.

She tries to shove the Sheeghr holding Sophia aside. "Let her go!"

One of the furry beings twists and pounces on her, driving Jennifer to the ground.

Oh, hell no. Rage fuels my steps as I move forward.

The Sheeghr scatter out of my way, chittering angrily. Something small and hard thunks against my bare chest, followed by another against my thigh. Two Sheeghr near the edge of the clearing are wielding slingshots. They each fire again, hurling prickly yellow objects that barely sting, even without me taking time to harden my matrix.

Jennifer screams, trying to push the Sheeghr off her.

I dismiss the pitiful missiles and grab the being who has her pinned, easily tossing him aside. More missiles bounce off my flank as I help Jennifer to her feet. They're annoying, making my skin tingle, so I take a moment to harden my matrix, then use my body as a shield to keep any of the missiles from hitting her.

The Sheeghr now have Sophia bound to a pole. They hoist her between them, obviously intending to carry her away.

"Stop them!" Jennifer yells.

We're vastly outnumbered, but I try to do as Jennifer asks and reach for the nearest Sheeghr.

My leg gives out, collapsing me to one knee. I can't feel my foot. A strange sort of numbness creeps through my body, and I try to rise, but can't. I can no longer lift my arms. My head dips and lolls against my shoulder, and slowly, helplessly, I topple forward to the ground.

Kuzara. What is happening to me? This is bad. Very bad. Several prickly yellow balls that look like burrs or gigantic pollen granules lay on the ground in front of my unblinking eyes. *The missiles.* Their barbs must be coated with some sort of poison. No wonder they didn't hurt much. Their damage is much more insidious.

What if one hits Jennifer? I need to protect her, but I can't move. The scuffling sounds of battle continue around me. My matrix is almost completely numb, threatening to devolve into my resting state. I can't let that happen, or I'll be as helpless and vulnerable as an infant. I could even die. Forced to direct all my effort into maintaining my human form, I can only listen while Sophia's screams fade into the distance.

Hands roll me onto my back, and Jennifer's worried eyes peer into mine. "Nazhin? Oh, God. What's happening? Are you injured?"

I can't answer. My mouth won't form words. I can't even blink. In my peripheral vision, I watch her hands glide over me, but I can't feel them.

"Don't touch those yellow prickly things," Tazhio says, somewhere behind her. "They'll paralyze you."

Now he tells us? I wish I could grit my teeth. When I recover from this, that cocky pilot is going to get a piece of my mind.

Jennifer looks frantically around us and picks up a huge leaf. She uses it to brush at the missiles still stuck to my skin. Then she puts a palm against my chest, looking at me with pinched brows. I can feel her concern squeezing my *Iki'i*. It's a comfort to know she cares.

Tazhio appears at the edge of my line of sight, looking down at me.

"Will he be okay?" Jennifer's voice trembles as she glances over her shoulder at him.

"I recovered fairly quickly the first time I was hit," he says with a shrug. "But I only took one missile before I shielded myself. He was hit by a lot of them." He radiates slight concern, and I find myself relieved. If he's not worried, perhaps I shouldn't be, either.

Jennifer sits down and cradles my head in her lap. "Don't you dare die on me, Nazhin." Her worry is still strong, but she smiles tremulously. "I was just beginning to like you."

Kuzara, I wish I could smile back.

14

JENNIFER

I remain close to Nazhin while he recovers, relieved when he finally blinks in response to my murmured assurances. I'm more relieved than I like to admit that he's not dead. The emptiness that invaded my chest when I saw his unblinking eyes is a feeling I never want to experience again.

Hanzhu, Ubi, and Erud are already up and moving, and Erud insists we need to go in search of Sophia immediately.

Tazhio shakes his head. "There's nothing we can do for her if we find her. We don't have any medical equipment to remove the parasite eggs."

"But why did they capture her instead of kill her on the spot?" Ubi asks.

"I'm guessing they'll do something with her body to be sure the eggs can't emerge." Tazhio grimaces and closes his eyes tightly. "I'm sorry I got us into this."

Tamara puts an arm around his waist and leans close. "It's not your fault, remember?"

I shudder. I wasn't Sophia's biggest fan, but I don't wish her ill. Hopefully, the fate the Sheeghr deal her is swift. My heart is heavy as I curl up next to Nazhin for a much-needed rest.

I'm half dozing when I hear a familiar barking somewhere in the forest. Sitting bolt upright, I spot Tamara already on her feet, peering between the trees.

"Beanie, come!" she cries.

I glance down at Nazhin. He's still naked from our encounter with the Sheeghr, and I can't help letting my gaze flick toward his well-endowed crotch before focusing on his face again. He smiles at me, and a flush rises to my face while relief also fills my chest. "Hey there. Feeling any better?"

"Yes." His voice is brittle as he struggles to sit up.

I move to help him, but he squeezes my hand and says, "Just hand me my clothes, please. Then you can go see if they need help."

While handing him his clothes, I lean over and give him a kiss. "I'm so glad you're okay."

"Me too." He smiles, though his expression seems weary.

I rise to join my sister, who continues calling for her dog.

In a few minutes, a tiny chihuahua bursts from the bushes, barking and wiggling. He's a bit scruffy, and there's a bare patch of skin on his rear leg, but overall, he looks remarkably well.

Tamara scoops him into her arms and sobs while he covers her face with tiny pink kisses. "Oh, Beanie, you found me. What happened to you?"

Then another voice among the trees calls, "Hello? Tamara?"

My breath hitches. I'd recognize the voice of my older sister anywhere. Both Tamara and I shout, "Suzanne!"

A moment later, Suzanne appears between the trunks, her red-gold hair a tousled mane around her face. Kiozhi, the Kirenai who sat with us on the shuttle, is leaning on her shoulders, apparently having trouble keeping his balance. The pastel scarf Suzanne originally wore around her head is wrapped around her free arm and spotted with blood, but aside from that, she looks okay.

I rush forward, throwing my arms around her. "I knew you'd find us!"

Tamara joins the embrace, squishing Beanie between us. The little dog wriggles out of her arms and runs over to Kiozhi, now sitting among the leaves. Beanie climbs onto his lap.

"Is he all right?" asks Tamara. I'm not sure if she's asking about Kiozhi or her dog. She looks like she might be a little jealous that Beanie left her to go to someone else.

"I'll be fine," answers Kiozhi, petting Beanie's small head. The chihuahua pants, mouth slightly parted in a doggy smile. "But if you see a tall plant with what looks like gold berries on it, stay far away."

"Good to know," I say, and turn back to Suzanne. My relief at finding my sister is turning quickly to excitement to get the beacon up and running. Now that we've found each other, we can focus on getting rescued. "Where's your phone?"

"Seriously, Jennifer? Is your astronomy project all you think about? You have such a one-track mind." Suzanne crosses her arms and glowers at me.

"This isn't about my project." I scowl. "I'm making a rescue beacon."

"That can wait a few minutes," Tamara says, glaring at me before she turns back to Suzanne. "Have you encountered any monsters? Flying monsters, specifically?"

I grimace, realizing the one-track mind comment was on point. Getting off the planet is of prime importance, but if the parasite has infected Suzanne, we need to deal with that first.

Suzanne's eyes get wide. "Oh, God, are there flying monsters on this planet, too? I thought the gargantuan centipede thing was horrible enough."

"So, no flying creatures?" I ask.

"No, nothing like that."

"Oh, thank God." Tamara wraps her in another hug.

I'm glad to hear she's not in immediate danger, and give her a quick squeeze before repeating, "So… about your phone?"

Suzanne shoves her purse toward me. "In there. But I think it's dead."

I pull out her phone. As she thought, it's dead, but my power pack has enough juice left to bring it back.

We return to the fire, and Erud fluffs a stack of leaves next to him, grinning hopefully at Suzanne. Kiozhi glares daggers at him, and Erud's whiskers droop with disappointment. I'm starting to feel sorry for the guy. Hanzhu and Ubi take the hint that Suzanne must be spoken for and politely but distantly offer food and water.

While Tamara explains about the parasite, I move away and sit next to Nazhin, laying all three phones out in front of me. I dig my power pack from my purse and plug in Suzanne's and my phones. Tamara's battery still has a decent charge, so I tap the app on the display to open it.

"Can I help?" asks Nazhin.

I give him a wary glance. Arthur seldom offered to help, and I'm used to doing things on my own.

He's not Arthur, I remind myself. The feeling that thought invokes is good and warm and makes me want to smile. "That would be great." I get my spectrometer from my bag and hand it to him, glad I grabbed it from my equipment case when we first boarded the shuttle. "I'm going to try to increase our broadcast frequency. Watch the meter and tell me when it approaches three megahertz."

He accepts the device. "I don't think that'll be enough to both penetrate the canopy and get through the ionosphere to orbit."

I frown, knowing he's probably right. But I don't think I can boost the signal above three. I look toward the darkness overhead. "What if we climb one of these trees so the beacon doesn't have to go through the biomass? We can tie vines together for rope, figure out something to use as carabiners, and…"

I taper off, realizing I don't even know what all we'll need. Climbing a humongous alien tree is probably a lot different from using a climbing wall, which I've only done a few times as it is.

Nazhin lifts his chin, regarding the dark canopy overhead. "A Khargal could simply fly up."

I don't recall seeing any of the gargoyle-like aliens on board the shuttle, but I was focused on my telescope, not the other passengers. Then I realize Nazhin might be saying he can do it. Kirenai are shapeshifters, after all. "Is that something you can change into?" I ask hopefully.

He nods slowly. "I can, but assuming a form and using its attributes are two different things. I've never flown before."

I chew my bottom lip. He's also probably still weak from being paralyzed. And flying a mile up into the trees is bound to be a lot of work. My gaze shifts to the other three Kirenai shapeshifters now sitting near the fire. "Do you think any of them could do it?"

From the corner of my eye, I see his hands ball into fists on his thighs. "I suppose if one of them has experience flying, they would be a more logical choice."

I sense he wants to be my hero, which I appreciate, but there's more at stake here than his pride. Standing, I approach the group at the fire. The mood is tense, and both my sisters' eyes are red, as if they're holding back tears. I assume they've been talking about Sophia's demise, which makes my eyes prick with tears, too.

I quickly shove my sorrow aside. I can't save Sophia, but there is still a chance for the rest of us. "Everyone, I may have a way to set up a rescue beacon, but we need to position it as high above the canopy as we can." I look between Tazhio, Kiozhi, and Hanzhu. "Do any of you have experience flying?"

"Sure," Tazhio's mouth quirks into an amused grin. "I've been around the galaxy a few times."

"No, I mean physically," I clarify as Tamara punches his arm playfully. "Like as a Khargal."

They all shake their heads no, but Kiozhi offers, "But I'll try if it means a chance for Suzanne to escape this planet."

I feel Nazhin at my back before I hear him. "I'll go."

I turn to face him, my eyes widening as I take in the massive, bat-like wings spread behind him, each tipped with a sharp claw. He has seven small horns like a crown around his bald blue head, and his fingers and toes now end in hooked claws as well. But his eyes are the same, a silvery hue that makes me think of light reflecting off twin moons. *Vin Diesel with wings.* Badass, clawed bat wings that send a delightful shiver down my spine. Who knew wings could turn me on?

"I'll practice flying while you work on the beacon," he says. He flaps his wings once, lifting slightly off the ground, a long tail twitching behind him. His pants are off again, but he's done something with his shapeshifting to make it look like he's wearing a Speedo. He actually pulls off the look, and I catch Suzanne giving me a knowing wink.

"Okay." I nod at him, trying not to look like a drooling idiot as I return to where the phones are charging. I sit down and pick up Tamara's phone again, but it's hard to concentrate on coding when Nazhin's swooping about the clearing and the other Kirenai are shouting advice.

Finally, I think I have the settings right, and look up to realize Nazhin has stopped his practice. He's with the others near the fire. Tamara and Suzanne have their heads together, and it looks like they may be arguing, but I don't have time for sisterly squabbles right now. The longer we wait, the less battery power the phones will have, so we need to get going.

I place all my equipment in my messenger bag and stand. "I'm ready whenever you are."

Nazhin rises and strides over to me, holding out one clawed hand. "What do I need to do?"

I stare in confusion at his outstretched hand before looking back at his face. "Take me above the tree line."

A worried look flashes over his face. "You? I thought I was taking the beacon."

I bite my lip. I guess I hadn't been completely clear about my plan. What if he's not strong enough to carry me? "I have to go with it. I need a reading of the ionosphere to calibrate the transmission frequency."

"I can handle calibrations." He straightens his shoulders. "I do own the biggest sensor manufacturer in the galaxy, after all."

Pursing my lips, I raise one eyebrow. "That may be so, but I'm pretty sure none of your products are programmed in English."

His smirk disappears. "*Kuzara.*" Tilting his head, he gazes upward. "Carrying you… That's a long way to fall if something goes wrong."

My stomach flip-flops. I've been so focused on getting the app working, I never took time to consider the perils involved with flying. But this is the only option I can see to save us. I put one hand on his arm. "I trust you not to drop me."

15

JENNIFER

I hug my sisters one last time and promise to be back soon, then step into the harness we created out of vines to bind me against Nazhin's chest. Not that I think he'll drop me, but Nazhin insists that it's better to be safe than sorry. Can't say I disagree.

I wrap my arms and legs around him, appreciating the solid feel of his body. But I don't have time to dwell on the intimacy of our position as he leaps into the air, pumping his powerful wings to push us up, up, up between the massive trunks. My sisters and the others quickly disappear from sight, leaving me to admire the forest's glowing understory. It's quite beautiful from up here, a patchwork of neon color and texture…

We drop unexpectedly, and my stomach lurches. "Sorry," Nazhin says, pumping his wings harder. "Just getting used to my new center of gravity."

"Don't worry about me." I let out a shaky laugh. "I'm impressed you're flying at all."

He doesn't look at me, keeping his focus above us, and I decide it might be best if I remain silent so he can concentrate.

Before long, we're flying in near darkness. We reach the first layer of the canopy by bumping into it, and my heart races as we drop a few feet. I wrap my arms and legs tighter around him, squeezing my eyes shut.

Nazhin regains his upward momentum and digs his claws into the bark of a massive horizontal limb. After pulling us awkwardly to the top of a long, flat branch as wide as a king-sized bed, he pauses, his chest heaving with exertion.

"That was incredible," I say, breathing hard as well. I feel shaky with nerves, but he doesn't need to hear that right now. Dropping my legs from around his waist, I stand on my tiptoes, hoping to take some of my weight off him. "Do you need to rest?"

Patches of what might be dimly glowing yellow moss scatter the top of the branch, but don't give off enough light to actually see anything. A low, whooshing roar rises and falls all around us, as if the forest is breathing. I have a sudden thought about the Sheeghr mentioning the parasite lives in the trees. *Could one be watching us from the darkness?* My arms tighten around Nazhin's neck.

His arms are still firmly around me. "I can continue. Are you ready?"

I look up, seeing only more darkness. "I wish I'd thought to bring a handful of those glowing leaves. Can you see well enough to fly?"

I feel him shrug. "No, but up is up. And I'm slow enough to move by feel."

If by feel he means bumping into branches, I guess he's right. And we haven't plummeted to our deaths yet, so I'll have to trust him. I wrap my legs around his waist again, breathing in his warm, masculine scent. "I'm ready."

He launches us upward to the next branch. Again and again we repeat the cycle of Nazhin clawing us on top of a branch, pausing a moment to breathe, then taking off again.

The branches grow closer and closer together the higher we go, and the wind grows more brisk. I thought having more branches would mean more wind protection, but it's strong enough to take my breath away. Leaves and other bits of debris sweep by, stinging my bare arms and legs. I don't know how Nazhin can continue exerting himself like he is. Each time we land, I swear our perch feels less steady, and the air feels colder.

We're airborne when I spot the first slivers of pinkish light overhead through the network of interwoven branches. "I think I see sky!"

A gust of wind sets us spinning, and Nazhin's arms tighten almost painfully around my ribcage. It feels like we're in freefall. Voice locked in my throat, I just squeeze my eyes shut and pray. We slam to a sudden stop, knocking the breath from my lungs. It's a good thing I don't get sick like Tamara does, or I'd be yakking all over Nazhin's chest right now.

After a second of terror, I crack my eyes open to see we've landed on yet another branch. My relief is short-lived, however. The wood is hollowed into a small bowl about the size of a compact car and filled with dry leaves. It seems to be sheltered from the wind, though the entire limb creaks and sways. "Is this a nest?" I ask, heart thundering against my ribs.

Nazhin rests on his knees, obviously exhausted. He glances around. "I'd be surprised if anything made its nest this high. It's pretty cold, and the wind up here is brutal."

Somewhat relieved, I let my legs fall from his waist. He falls forward on top of me into the hollow. Pinkish light from above outlines his wings and the back of his head, catching on his small crown of horns.

"This might be a suitable spot to set up your equipment," he says, breathing hard. "Are we high enough yet?"

I grimace, uncertain, and stare past him toward the branches. "The beacon can probably get through from here, but my spectrometer needs a clear shot of the sky for a proper reading. If our frequency is off, the signal might bounce off the ionosphere instead of reaching orbit."

"Is the spectrometer something I can use for you?"

"Well, yes, but—"

"Then let me do it." He tugs the knot on the harness behind his neck. The vines release, and he sits back on his knees. The sudden loss of his weight on me makes me feel naked and alone. He reaches into my messenger bag, pulling out the spectrometer. "Show me what to do."

Still uncertain about this plan, I instruct him. My weight is obviously becoming a burden, and the increasing wind only makes flying harder. All I need is a reading from the spectrometer and I think I can make the beacon work.

Nazhin listens carefully, then runs through the steps again with me before tucking the device into the harness belt. "I'll be back soon."

Before he can stand, I grab his clawed hand. "Be safe, okay? Come back to me."

He nods, then he's up and away, leaving me shivering and alone in the hollow.

Without him to block it, the wind bites into my skin, and I soon grow chilled. I sit with my back to one sloped edge of the hollow and pull leaves up around me, but I'm shivering from loneliness and worry as much as cold. The pink glow overhead has grown stronger since we arrived, and I assume it must be the planet is rotating into daylight. *God, I miss seeing the sky.* I bet it's glorious.

My stomach growls, and I dig into my messenger bag for one of the purple fruits we brought along and a cooked mushroom. The food warms me, and I sit back to watch the growing light. What's taking him so long? A list of potential tragedies fills my head as I wait. He's blown off course and can't find me again. He freezes to death before he can get back. He falls to his death…

My stomach is in terrible knots by the time Nazhin returns, and I shoot to my feet to grab him in a hug. "I thought something might've happened to you."

"It was rough up there," he says, putting his arms around me. His teeth are chattering, and he's like a block of ice against me. "I lost your spectrometer."

My heart falls, but I shake my head and drag him down into the leaves, pulling them up around us. "That's okay." I'm actually surprised at how okay I am with it. "I'm just glad you came back safely."

"I took some readings on my ICC that you may find useful." He lifts his arm and brings up the hologram, but he's shivering too badly for me to focus on the image.

"Don't worry about that now." I pull his arm back down into our smothering of leaves. "We need to wait until nightfall to start the beacon, anyway, when the ionosphere isn't already zinging with energy from the sun. That's the optimal time to get a signal through, and I'm worried the batteries won't last very long once I turn it on."

"Okay," he agrees and snuggles closer to me.

I wrap my arms and legs around him to help warm him. He's big, and his wings make him seem even bigger. He wraps them around us like a cloak. Slowly, warmth fills the space around us. In the growing pink light, I examine his features. His Khargal horns are interesting, though his face is mostly the same as his human one. Yet I feel as if I'm seeing him with fresh eyes. "We've been through a lot together, haven't we?" I ask, not really needing an answer.

"Our adventures aren't over," he says, his face somber. "It could be a while before we're rescued—if a rescue ever comes at all."

I gulp. He's right. And while we wait, we have to survive the parasite, the Sheeghr, and God knows how many other monsters we have yet to meet. Heck, if the wind picks up, we might not even make it back down to my sisters alive.

Sudden resolve fills me. *I refuse to die without experiencing Nazhin.* I've been attracted to him from the first moment we met, and that attraction has developed into genuine affection. Maybe something more, though I'm not sure I'm ready to go there yet. But I know what I want right here, right now.

I put my fingertips against his cheek. "Nazhin, I don't want to die without being with you at least once."

He smiles softly and sighs. "I want you, too, Jennifer. But I can't be with you and not claim you, and you've been very clear that you don't want a mate."

I frown and shake my head. "If we die, none of that will matter."

"But if we live, I don't want you to have any regrets." His gaze is intense and gives me flutters deep in my stomach.

I love that he understands me so well. His refusal only makes me more certain that *not* being with him would be one of my life's biggest regrets, maybe even bigger than my defunct career or my stolen research. "You're right," I say. "I don't want a mate, not in the traditional sense of making a home and raising kids. But I do want a partner who is always there for me, who respects what I want, yet also stands firm for what he needs. I want you, Nazhin."

"And what happens when what you want and what I want are completely opposite?" His eyes are wary, but he doesn't pull away.

"I guess we find a compromise." I lace my fingers with his, careful of his claws. "Is that something you can live with?"

As an answer, he cups the back of my neck and draws me toward him for a kiss.

16

NAZHIN

Jennifer's words echo in my head. On some level, I know I should stop now. Push her away before she makes a choice she'll later regret. But I can't bring myself to do it.

Once I take her, once I plant the genetic markers that make her mine, there will be no escaping this bond. And humans don't feel the tie like Kirenai do. If she ignores our union, it could drive me insane. But as my lips move over hers, I'm helpless to deny myself.

She wraps her arms around my neck, pressing her breasts deliciously against my chest. I explore every corner of her mouth, staking my claim as my fingers trace patterns down her shoulders to the base of her spine.

Her muscles shift beneath my touch, and she throws her leg over mine, straddling my hips. The need to be inside her is overwhelming. My *Iki'i* senses she feels the same way as she pulls me tighter against her heated center. When I assumed this Khargal form, I shed my pants so I could make use of my tail while flying, but had adopted a modesty shield to obscure my genitals as humans prefer. Now both of my shafts burst free, pushing my matrix aside to make themselves known.

She gasps as I throb against her, then her hand works its way between us, grasping my primary shaft as she'd done during our previous intimacy.

I hiss, "*Kuzara*, Jennifer. I won't last long if you keep that up."

She pulls back, reaching down to lift the hem of her blouse over her head. Her nipples are already hard, her breasts perfect mounds of softness I can't wait to taste. I lean in and capture one nipple, circling it with my tongue until she arches her back and moans, both hands clutched around my head.

Her thumb runs across the Khargal horns, and I shudder. I nip the stiff bud of her nipple before I slip my hand between us to cup the heat between her legs. She responds immediately by flicking open the front of her shorts. After a moment of contortions, she sheds both shorts and panties. I can wait no longer. I roll her onto her back and position myself between her legs, the head of my shaft poised at her entrance. "Are you certain?" I offer one more time.

Jennifer nods, eyes glittering with heated desire. "Take me."

I enter her slowly, her tight flesh gripping me in exquisite heat and wetness. I have to breathe slowly to keep myself from finishing before we've even started. Once I've sunk completely inside her, I press my tickler against her clit.

"Oh," she growls, her voice filled with a sultry need that makes my blood sing.

Controlling my tickler takes finesse, but soon I have her writhing beneath me as her engorged clit pulses, her juices surging around our joining. She gasps and shudders, and I know it's time.

Pulling out partway, I slam into her again, pleasure driving me like an animal. My mating shaft is pulsing and ready, prodding her ass with every forward thrust. She bucks up to meet me, her breath coming in tiny, panting gasps as our rhythm increases. I feel myself nearing the brink and slow my thrusting, wanting to make it last longer.

She digs her nails into my back. "Don't stop. Don't stop!"

Happy to oblige, I thrust again. This time, my mating shaft sinks into her ass. I can no longer hold back, my release rolling through me like lightning. Her inner walls tighten to almost painful strength, her orgasm colliding with mine as we both shudder and moan, the groaning of the wind and trees a counterpoint to our intensity. The pleasure seems to go on for an eternity as I pulse inside her, each shaft filling her and making her mine.

I sag on top of her, my wings spread over us like a protective blanket. Her fingers stroke my lower back and ribs.

"Tell me you're my mate," I say. I need to hear her say it.

"I'm yours, Nazhin." She kisses the side of my neck and along my collarbone. "Your mate."

I nuzzle against her ear and speak the words I've been dying to say for so long. "I love you, Jennifer."

She makes a soft, happy sound and runs one hand along the inside of my spread wing. "Will it be like this every time? Or only when you're a Khargal?"

Then I realize what has—or rather hasn't—happened. My form isn't settled. I'm not bound as a human. I lift a clawed hand to my forehead and touch my horns. *Curious.* "Most Kirenai assume the male form of their mate's species upon bonding."

Disappointment sours the air. "But you're obviously still Khargal. Does this mean… we're not mates?"

I glance at her sharply. "We are most definitely mates."

"How can you be so sure?" Her eyes are tight with worry.

"My *Iki'i* doesn't lie."

I push onto my knees, letting the wind tug at my wings. "Perhaps it's because you prefer me as a Khargal."

She laughs. "The wings are sexy, but I liked your Vin Diesel form, too. Can you still shift into that one?"

I stretch out my hand and try to retract my claws. Only when I focus all my energy on a single digit can I make the change happen, and the nail quickly resumes its Khargal shape when I stop concentrating. "There are legends about Kirenai who don't assume the shape their mate prefers, but only when the mating is under great duress."

Jennifer reaches for her shorts and panties, which have ended up precariously close to the edge of our perch. "Well, our situation probably qualifies. I mean, if you lost your wings right now, we'd be fucked."

My blood turns to ice. "*Kuzara*, I never even considered that." I'd been too swept up in the moment to consider there might be consequences to our joining under these conditions. "I'd better not try a full shift just yet. Just in case I can't shift back again."

She snuggles against me. "Well, if you can't shift back, I'll take you in whatever form you have to be in. Wings, no wings, whatever."

"That makes me so happy, *bareshi*." I lay down beside her and cover her with my wing.

"What was it like up there above the trees?" she asks. "I bet it was glorious."

"I wish I could take you to see it. The entire sky is an aurora. Lots of red and purple and orange, like a river of sunsets. But the storm..." I inhale deeply, recalling the moment I lost her spectrometer. The wind drove me back down into the trees with crushing force, bouncing me halfway toward the forest floor. But I don't want to scare her with details. "I can see why ships choose not to land here."

I bring up my ICC, pleased I had the foresight to turn on my sensor before cresting the tree line. Jennifer leans close, trying to see the information. "I can't read it."

"Let me show you." I pull her onto my lap, showing her the symbols and graphs.

She's a quick learner, and soon has her phone in hand, adjusting the settings on her beacon. "This is exactly the information I needed."

I love how excited she is about her work. She could accomplish so much with the equipment my company could provide. I really hope we get rescued so I can be at her side while she explores the universe.

When she finishes with her phone, she sets it aside and gives me a naughty smirk. "Now we just need to wait for nightfall. Any thoughts on how we might kill some time?"

With a growl, I roll her onto her back among the leaves.

17

JENNIFER

*N*azhin and I make love twice more while we wait for the daylight to fade, pausing only to snack on purple fruit and mushrooms. Eventually, the glow overhead deepens from pale pink to maroon, indicating darkness is coming. I set the phones in the center of the hollow.

"Here goes nothing," I say, and engage the beacon.

We wait a few minutes, as if expecting something to happen. When I realize I'm holding my breath, I let it out. "Well, that's it. All we can do now is wait. Do you think anyone is in orbit to hear it?"

Nazhin hugs me to his chest and sighs. "The real question is whether anyone will try to come for us if they do hear it. We've done everything *we* can to get off this planet."

I nod against his warmth. "At least we have each other now." I've thought a lot about our future. Whether we remain stranded here or not, I'm glad to have Nazhin at my side.

He kisses the top of my head. "We can face anything together, my *bareshi*."

I loop the strap of my messenger bag over my head. It feels strangely empty now. No phones. No equipment. Not even any food. "Let's get back to the others before we freeze to death."

Once again in my harness, I wrap my arms and legs around Nazhin as he jumps from our branch. The wind stings my skin and steals my breath, so I close my eyes as we dodge the massive limbs. When we reach the thickest layer, Nazhin resorts to hopping from branch to branch, sometimes walking along a limb before we can find a spot wide enough to squeeze through.

"I don't remember it being this difficult coming up," I say as we pause. The darkness here is eerie, and I glance around, worried something might be watching us.

"I think I'm just tired," he says.

Not wanting him to think I'm criticizing his efforts, I brush his lips in a kiss. "I think I'm just eager to be back. You're freaking amazing."

He kisses the tip of my nose. "Save the congratulations until after we get back safely."

His concern is unwarranted, and we soon clear the last of the massive, horizontal branches. Massive trunks still block most of the view, but I look down over the glowing neon colors of the understory while Nazhin glides between the trees. His wings tremble, and our course feels a little unstable. Plus, he's breathing hard.

Circling a massive trunk, he says, "I don't think we came down in the same spot."

Worry fills my gut, and I scan the ground below us, looking for any sign of the camp. Without our phones, we have no way to track each other. "How far off course might we be?"

"I'm not sure." He drops toward a pond, but there is no sign of a camp, so he pumps his wings to gain altitude again.

"Maybe we should land and rest," I suggest.

"No, I think I smell smoke," he says, looking around. "Can you tell where it's coming from?"

We circle a few more times before I spot a brighter glow among the bioluminescent foliage. I point. "There. I think that's our fire."

With stomach lurching speed, we drop to the clearing. People immediately gather around, and I see several unfamiliar faces crowding around. I pull the knot on my harness to free myself and proudly announce, "The beacon's set."

But this doesn't receive the hopeful response I expected. Instead, Tamara pushes past Erud with Beanie in her arms. Her eyes are puffy and her cheeks are red. "Oh, Jennifer!"

Concern flares in my chest. My sister has always been prone to anxiety, but something obviously happened while we were gone. "What is it?"

Her face creases with agony, and she chokes out, "Suzanne is missing."

I look around, realizing my oldest sister's strawberry blonde hair is nowhere in sight. "Have you looked for her?"

"Of course we looked for her." Tamara's voice is an octave too high. "She's gone. What if the parasite took her?"

"Or the Sheeghr?" Erud adds, his red mustache and eyebrows drawn into a tight scowl.

"Or one of those monsters with so many legs?" asks a Kirenai I don't recognize.

My stomach suddenly feels filled with rocks.

KIOZHI

I REFUSE TO BE STRAPPED TO A SINGLE
MAN EVER AGAIN. BUT A HOT BLUE ALIEN
SEEMS TO THINK A ONE-NIGHT-STAND
MEANS FOREVER...

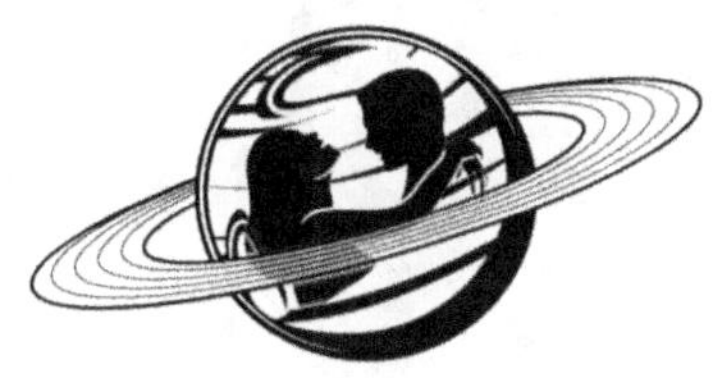

1

KIOZHI

"You look like you could use a swig or ten of something strong," I say to Tazhio as we step onto the crowded observation deck.

This is the first night of the Intergalactic Dating Agency's inaugural cruise with human passengers, and the effervescent sensation of hundreds of emotions prickle against my empathic senses. The nebula shining through the dome overhead bathes everyone in an aurora of pastel colors, and a small band plays an upbeat Fogarian waltz while people on the dance floor spin and sway.

Tazhio has the worried look of an old man who's lost his way. He snags two glasses of Lensoran bubbly from a passing tray. "Got it covered."

He didn't want to be here tonight, but he's a good friend and agreed to be my *wingman*, a human term for one male who supports another during courting. Like me, he's Kirenai, but he's in his Hypawan form, which looks mostly human except for overly large eyes and very thick hair. As part of the crew, he wears a white uniform that stands out amidst the mostly black clothing worn by everyone else.

I smile, take a glass for myself, then turn my attention back to the humans. My human-style finery—a "tux", the tailor called it—fits my current human form perfectly; broad shoulders, tall straight spine, muscular legs ending on flat feet. The Intergalactic Dating Agency assured us this template is the most pleasing to human females. It took many cycles after Nanaia's passing, but I've re-trained my matrix to assume the shapes of other species, and can modify my features to please whichever woman I might find pleasure with this evening.

Many of the females stand in small clusters surrounded by male suitors from every race across the galaxy. The females have so many lovely shades of skin; deep brown, golden, and some who are as pale as starlight. The women all wear different fashions, from gauzy to svelte, though most seem to favor the color black, and the smells of so many perfumes are almost overwhelming.

A light-skinned female strides past me in a knee-length black dress with a cutout back panel that exposes the ridge of her spine. A unique hair clip with a spray of gems that look like stars holds her dark brown hair away from her face. I gaze after her appreciatively until a Kirenai following close on her heels with an enormous case in his arms glares at me, his aura radiating menace.

I understand immediately. It was that way with Nanaia when we met, an all-consuming desire that couldn't be ignored. The devastating accident that took her from me sent me into a depression that ruled my life for many cycles.

I jerk my attention away from that particular female—I won't interfere with someone finding a mate. I'm not here to replace Nanaia—that would be impossible. Kirenai mate for life, and finding my true mate had been a one-in-a-million chance, anyway. But my body still has needs, and I can afford to treat any female who wishes to be with me like a princess.

My attention stops on a pretty brunette talking to several other women. Her hair is piled on top of her head, cascading down in a mass of curls. Her lips have been painted with a glistening red substance that reminds me of fruit. A slit in her long black dress exposes a length of golden thigh I'd love to explore further.

I step forward, running my gaze up and down her curves. "Hello, ma'am."

The woman turns to me with an assessing glance, eyes narrowed. "Ma'am? Do I look like a ma'am?"

The IDA told us we should use the term in polite human conversation. Apparently, they were wrong. "My apologies. I was informed the title was honorific. What shall I call you?"

"I'm Amanda, and this is Genevieve and Flora." She gestures toward a tall blonde and a petite brunette. They nod in greeting.

"I'm Kiozhi." I take her hand, turning her palm up to brush a kiss across her skin. My *Iki'i* senses the giddy thrill racing through her at my touch, yet she firmly pulls her hand free of my grip. I don't allow this to stop me—this is most likely why the literature about humans suggests bringing a wingman while courting. "This is my friend, Tazhio. As you can see, he's Kirenai too."

Tazhio is looking out at the crowd, not paying attention to the women at all. I elbow him and he jerks his gaze back to Amanda. "Oh, yes, greetings."

The women all giggle and nod appreciatively at him. I frown. The guidebook said nothing about the wingman competing for female attention. Perhaps I shouldn't have brought him after all.

"So," the other brunette drawls, "what are you two looking for in a woman?"

I seize the opportunity to remove Tazhio from consideration. "Tazhio's not allowed to date the passengers. But I would be happy to explore a night of pleasure with you."

She places a finger against her chin thoughtfully and looks me up and down again. "Oh, I bet you would," she says, her voice heavy with sarcasm. "But we're here looking for relationships, not one-night stands."

I blink, not fully understanding her terminology. She seems to interpret my confusion as confirmation of her judgement and turns away. *Kuzara.* Finding companionship among these humans isn't going to be as quick and easy as I imagined.

I turn to complain to Tazhio but find he's abandoned me, disappeared somewhere into the crowd. I sigh. So much for my wingman.

On the dance floor, several beautiful women are moving to the music, laughing, flirting with their partners. I move forward to watch. Each female is divine in her own way, though I can't help comparing each one to my Nanaia and have to determinedly redirect my thoughts. I divert myself by imagining what it might be like to entwine myself with one of these females, to feel her body pressed against mine, our tongues dancing together in passion. Though my mate is gone, my sex drive is not, and providing pleasure gives me joy and helps keep my lingering depression at bay.

A laugh catches my attention. It reminds me of a clear waterfall chiming against the crystal cliffs on my home planet of Alkavar III. *Who is that?* A longing rises through me. I want to be the one making her laugh.

Intrigued, I follow the sound and discover a female with ivory skin and the most delightful shade of hair I've ever encountered —a light red-gold that reminds me of a sunset. She's twirling across the dance floor in the arms of a Kirenai my *Iki'i* doesn't recognize. Her short black dress is covered in small scales that catch the light with pearly iridescence. The glimmer accentuates her curves in a way that makes my heart pound faster.

She spins past me, brilliant green eyes connecting with mine for an instant. My mating shaft stirs, a long-forgotten ache flaring low in my belly. I stumble back in confusion. I haven't felt this sensation since Nanaia died.

The female tosses her hair and looks away, an amused grin on her face as the other male guides her across the dance floor. Normally, I'd approach her without hesitation, but I need to understand what's happening first. This sensation can't be normal.

I push through the crowd to keep up with her, trying to remain a mere a shadow in the distance. My breathing quickens as I watch her hips sway. I feel like a youth again, eager and impulsive. She's mine, I know it. I must win her away from this other male.

2

SUZANNE

I tip my head back and laugh as I spin across the dance floor in the arms of yet another tall blue alien. So far, I've danced with at least six Kirenai, a short, hairy alien called a Fogarian, and a tall, stone-like beast of a man with wings and horns. After seventeen years trapped in a co-dependent marriage, I'm finally free, and I made a promise to myself that I wouldn't dance with the same guy twice—though telling the uniformly good-looking blue aliens apart might be a challenge. I haven't had this much fun since before I got knocked up in high school, and now that the kids are grown and gone, I'm determined to make the most of this two-week singles' cruise through space.

The song ends, and I snag a glass of whatever this stuff is that passes for alien champagne from a passing server's tray. I pull my arm free of my dance partner's. "Thank you for the dance. I need to catch my breath."

He opens his mouth to respond, but I duck behind a couple doing a flailing approximation of swing dancing and move away. The room is filled with all sorts of aliens, from handsome blue Kirenai with action figure bodies to short, frail-looking Area 51 beings with gray-green skin and huge dark eyes.

Overhead, multicolored ribbons of light speckled with thousands of glittering stars illuminate the domed ceiling. Sipping the bubbly, fruity drink and smiling at every hot alien who glances my direction, I move back toward where I left my sisters at the edge of the dance floor. I feel self-conscious in my silky black cocktail dress with iridescent sequins but force myself to have positive thoughts about being sexy and keep my chin high.

All around me is laughter and talking in a hundred different languages. I'm still wrapping my head around the fact I can understand them all—alien and human alike—thanks to a translator implant I get to keep when the trip is over. Maybe I can use it to land a job as a corporate translator when I get back to Earth. Wouldn't that be something?

I pass by a hulking gray dude with wings, horns, and a tail who gives me a once-over before breaking into a sharp-toothed grin. His bod is rock-solid, though his features are a bit too chiseled for my taste, and he carries himself like a conceited asshole. It's that last part that I turn away from. I've had enough of men who think they're God's gift to women—my husband used me to get through med school, then divorced me for a hot young blonde he was having an affair with.

Fucking bastard.

I dodge another alien who's looking at me with a proprietary gaze and search for my sisters. I want to see if they're having fun too. Lifting my chin, I locate Jennifer fiddling with her telescope at one edge of the observation deck. She's insisting on using this trip to gather astronomy data for her doctoral thesis and is somehow successfully ignoring the constant stream of alien men asking her to dance. It probably helps that the tall, bald Kirenai who's been hauling her equipment around glares daggers at anyone who comes near.

I'd prefer not to be dragged into one of my brainy sister's dissertations about random star systems, so I keep looking. I spot Tamara's copper curls among the crowd. She's heading to the dance floor with an alien who looks like a dwarf who's been dipped in red paint. *Good for her.* She's usually so shy, I'm glad to see she's having fun.

That only leaves our baby sister, Bethany. I know just where to look for her—near the kitchen, stalking an alien chef she wants to host on her cooking show. Spotting her next to the service doors where tables are laden with appetizer trays, I swoop over and take her hand. "God, I'm having such a good time. Take a break and dance with me."

"Stop, Suzanne." She yanks her hand away, planting it back on the hip of her deep wine-colored cocktail dress. "There's a Nebula Chef on board, and I'm waiting to speak with him. I wish they'd just let me go talk to him in the kitchen."

I sigh. Just like Jennifer, Bethany has a one-track mind when it comes to her career. I examine the alien appetizers on a nearby table and pick up something that looks exactly like a small red penis. "Maybe they're not letting you in the kitchen because they don't want you to find out their alien dicks aren't fresh." I waggle my eyebrows suggestively.

One of the small Area 51-looking servers stumbles slightly, obviously overhearing me. I flash him a naughty grin, sure his cheeks turn pink underneath all that gray skin before he turns and scurries away.

"Quit joking around. This is serious." Bethany scowls, snatching the food out of my hand and taking an aggressive bite. She waves the other half in my face. "You're the only one who insisted this trip was all about meeting hot aliens. Dance with one of them." She gestures toward a nearby Kirenai.

Most of the blue aliens look similar, but there's something about this one that makes my engine rev. Perhaps it's the magnetism of his midnight dark eyes. I'm not sure if I've danced with him before, but he's hot enough I might consider a second turn around the dance floor, promise to myself be damned.

He moves forward and holds out a hand. "I noticed you from across the room." His rumbling voice cuts below the music. Ok, I know I haven't danced with him because I would've remembered that voice. "My name's Kiozhi. Would you care to dance?"

"Sure." I shrug, trying not to appear eager as I start past him toward the dance floor.

He stops me with an arm around my waist. Pulling me closer, he starts to sway to the music. Maybe it's the slightly crooked way he smiles, or the subtle, almost chocolaty scent of his cologne, but I find myself looping my arms around his neck. "Something wrong with the dance floor?"

Guiding me in time to the music, he leans close to my ear. "There are too many people there. I want you all to myself."

Oh, boy. That deep voice really makes my girly parts flutter. The TV shows on Earth make Kirenai out to be mind-bogglingly exceptional lovers, which I always assumed must be fiction. Now's my chance to find out for real.

I've never had a one-night stand, but I'm starting to think tonight is the night. It's a big step for me. *You are allowed to have fun.* I repeat the self-talk my therapist encouraged me to use.

Tilting my head back, I meet his gaze. "That's hard to do in a room full of people."

He pulls me tighter against him. Heat pools between my legs as I feel the throbbing length now trapped between our bodies. "Yes, very hard."

I don't even recall his name, but I don't care. I close the distance between our lips. His arms fold around me like a cloak as his kiss ravages my mouth. His fingers toy with the hair at the base of my neck, sending shivers down my spine. I wrap both arms around his ribs and let my hands play up and down the broad muscles of his back. Our tongues tangle until I've lost all sense of space and time.

I'm panting with desire and my nipples ache inside my dress by the time he pauses. I want him to touch me all over, skin to skin. Voice raspy with need, I ask, "Should we take this back to your room or mine?"

3

———

KIOZHI

The moment the female—Suzanne, I heard her sister call her—presses her lips against mine, fire ignites my blood. I still find it impossible that I've discovered another mate, but there is no denying the surge of my mating shaft or the surety in my heart. I pull her tightly against me and let myself revel in our connection. Never did I expect to feel this way a second time.

She takes my hand and hurries us toward the lift. I let her lead, still in shock from my roiling sensations. As the lift descends, she faces me again, both hands around my neck, nipples hardened to points I can feel even through our clothing. Her tongue invades my mouth, and I open for her, letting her take all she desires. She's sweet and intoxicating, our tongues engaging in a battle neither of us can win nor lose.

By the time we reach her room, she has already removed my tie and opened my shirt to run her hands over my pecs and abs. I don't know how much longer I can wait to bury myself in her heat. But I recall reading that humans prefer a slow courtship, and I want Suzanne to treasure our bonding moment. We'll have hundreds of cycles together once I claim her, so I don't need to rush this now.

The cabin door has barely spiraled shut before she reaches behind her and opens the back of her dress, letting the silk folds slide into a puddle around her ankles. Her body is magnificent, clad in nothing but a thin triangle of cloth covering her sex. I want to taste her full, rosy nipples. Her hips are wide and curvy, and her sunset hair curls wildly around her shoulders.

"*Oritsu*," I breathe. "You are magnificent."

She grins wickedly and uses both hands to shove my jacket and shirt off my shoulders.

I unfasten the front of my pants, relief washing through me as my cock is allowed to spring free. Then I firmly push her back onto the mattress and kneel on the edge of the bed so I can look at her. I'm doing my best to increase the anticipation, but it's becoming difficult to restrain myself.

Her eyes are dark, and she raises both arms to welcome me. "Come here."

I can't resist. Lowering myself against her softness, I kiss her again, letting one hand roam the bounty of her curves. She moans when my fingers slide between her legs. Her heat is like lava through her panties.

"Please," she begs, flexing her hips toward my touch.

I don't need to be asked twice. Ripping her panties from her body, I slide a finger inside her. She moans louder, and my *Iki'i* revels in the growing frenzy of her pleasure. A certain spot inside her seems to drive her wild, so I focus pressure there, finding the rhythm that pleases her most.

When I press my thumb to her clit, her head thrashes back and forth. She's lost to sensation, no longer capable of returning my kisses. I grin and nibble my way down her neck until I reach her breasts, licking and sucking. She grips the covers on either side of her, writhing and gasping, her inner walls fluttering on the verge of release.

"Come for me," I say.

My beautiful Suzanne complies, her body arching up from the mattress as her channel convulses around my fingers.

When her shuddering subsides, I withdraw my finger and feather her face with kisses. She's flushed and panting, her satisfaction like a salve on my *Iki'i*.

After a moment, she regains enough strength to turn her lips to mine, and our tongues resume their dance. Her delicate hands travels down my rib cage to my waist, and one slides between us to find my primary shaft. I groan as her fingers close around it. Her thumb rolls over the head, spreading slick pre-cum in a small circular motion that almost makes me lose control.

She murmurs into my mouth, "I want you inside me."

I'm ready too. More than ready. But I know if I take her from the front, there will be no controlling my mating shaft. I wouldn't be able to stop myself from claiming her here and now, and I want to give her the courting she deserves before we seal our bond. Gripping her hips, I roll her onto her stomach, then pull her back so she's resting on her knees.

I can't resist the urge to look at the puckered hole of her ass, so I spread her cheeks gently and let my thumb press against her tightness. She's slick there from the juices drenching her pussy, and she gasps and tightens as I press more firmly without quite entering.

"This is for later," I growl before bending down to nip her ass cheek.

Then I position myself behind her. She opens her legs wider when I settle between them, and I grasp her hips to hold her still. The tip of my primary shaft presses into her channel, and she exhales with a low moan. She's so wet, I have no trouble sliding my length inside her, adjusting my shape and size to fill her completely. My mating shaft, thwarted from entering her ass, glides across her clit.

I shudder at the stimulation, rocking my hips back and forth a few times. It won't be enough to provide the double ejaculation I crave, but it feels good, especially when she arches her back to accept each deep thrust. I can feel her tightening around me and know she's close.

Pistoning forward, I drive into her again and again until she explodes, straining back against me. She cries out, her juices flowing in heated rivulets over my balls.

I can't stop myself. "Suzanne," I hiss her name, every muscle in my body tightening as my release shoots deep inside her.

She moans, spasms of release still rolling through her, milking me of everything I have. I pulse and throb, trapped in her body's tight embrace. All I can hear is the sound of my breathing, the beat of my heart, the rush of blood in my ears. All I can smell is the sweet scent of her pleasure.

When I finally return to my senses, I take a moment to enjoy the perfect sway of her back. Her hands loosely clutch the bedsheets, and her pale red-gold hair is plastered to her cheek with sweat. She's the most phenomenal sight I've ever seen. *My mate.* I can only imagine what pleasures our actual bonding will bring.

With her lovely, heart-shaped ass still securely against my hips and my shaft still inside her body, I roll us over and wrap my arm around her, breathing in the floral perfume of her hair.

"That was incredible," she whispers, her ribs rising and falling with breath.

I nibble her ear, loving the way she shudders and snuggles closer. "That was only the beginning, my *kikajiru.*"

4

————

SUZANNE

I wake feeling boneless and sated; the propaganda about Kirenai lovers is not an exaggeration. I never even learned my alien lover's name, but I'm still high on the aftermath of our night together hours after he left my cabin. He worshipped every inch of my body at least twice, and I lost count of the number of times I climaxed.

I stretch languidly between the soft sheets and let my gaze wander around the room. It looks like almost any other hotel room, with a bed, vanity, and chest of drawers. The walls are a soft gray, and the rest of the room is decorated in pearl fixtures with deep purple accents. Not my favorite colors, but elegant and sensual. The sheets still smell like our lovemaking, and I'm filled with a twinge of longing. "Get it together, Suzanne," I mutter to myself. "He's supposed to be just another notch in your lipstick case."

My attention snags on a brilliant green and orange flower arrangement on my vanity. *Where did that come from?* The steward must've delivered it while I was asleep. I glance toward the closed door, feeling a bit creeped out, but these are aliens, so I guess they might not understand etiquette when it comes to privacy. A card pokes from the center of the bouquet.

I fling the sheets aside and stand, pulling on the fluffy white bath robe provided with the room. The bouquet smells like bergamot and peppermint, and the shapes of the blooms are fascinating, like a cross between a bird of paradise and sea holly. I reach for the card and flip it over. *Thank you for the extraordinary evening. Let's meet for lunch on the observation deck. I look forward to furthering our acquaintance. Sincerely, Kiozhi.*

Excitement and terror wage war within my chest. I'm flattered he liked me enough to want more, but I'm not here to latch onto the first guy I meet. I know myself too well; if I accept the invitation, I won't so much as glance at another guy for the rest of the cruise.

"At least I know his name now," I mutter, tossing the card on the bed. Heading to the shower, I wash off all traces of the previous night before getting dressed to join my sisters for lunch.

Bethany wants to try one of the little specialty restaurants, so we head below deck and wind our way through the halls to the nearest lift. The *Romantasy* is shaped like a donut with multiple levels, and we could walk for hours without recrossing our path, but every lift has a button that takes us directly where we want to go. I have no idea how it works, but it's pretty cool.

The restaurant is filled with the din of other guests, a chorus of voices that rise and fall in pitch and volume. Legless tables hang from the ceiling by large cables, and the floor is tiled in red and black geometric shapes. Surprisingly, the air smells of cinnamon and vanilla—not alien at all—as we take our seats.

Bethany chatters about her upcoming birthday and how she's convinced one of the cruise chefs to make her a special cake as a demo for her new cooking show. "I booked this entire restaurant for the party," she says gesturing to our surroundings. "I'll film a demo my producers can't resist. Go big or go home, right?"

"I don't know, Bethany," Jennifer shakes her head. "Are you sure you should put all your eggs in one basket like this? I mean, you haven't even met him."

"It's fine! I'm not worried about the food—this guy's a Nebula Chef. Plus, he's Kirenai, so he'll look hot for the camera." She taps a finger against her lips. "But I'll ask him create a face with character. I don't want him to look like the generic Ken dolls around here." Bethany turns to look at me. "Speaking of Ken dolls, how was your night? What do these aliens look like under their clothes?"

"He definitely wasn't a neutered doll," I say. My sisters giggle appreciatively, and I smirk. Leaning in close, I fill them in on the details. "He sent me flowers and a thank you note this morning. I may have to try one of those guys with horns and wings next to get Kiozhi out of my system."

Even as I say it, an uncomfortable feeling roils in the pit of my stomach. I may not be cut out for this bed-hopping thing. But at least I did it once, and it was a hell of a ride. Even if I don't take another lover for the rest of the trip, I can honestly say I had fun.

When we finish eating, I head back to my cabin. A ribbon-wrapped box of chocolates waits on the end of my bed. *Another gift from Kiozhi?* I pull the note off the box and turn it over. Carefully drawn calligraphy sweeps over the thick card stock.

My sweet Suzanne, the note begins. *I'm sorry we missed each other at lunch today. Please accept my invitation to dinner this evening at a private booth in the Amorous Starlove Solarium. I'll be at your cabin at eight to escort you. With sincere affection, Kiozhi.*

The Amorous Starlove Solarium—ASS for short, which put me and my sisters in stitches when the cruise director first introduced it—is the most expensive restaurant on the ship, the only dining that isn't included in the cruise package. Hands trembling, I shove the card back under the ribbon. *Bethany is going to kill me for refusing.* But I can't accept, no matter how elite the invitation.

I summon a ship's steward and ask him to return the chocolates.

The small gray alien who arrives at my door gazes longingly at the box and licks his lips. "These are exotic delicacies," he says, slowly blinking his large eyes like Puss in Boots. "Would you like a credit at the gift shop?"

He looks so pitiful and hungry, I'm tempted to tell him he can have the candy. Except I can't, because I need to be sure Kiozhi knows I returned his gift. "No, thank you. I need you to refund the purchaser's account. His name's on the card."

The steward nods, and I close the door. I really hope Kiozhi takes the hint now, because this cruise is supposed to be the "Hot Girl Summer" I never had. My kids are grown and out on their own, I'll have an apartment to myself for the first time in my life, and I've already signed up for classes to get my horticulture degree. I'm still young enough to start over, and that's exactly what I'm going to do.

No way am I falling for the first guy I take to my bed, no matter how amazing Kiozhi looks or how good he makes me feel.

KIOZHI

The glass of something called whiskey sitting in front of me smells warm and slightly spicy. It burns pleasantly when it goes down. Right after I left Suzanne's cabin, I looked up everything I could about her, then re-read the IDA's information packet about humans, absorbing everything I can about my mate's culture. The packet indicated human females prefer knowledgeable males, so I'm sampling everything on board related to Earth so I don't look like a fool when I see Suzanne again.

Right now, I'm sitting in the ship's forward lounge—a circular area with lots of metal and glass, from the shelves holding bottles of imported Earth liquor to the gleaming metal stools set around high top glass tables. To either side of me at the bar, clusters of unattached males stare longingly at the couples scattered about the room. There are fewer females than males on this cruise, and only a lucky few will return home with mates.

I smugly take another sip of whiskey and continue surveying the shelves of bottles. Soon I'll also be receiving envious stares from unmated males. I still can't fathom my fortune in finding Suzanne; second mates are beyond rare. I even doubted my senses at first, but our physical intimacy last night made me more than certain it's true—my *Iki'i* can't lie. But I also need to respect the human custom of taking things slow. Human females enjoy what they call an engagement period, so I'm going to use our time on board the ship to make sure she knows just how precious she is.

My Integrated Circuit Chip pings, and I tap my arm to bring up the ICC interface. I scowl when I see it's a return receipt from the gift shop. I was very specific with my instructions. Why are they refunding my money? When I scroll down, my heart seizes in my chest. *Suzanne rejected my gift?*

I glance around, no longer smug at the sight of so many couples staring lovingly into each other's eyes. At a table across the room, a female holds up one hand, beaming at a gem-studded ring. The male across from her is grinning like a fool, their happiness strong enough to make every nearby Kirenai smile too.

I don't smile. I can't. The information packet said flowers and chocolate are standard exchanges humans use to communicate affection. Suzanne didn't reject the flowers. Is she a rare female who doesn't like chocolate?

Confidence returning, I allow myself to smile. *My mate is special.* I'll have to try harder to learn what she likes. Dinner tonight will help me understand her preferences in food. And perhaps I should also look into some jewelry.

Downing the remainder of my drink, I head to the gift shop to peruse the gemstones on board. I'll present her with a lavish bauble when I see her at dinner tonight.

SUZANNE

I step out of my cabin and nearly bump into my sister Jennifer. Her usual, massive blue porter stands a few steps behind her holding her astronomy case. She's in denim shorts and a black t-shirt filled with stars and the words *I need my space*. As always, she has her beat-up messenger bag hooked over one shoulder.

I raise an eyebrow. "Are you bringing that thing to karaoke?"

"No," she scowls. "The karaoke bar doesn't have any viewing portals. I'm on my way to drop this stuff off at my cabin first. These social evenings are such a waste of time."

"Cut loose and have some fun," I say, sliding a glance toward her porter. I swear he looks more like Vin Diesel every day, and I know my sister has a thing for the hunky actor. "It's just for a few hours."

"Hours I could use in far more productive ways." She waves a hand and tromps by me and unlocks her cabin. "You guys go on without me. I'll meet you there."

I shrug and knock on Tamara's door. I'm waiting for her to answer when I hear my name from down the hall. A handsome blue Kirenai in a tuxedo strides in my direction. Though he looks the same as most other Kirenai on board, I know in my heart it's Kiozhi. I gulp, heart fluttering like an army of butterflies.

"Shit," I mutter, wondering if it's too late to pretend I didn't see him and go back to my cabin.

Kiozhi comes to a stop next to me, his warm, masculine scent taking me back to the bliss of last night. Voice low and intimate, he says, "Suzanne, you look absolutely stunning."

My entire body heats at the compliment. I'm not usually a dressy person, but I bought all new clothes for this trip. Tonight I'm wearing a gold sequined tank top, Spanx tuxedo leggings, and black stiletto sandals, ready for the promised karaoke on tonight's social calendar. After years of keeping my strawberry blonde hair tucked up and away from my face, it now hangs loose around my bare shoulders.

I smile tightly, not quite looking at Kiozhi. My ex would always qualify his praise with something backhanded, and I can't help the instinct to brace myself for the other shoe to drop. Staring at my sister's door, I opt for a simple, "Thank you."

"Are you ready for dinner?" Kiozhi holds out an elbow as if expecting me to take it. "Or would you prefer drinks first?"

Relief floods through me as the door spirals open, revealing Tamara. Her gray eyes widen, taking in Kiozhi's well-cut figure. "Oh."

I push past her into the room. "Sorry, Kiozhi. I have other plans tonight. Thanks for the invitation, though."

I refuse to turn around until I hear the door spiral closed again.

"Is that your stalker?" Our youngest sister, Bethany, asks from inside the room. She's standing in front of a full-length mirror next to the bed, a curling iron in one hand. Her elegant silver cocktail dress is slit up one side, nearly to her hip. I always wished I had a body like my baby sister's. I don't know how she can stay so fit when she's always sampling food for her cooking show.

"Hush." I sit on the end of the bed next to Tamara's chihuahua, Beanie, who is happily chewing a stuffed animal. "He might be listening."

Bethany goes back to curling her auburn hair. "So? Sometimes you have to hurt someone's feelings to get them to take a hint."

I sigh. I'm not usually a fan of my baby sister's brashness, but she has a point. Yet the thought of hurting Kiozhi makes my insides feel all squiggly and uncomfortable.

Tamara picks up her dog so she can sit next to me. She's dressed in a green peekaboo blouse and black leggings that are quickly covered with dog hair. "I bet he'll be at karaoke tonight."

"He'll take the hint soon," I say. "I'm sure he'll find another woman for his affections at the party." That would be the easiest solution. So why is my stomach tight at the thought of seeing him with someone else?

"Aren't you the one always telling us to be direct about what we want?" asks Bethany, a snide smirk on her lips.

I stick my tongue out at her. "Yes. I'll be direct the next time I see him." At least, I hope I will. The memory of his hands on my body, the warm, almost chocolaty scent of his skin, the feathery kisses as we enjoyed the afterglow make it difficult to be firm in my rejection. I shake off my longing. "Everyone ready to go?"

We head to the party, taking the lift to another of the *Romantasy's* many decks and following the corridor toward where I can hear someone belting out the lyrics to "Faith" by George Michael. Inside the darkened bar, a disco ball flashes multi-colored lights over the crowd. Aliens of all shapes and sizes cluster around gyrating human women.

The only requirement that came with our free cruise tickets is that we attend nightly social events with the aliens. No problem. Each alien is hunkier than the last, depending on your taste in men. I'm partial to the somewhat generic GQ look most of the Kirenai seem to have adopted, and yet the moment I spot Kiozhi at the bar, every other guy might as well be hamburger. He's still in his tailored tux, his blue hair in a stylishly tousled French crop I vividly remember clutching while his face was between my legs.

Dammit. What is wrong with me? He has no right to consume my thoughts like this. I must have sex on the brain because I had such a long dry spell after my divorce. Yes, that's it. Any of these hot guys would make me feel the same way.

Beside me, Tamara stands on her tiptoes, searching the crowd. "Do you see him?"

I can barely hear her over the gravelly voice of a winged alien attempting to sing something that reminds me of a sea shanty, but I know she's looking for her hot shuttle pilot. I glance around the teeming crowd, nearly blinded by the flashing lights. Leaning close, I shout. "Not yet, but let's keep looking!"

Bethany taps my arm and gestures toward a row of tables where a Kirenai in a chef's hat has his back to us. "I think I see my chef. I'll be over there."

I nod at her and spare another glance toward Kiozhi. He's chatting with a waif-like woman with straight black hair that hangs well below the short hem of her red cocktail dress. Her stilettos are impossibly high, and the muscles of her perfectly shaped legs gleam in the disco lights.

Jealousy actually lodges in my throat. I swallow it down. *What the hell is wrong with me?* This is not at all what I should feel. I should be relieved he's found another woman who's happy to be the focus of his attention.

My loyalty issues are getting out of hand. I need to distract myself, fast. I latch on to the nearest blue alien and ask him to sing with me.

His dark eyes light eagerly, and he puts an arm around my shoulders. "I have just the song for us."

As he leads me toward the stage, I resist the urge to shrug off his arm. His skin feels tacky and overly warm against mine.

We climb onto the short platform and the opening notes to "I Got You Babe" by Sonny and Cher start to play. I clumsily follow the words on the screen, while my partner seems to have this song well-rehearsed, replicating Sonny's tenor notes perfectly and making a point of grabbing my hand every time the main chorus repeats.

I try my best to keep my focus on Tamara in the audience, but my attention wanders to the bar where Kiozhi stands with his arms crossed. I can't tell if he's hurt or angry. Do I care? My head says no, but there's an uncomfortable twinge in my chest. *Dammit, do not let yourself fall for puppy dog eyes.* Yes, that one night was great, but it was only one night. This guy singing with me could be great too.

To prove it, I smile at my duet partner and loop my arm through his as we step off the stage to mild applause. "Buy me a drink?"

"It would be my pleasure." Unfortunately, he guides me straight to the bar where Kiozhi is standing. I position myself with my back to Kiozhi as the bartender hands me my drink—a flowery green thing that's overly sweet. I'm pretty sure my karaoke partner just told me his name, but I can't seem to focus. I swear I can feel Kiozhi's stare on the back of my neck.

After a few moments of nodding at small talk, I can't take it anymore. I glance over my shoulder.

Kiozhi is gone.

I look around the bar but can't find him. Did he finally give up on me? I should be glad, but my hands are shaking and my heart races. I set my barely touched drink on the bar. "I'm not feeling very well," I say. "I'm going to retire. Thank you for the song."

"But wait, you—"

I dart for the door without waiting for him to finish. Once I'm safely in my room, I text my sisters that I left the party. Then I flop back on the bed where Kiozhi and I made love not all that long ago. I run both palms over the coverlet and sigh, squeezing my eyes shut at my mixed emotions.

I never expected my quest for freedom to feel this awful.

6

KIOZHỊ

I lean back in the co-pilot seat and look around the sparse shuttle cockpit. The view screen dominating the front wall shows the *Romantasy's* shuttle bay doors open to the stars, the golden glimmer of the atmospheric force shield flickering now and then. Through the open portal to the rear of the compartment I can hear the low voices of guests boarding the shuttle.

I pivot my chair to face Tazhio in the pilot seat. "Why am I here again?"

"An excursion to the Singing Planet is guaranteed to take your mind off your other problems." Tazhio keeps his attention on the control panel, prepping for our upcoming flight. "You'll love it, I promise."

I make a doubtful sound at the back of my throat. Tazhio's always working, always able to keep his mind off his troubles.

Not for the first time, I envy him. All I can think about is Suzanne's amazing voice as she sang last night, her promises of love directed at someone other than myself. I really need to find something else to focus on. "Is there something I can do to help?"

He barely glances at me. "Not unless you want to calculate shield modulation for friction induced plasma ionization."

"Pretty sure I skipped that class in school," I say wryly.

He chuckles, then abruptly silences. His alertness triggers my *Iki'i*, and I turn toward the sound of voices coming from outside the cockpit.

"Thank you, no." A woman's soft voice reaches me. "I'm with my sisters."

A gravelly voice replies, "We can make room for them…"

I stop listening at that point, conscious of my friend's reaction and the roiling jealousy now bombarding my *Iki'i*. I'm not the only one trying to distract myself from female interactions. One of the humans on board has gained his attention too, but he's not allowed to pursue her; the crew isn't allowed to look for mates among the guests. But finding a mate is so rare, I think he's being an idiot not to act, consequences be damned.

"Is that her?" I ask.

"Yes," he says, his voice raspy.

"You need to go see her," I say. "At least let me live vicariously through you. Go!"

"Are you trying to make me lose my job?" he says through gritted teeth. "You know my contract prohibits me from pursuing a mate among the guests."

"*Kuzara*." I fling my hands up in exasperation. "Just say you're checking on the welfare of your passengers. If you get fired, I'll hire you as my private shuttle pilot."

He scowls. "I don't want your charity."

Yet he stands and moves toward the door as if unable to help himself. Moments later, he returns with a copper-haired female. I recognize her. She's one of Suzanne's sisters. *If she's on this tour, maybe Suzanne is too.*

I shoot to my feet. "Aren't you one of the Bloom sisters?"

She nods, glancing around the cockpit. "I don't mean to intrude…"

"Nonsense." I gesture toward the chair I just vacated. "I'm more than happy to exchange seats."

Before she can speak again, I squeeze past her into the passenger area, scanning the banks of plush red seats for Suzanne's familiar red-gold hair and pale skin. She's seated near the back, and the seat paired next to hers is empty. Grinning, I stride down the aisle toward her.

Her green eyes meet mine and a pretty flush rises to her cheeks. My *Iki'i* senses her attraction and draws me forward like a magnet.

Taking the seat adjoining hers, I lean over the shared armrest and give her a wink. "I hope you don't mind, but your sister traded seats with me."

Suzanne turns her shoulder away from me and crosses her arms. "I absolutely do—"

A voice over the intercom interrupts the rest of her words. "We've closed the hatch and are preparing to depart. Please remain seated until we clear the docking bay doors."

I give Suzanne a sly grin. "Guess you're stuck with me this time." I'm not going to let her push me away again. We have an entire excursion to spend together, and I plan to make the most of it.

"Oh, goodie," she mutters, still staring out the viewport.

The shuttle shivers momentarily as it lifts from the flight deck, then sails smoothly between the *Romantasy's* bay doors. Tazhio's an excellent pilot, and I bet he's pulling out all the stops to show off for his lady. I just need to find a way to do the same.

Keeping my voice low and intimate, I say, "I'm sorry you don't enjoy chocolate."

"Who says I don't like chocolate?" She glares at me from the corner of her eye.

"You returned my gift."

"I was trying to make a point," she says, exasperation clear in her tone.

"What point?" I ask.

She turns to look directly at me. "I'm not interested in you, Kiozhi. Stop stalking me."

Confusion fills me. Why is she lying? She can't hide her attraction to me. My *Iki'i* knows she feels it, the same way I know she gets aroused when I deepen my voice. Perhaps this is part of the human courting game. I make the decision not to back down. Looking directly into her amazing green eyes, I state, "No."

"Wh-what?" Her eyes widen, and surprise flickers across my *Iki'i*.

"I'm not stalking you," I clarify. "I'm courting you. I've been told human females enjoy this. Tell me what you want, and I will provide it."

"Never again." She crosses her arms and stares straight ahead.

I don't know what I'm supposed to do when my *Iki'i* is sensing one thing, and her words are telling me another. I glance at the Kirenai male across from me. He's leaning over the lap of another Bloom sister—Jennifer, I believe she's called. They seem to be having an intimate moment of attraction as she smiles at him, her fingertips lightly pressed to his arm.

I'm pretty sure he and I have met a few times at parties, though not in our current forms. He looks human, but much broader than the template the IDA provided, and he's completely bald. I assume that's in direct response to Jennifer's unspoken preferences. If so, it means he's been able to spend extensive time with her. A flicker of jealousy rises in me that he's had better luck. *Perhaps he can offer me advice.*

"Hey," I call to him. "You're Nazhin, the owner of Demod Industries, right?"

He stares at me. "Why would the owner of a corporation need to work as a porter?"

His words aren't exactly a lie, but I definitely get the sense he wants me to shut up. I glance toward Jennifer. Does he not want her to know who he is? But why? He's almost as wealthy as I am. Perhaps he's having difficulty courting too. Yet if Jennifer's current responses to him are any indication, he's doing something right. I'll have to ask him about his tactics later. For now, I'll let him continue his disguise.

"My mistake." I recline in my seat and wave a dismissive hand. "Back to your portering or whatever." Then a thought occurs to me. I lean closer to Suzanne. "Do humans have something against rich guys? Is that why you keep rejecting me?"

"Could you be more full of yourself?" she snaps before focusing her attention on her sister and Nazhin once more.

Kuzara. Will I ever get a straight answer out of her?

"What's Demod Industries?" Jennifer asks.

"A company that designs high-end sensor equipment," Nazhin supplies. "I believe they're currently the largest manufacturer in the galaxy."

Interest sparks in Jennifer's eyes. "Like astronomy equipment?"

"Certainly," he says. "But I'm afraid humans are banned from purchasing advanced technology until your planet is no longer on probation."

Suzanne drums her fingertips against her thigh, eyes narrowed on Nazhin's face. Suspicion pulses off her, and I get the sense she's going to call him out at any moment. If she blows his cover, it will be my fault, and I don't want that. I smile broadly and lean forward, trying to draw their attention. "I could probably smuggle you a few things."

"Really?" Jennifer grins, eyes full of excitement.

An idea blinks like casino lights in my mind. *Can I sweet talk Jennifer into putting in a good word with her sister?* "Of course." I shrug nonchalantly. "Just tell me what you need."

Suzanne rolls her eyes. "Don't encourage him."

Jennifer ignores her. "Could you get me a sensor that can calculate the Roche limit of a planetary body?"

I have no idea what any of the words she just said even mean, but I say, "I'll ask my contact once we get back to the *Romantasy*." I turn to face Suzanne. "Is there anything I can get you?"

Just then, multi-colored light fills the cabin, and everyone turns toward the viewport. Outside, a braided tangle of brilliant pink, green, and yellow light flows against a backdrop of velvet-black space.

"This is your captain." Tazhio's voice comes over the speakers as the seat cushion softens beneath me. "I've engaged the cabin's safety features. It's normal to encounter some turbulence during this excursion, so please sit back and enjoy the galactic symphony."

Golden streamers of light float through the cabin, followed by a high, sweet note I can feel to the depths of my matrix. The lights are amazing, but I'm more enraptured by Suzanne's soft gasps of wonder. She made such noises during our lovemaking, and I yearn to tease those sounds from her once more. It takes all my willpower not to reach out and trace the trails of light playing over her skin.

Purple and red lights explode against the view screen, coating us in a garish glow as the music dips into a low, mumbling groan. The ship jolts once. Twice. Then the deck starts to shudder.

The mood in the cabin shifts from wonder to nervousness bordering on panic. The once-lovely melody crescendos into a shrieking whine. *Something's wrong.* On instinct, I throw an arm over Suzanne just before wind blasts through the cabin and the air is spiked with the scent of ozone.

7

SUZANNE

My heart feels like it's going to explode from my chest. One minute I'm enjoying the amazing light display, and the next Kiozhi throws an arm over me and we're completely encased in foam. I can't see a thing. I can't even twitch a finger. At least I can breathe, despite what feels like foam up my nose, but my stomach is doing flip-flops because it feels like we're falling.

Holy fuck, are we about to crash?

My entire life flashes before my eyes. My parents, my sisters, my children… Why didn't I make one last call to my kids when I had a chance last night? I want to cry, but I'm too afraid.

Then we jar to a sudden stop. Like a vacuum seal releasing, the foam pressing around us lets go. I suck in a reflexive breath, eyes wide in the surrounding pitch darkness. At least the comforting pressure of Kiozhi's arm still wraps around my torso like an extra layer of protection. I really hope this is part of the show, but I know in my gut it probably isn't.

I squirm, pressing my arms against a flexible shell about an inch or so away from my body. I've never been claustrophobic, but I could easily develop a case of it right about now. Sliding one hand down to grip Kiozhi's arm, I speak into the darkness. "What's happening?"

The chiseled muscles of Kiozhi's arm flex, his deep voice sounding deliberately calm. "The safety foam only expands in the event of a crash."

My rapidly pounding heart squeezes in fear. *We crashed on an alien planet.* "Is the air out there breathable? Where are my sisters? Are they all right?" I realize I'm babbling, my voice getting shriller with every word, but I can't stop. My hands bat uselessly against the surrounding cocoon. "I need to get out of this seat. How do we get out?"

"I'm not sure." Kiozhi pulls his arm from my waist. "The safety pod should open when the foam dissolves. It seems to be malfunctioning."

I sense him pushing at the shell around us and join him, thinking this must be how baby sea turtles feel when they hatch. And just like those little turtles, we have no idea what sort of danger awaits us outside this shell.

Something cool sloshes around my ankles. Is it the dissolved foam? It feels like it's rising. "Is there supposed to be liquid in here?"

"No," Kiozhi grunts, straining harder. "There must be a crack in the emergency hull. I think we landed in water."

Dread fills my stomach. I push more frantically, trying to dig my nails into the material keeping us trapped as water rises up my shins. I realize I'm repeating, "Oh, God." My breath hitches. "I never called my kids. I don't want to die. Please don't let me die."

"Stay calm." Kiozhi's hands touch my face, turning me to face him, though I still can't see a thing in the darkness. "We must've landed in water, but I promise I will get you out of here."

I suck in a shuddering breath and nod fiercely as he withdraws his arm. I know I need to get myself under control, but I've never actually faced my own death before.

"What are you going to do?" I slide my hand across the seat, seeking his touch, but he's not there. Instead, something soft and spongy ripples beneath my fingertips. I recoil. *What the hell is that?*

Water climbs up the backs of my thighs and ass. It smells rank and swampy, like the time my kids came back from summer camp with wet swimming suits in their suitcases. My seat rocks violently, and I grip the arms of my chair. "Kiozhi!"

No answer. I slide my hand over to find my purse, which is wedged in the seat next to me, frantic to find anything that might help me escape. For almost two decades, I had a classic mom-purse full of everything under the sun. Of course for this trip I scaled down, and all I'm carrying now is a tiny cross-strap purse barely big enough for my phone, a tube of lipstick, and my sunglasses.

The water reaches my armpits, and I choke back a sob. *I'm going to die.*

Suddenly, the shell splits open and water rushes in. What feels like serrated teeth clamp onto my arm, and I'm dragged from my seat. Water goes up my nose and stings my eyes. I break the surface abruptly, and whatever was holding my arm releases me. I go flying through the air and hit the water again flat on my back, driving the air from my lungs.

Flailing, I try to rise to the surface. I reach it, choking and sputtering and blinking. Violent splashing draws my attention as I tread water, and I spin to see what looks like a gargantuan centipede with writhing legs. And it's coming straight for me.

With a choked yelp, I turn and paddle in the opposite direction. I can see what I think is the shore, but it feels a million miles away. Glow-in-the-dark plants line the bank, and massive trees climb toward the dark sky overhead. It's hard to breathe, and my arm stings. *This can't be happening.*

Something circles my foot, pulling me under. Water stings my sinuses. I can't see anything in the murky depths. I kick out with my other foot, dislodging whatever has hold of me. Bobbing to the surface, I swim for all I'm worth toward shore. My lungs ache and my heart knocks painfully against my ribs. Finally, I drag myself up the slippery bank, using handfuls of glowing foliage to pull myself free of the treacherous water.

Turning, I see the centipede monster rise from the surface. My jaw drops. Kiozhi is straddling it like an enormous mount.

"Run, Suzanne!" he shouts.

I turn, ready to flee, but then hesitate. I can't just leave him to fight this thing alone. Spotting a long, splintered branch, I grab it and hold it in front of me like a spear. No way I'm going back in the water, but if it comes my way, I'm going to do what I can to help.

The creature writhes and twists, mandibles clacking as it tries to dislodge its rider. Kiozhi's teeth are bared, and he rips one of the creature's antennas right off its head. The thing screeches and drops back into the water, taking Kiozhi with it. The surface ripples and bubbles.

One breath.

Two.

My heart jackhammers in my chest.

Still no sign of Kiozhi.

My arms start to tremble. This isn't possible. He can't have drowned. I hold my breath, waiting for him to emerge. A black tentacle whips up from the depths, smashing the near bank with a deafening crack. Water rises in a wave, cresting the bank and washing my feet out from under me. I land hard on my side, slipping in mud and leaves. Rolling to my knees, I see Kiozhi rising from the water. He's holding the creature's severed head by one antenna.

Tossing it aside, he steps onto the bank and kneels next to me, reaching for my arm. "You're hurt."

"Me? What about you?" I gape at him, surprised that he seems unscratched. Then I glance down at my arm.

A jagged gash circles my biceps where the thing must've grabbed me. Blood runs down my elbow and drips from my fingertips. Suddenly, my arm throbs and my fingertips feel numb. *Oh, God.* I've never been good with blood. My vision narrows, tightening to a pinprick. I glance back up to see Kiozhi's concerned eyes looking into mine. Then the world goes black.

8

―――――――――

KIOZHI

I catch Suzanne before she hits the ground, lowering her limp body gently to the mossy bank. My hands are covered in alien goo: a slippery purplish ooze that's more like mucus than blood. I don't want to foul her with it, but washing in the pond won't get me much cleaner, especially with the carcass now floating in the middle.

I'm still shaken from the attack. The creature hit me as I was resuming my human shape, and I barely hardened my matrix in time to defend myself. Then there was Suzanne, trapped in the pod while I fought. If the beast hadn't cracked the malfunctioning pod open with its thrashing, she might be dead now.

I scrub my hands clean on some nearby leaves and lean over to examine her unconscious form. She's pale, but her breathing sounds fine. The laceration on her arm from where the creature grabbed her doesn't appear to be deep, though she is still bleeding.

I sit back on my heels and survey our surroundings. We need a place to rest and see to our injuries. I know next to nothing about the Singing Planet, but it appears we've landed in a forest. Massive trees rise into darkness overhead, and multi-colored plants surround us, their leaves emitting a nebulous glow. Tree roots run like interlacing highways between the shrubbery, making line-of-sight impossible. I hope the other pods have landed nearby.

Standing, I call into the forest. "Hello? Can anyone hear me?"

Other than the soft creak of branches rubbing together, the forest is silent. My gut churns with worry. Our pod may not be the only one that malfunctioned. I bring up my ICC, but there isn't any signal. *Kuzara.* I guess it makes sense, since the planet isn't on the galactic grid, but it will make finding the other survivors extremely difficult.

I gather handfuls of large fallen leaves and scrub the slime from my body as best I can. Then I do the same for the cut on Suzanne's arm, removing the scarf she wears around her neck so I can use it as a bandage.

Once that's done, I glance at the floating carcass. Are there more of them in the area? I feel like we need to get away from here as soon as possible. I slide my arms under Suzanne's shoulders and knees to pick her up and carry her, but she rouses.

"What happened?" She sits up and looks around, her eyes widening when they settle on the pond. "Oh, God, it wasn't a dream."

"Unfortunately not." I gently touch the scarf on her arm. "How are you feeling?"

"It hurts, but I think I'm okay." She looks at me, stiffens, and turns her attention away. "Um, why are you naked?"

"Oh." With everything else going on, I hadn't considered it. I immediately have my matrix form a modesty shield over my genitals. "I had to use my amorphous form to escape the pod. My clothes are still inside."

Her eyes flick toward me, and my *Iki'i* senses her embarrassment shift to curiosity. "I forgot Kirenai could do that. Become… liquid."

Relieved I don't feel any revulsion coming from her, I chuckle. "Not liquid, exactly, but our natural state is semi-fluid. We don't use it very often because it's when we're most vulnerable. Other than that, Kirenai are impervious to most damage."

That seems to satisfy her, and she stands to look around. "Where's the shuttle?"

"I don't know. The escape pods must've jettisoned before it crashed."

She gulps and wraps her arms across her chest, shivering as if she's cold, though the air is almost stiflingly warm. "So everyone is scattered?" Her arms drop and she stands slightly taller, as if hit by an inspiration. "Hold on, my sister put an app on my phone. I might be able to use it to find her."

She opens the tiny bag hanging against her hip and the hope on her face collapses almost immediately. Tilting the small bag, she pours a stream of water from it, then pulls out a flat rectangle the size of her palm. "Dammit, it's soaked. It won't turn on." She shoves it back into her bag and spins in a slow circle. "Which way do we go?"

I look around and shrug. "Moving away from this pond is a good start."

We elbow our way through the bushes until we reach one of the massive roots humping up from the forest floor. She's about to pull herself on top of it when she cocks her head. "Do you hear that?"

I hold my breath and listen. There is a strange repetitive call echoing faintly between the trees. I think I've heard it before, but I can't place it. "Yes. Do you recognize it?"

"I think that's Beanie!" She hauls herself up onto the massive root. "Beanie! Here, boy!"

I climb up and follow her, using the wide curved top of the root as a trail. "What's a Beanie?"

"My sister's dog." She bends over to crawl across a massive root, and I can't help but admire her ass. She's wearing loose pants made of a flowing green material that is slit up the front nearly to the tops of her thighs. Far too elegant for our current environment, but sexy enough to make my shaft stir. I tamp down my lust. This is the wrong time and place to pursue my courtship.

I follow her along the root, which creates a path between the glowing brush. It curves gently, meandering over the ground. The gullies and swells between it and the other roots create a maze with glowing plants sprouting in every nook and cranny. We're forced to climb several more roots as we follow the sound of the barking, calling out for survivors at regular intervals.

We're both panting and tired when the root we're following makes a sharp turn to skirt the bank of another pond. Thick shrubs grow along the edges, jutting from the water and obscuring the transition between land and shore.

Suzanne sucks in a sharp breath and takes a step backward, bumping into me. I instinctively put an arm around her to keep her from tripping. She presses her back against me, and I can't help the satisfied feeling I get from having her this close, regardless of the circumstances.

She whispers, "Do you think there's another one of those monsters in there?"

Narrowing my eyes, I look over the glistening surface and expand my *Iki'i*. A large predator is bound to give off at least some primitive emotions. "I don't sense anything."

We stand in silence for a few more moments studying the surface before she whispers, "Beanie stopped barking."

"What does that mean?" I ask.

"Either Tamara calmed him down or…" She shakes her head as a small shudder rolls through her.

I know what she's thinking. Her fear is valid, but there is nothing for us to do except press on. "Let's try to go around."

She nods. We backtrack to another cross-root, then follow a trail perpendicular to our previous direction. The path ends back at the pond.

"Shit." Suzanne loops an arm around my biceps and hugs it against her chest. "I'm so turned around. Is this the same pond or a different one?"

I shake my head, as uncertain as she is. Then I spot ripples fluttering across the surface of the pond. Something is moving in the water.

9

SUZANNE

I clutch Kiozhi's arm, too terrified breathe. There is something moving in the water. Then, beneath a cluster of purple leaves dangling over the water on the opposite bank, I see a familiar fawn-colored muzzle and two dark eyes.

"Beanie!" I let go of Kiozhi's arm and step forward. The tiny dog is trying to climb the opposite bank. When he hears my voice, he turns and paddles toward us, whining softly. That explains why he stopped barking. He must've fallen in and can't get out.

I'm fearful something will rise from below and devour him, but he reaches our side without incident, scrambling to find a way up.

Dropping to my knees, I reach down for him, but my arms aren't long enough.

"Let me," says Kiozhi, laying down on his belly.

The dog is also out of his reach, but not for long. His arm stretches, becoming disproportionately long until he grabs Beanie and pulls him free of the water. He sets the dog down and Beanie shakes, sending a spray of droplets over our laps. Then his tail starts wagging furiously. He puts his front paws on Kiozhi then wriggles over to me, tiny pink tongue darting out to kiss my chin when I bend down to pick him up.

"Good boy. Where's your momma?" I stand and look across the pond. "Tamara! Jennifer! Hello?"

There's no answer, which makes my heart ache with dread. I give Kiozhi an anguished look. "Tamara is never without her dog."

His lips thin as he nods. "We'll keep looking."

I cradle Beanie in one arm as we continue our search for a way around the pond. I'm trying not to dwell on what finding him alone might mean, but worry for my sisters makes my insides tremble.

Eventually, we reach the opposite side of the pond, thankfully without incident, but there's no sign of my sisters or any of the other pods. We keep walking. There doesn't seem to be a division between night and day on this planet, but it feels as if we've been walking for hours by the time we come upon a cave-like hollow in one of the massive trunks. The interior is dotted with bits of glowing golden moss.

Kiozhi gently takes Beanie from my arms. "This looks like a good place to rest."

I hadn't realized how heavy the dog had become until I was relieved of his weight. I don't want to stop searching, but I'm beyond tired. I nod reluctantly. "Yes."

The cave isn't large—barely big enough for us to lie down—but it's better than being in the open. The floor is covered with a spongy layer of dry leaves, and I sink down onto them gratefully. My stomach rumbles, and I realize my mouth is parched, but I'm too tired to deal with either of those things. I lay down on my side, shivering slightly. Kiozhi places Beanie against my stomach, and the little dog walks a tight circle before settling against me with a wuffly sigh. I pet his soft fur and close my eyes against tears of frustration.

Kiozhi's warmth settles against my back, and when he wraps one arm tightly around me to spoon against me, I don't even complain. As much as I tried to dodge his attention on the *Romantasy*, I'm really glad he's here with me now. I'm not sure how well I'd handle being stranded alone on this alien planet. His other hand slides up to stroke my hair, and I doze off.

I wake some time later with Kiozhi's arm still around me like a weighted blanket. Beanie has deserted me to tunnel under the leaves nearby, only his nose poking out. After a few minutes of reorienting myself to our situation, I wriggle onto my back and look over at his sleeping face. The golden glow of moss bathes his features, highlighting the classic lines and angles. His lashes are thick, dark crescents against his cheeks, and his slight dimples make me want to see him smile. He looks too perfect to be real.

His eyes open slowly, and he blinks at me. "Hey," he whispers.

Realizing I just got caught staring, I'm not sure what to say, so I just whisper back, "Hey."

He smiles and brushes his thumb over my cheekbone before plucking something from my hair. "You have leaves in your hair."

I reach up self-consciously and smooth my palm over my tangled tresses. My ex used to gaslight me all the time about my looks, trying to undermine my confidence. I never realized it until my therapist pointed it out after our divorce. But Kiozhi just smiles as if he thinks I'm cute, not passive-aggressively telling me I'm a rumpled mess. I'm struck by the sudden urge to kiss him.

Before I can stop myself, I *am* kissing him. Deeply. Hungrily.

He pulls me closer as my tongue meets his. His hand slides over my thigh to cup my ass, squeezing gently as he rocks his hips against me. The solid length of his erection presses against my belly, and a jolt of desire races through my blood. I know what he can do, and I want to feel that pleasure again. To leave my stress behind, even just for a moment. I moan into his mouth, and he responds by sliding one hand between my legs and rubbing gently over my crotch. *God, he's good at this.*

I reach down to stroke his hardness, discovering the covering over his crotch is gone, exposing his shaft to my touch. It's solid and hot, throbbing against my touch.

He presses my clit through the thin fabric of my pants, and I gasp. My panties are already drenched, my core pulsing with a need for more. I want him inside me *right now*. Breaking our kiss, I untie my waistband and shove my pants down my hips. He helps pull them free of my legs before lifting my tank top over my head. He cups my breasts in his palms, thumbs circling my nipples until sparks of lust race through me.

I widen my legs, drawing him between my knees. With one hand between us, I guide his erection to my opening. I gasp as he fills me in a swift, sure stroke. He feels so perfect inside me. My inner muscles contract almost immediately in climax. Even as I spasm, he pushes me higher with his strokes, his rhythm building into something primitive and wild that makes my blood sing.

He moans and thrusts, his eyes never leaving mine. I can't deny the connection I feel to him. I'm on the cusp of another release, riding it, surfing like a wave that refuses to crest.

Just when I think it will never break, he does a little circle with his hips, and I'm thrown over the edge, clenching around his huge cock. This time, Kiozhi isn't far behind. He explodes with a shudder, heat filling me and sending an aftershock of pleasure through my body.

He holds himself tight against my hips, pulsing with heat as he looks down into my face. I swear I see love filling his eyes. *Impossible.* He can't love me. We barely know each other. We're simply feeling connected in this impossible situation and needing to de-stress.

He rolls over and pulls me to lie on his chest, warm skin against warm skin. Beanie huffs and pokes his head from under a nest of leaves, then burrows back out of sight. I blink and sigh deeply, sleep threatening to drag me under once more.

I know we should get up and continue our search, but I don't want to move, not quite yet. I gaze toward the back of our shelter, looking over the glowing moss and other small plants. Growing things have always been one of my passions, and these would make a spectacular moon garden back on Earth.

Back on Earth. Out of nowhere, a sob overtakes me. Will I ever see home again? My kids?

Kiozhi's arm tightens around me, and he kisses the top of my head, a gesture so sweet it makes me sob again. I don't like feeling this vulnerable and needy, especially with a guy who basically stalked me not too long ago. I push up to a sitting position and search for my clothes. "Stop being so nice to me," I grit through my teeth, feeling stupid as tears threaten to spill from my eyes. "This doesn't mean we're a couple. It was just a moment of weakness."

"Suzanne—"

I know I'm being a bitch, but if I look at him, I'll break down, and that's the last thing we need. "Come on." I stand and pull on my pants, moving out of the cave before I even have them tied in place. "We need to find the others."

10

———

KIOZHI

Stunned by Suzanne's outward reaction to my affection, I lay on the leaves for a moment after she departs. My *Iki'i* insists she enjoys my tenderness, but her words and body language indicate otherwise. Which truth am I to believe?

Rising, I stretch until my fingertips brush the cave ceiling. I feel better after resting, but my stomach feels like it's gnawing a hole through me.

The carpet of leaves rustles, and I remember the dog. Suzanne must be too agitated to remember he's with us, and those tiny legs won't be able to keep up well, especially if we have to do more climbing. I bend down and push aside the leaves. "Are you ready to travel, little man?"

Beanie shakes off the rest of the leaves and stretches, small mouth opening in a wide pink yawn. His hind quarters wiggle

298

furiously, and he prances in front of me, front paws batting the air with excitement.

I smile indulgently and pick him up. He's soft and warm, settling into the crook of my arm as I catch up to Suzanne.

She's studying an enormous branch laying across the root she's following. "It looks like this was recently broken, possibly from the shuttle."

I examine the purple bark and scattered leaves. The area looks exactly the same as everything else we've encountered. "How can you tell it's recent?"

"The sap is fresh. Smell it?" There is a slightly vegetal scent in the air nearby. She points at the splintered end of the branch with glistening beads of pinkish fluid. Then she points toward the canopy. "And there's a gash in that trunk that may be from a recent impact. See? It looks like it's bleeding sap."

I look up and nod. "That's good reasoning. I never would've noticed these details. Are you a plant specialist?"

A flush rises to her cheeks, and I sense a flicker of pride. "I took a few horticulture classes while the kids were in school, but I couldn't carry a full course load, take care of the house, and work a full-time job. Though I suppose I did manage to keep us fed and clothed, so I guess it was worth the sacrifice. Besides, I never was a straight-A student." She sighs and picks up the end of a thick vine tangled around the limb. "That's why I supported my ex while he got his M.D. Instead of the other way around."

Waves of self-loathing pulse from her, strong enough to make me nauseous, and my own thoughts are now in turmoil. She has offspring? I thought the IDA had specifically picked women who hadn't yet experienced mates and children. Not that it matters to me in the end. "Is this male you refer to as your ex the one who sired your children?"

She laughs, a pitiless sound. "That is an excellent description of him."

I don't like the change in her emotions when she talks about this male. "You supported him… but never the other way around?"

"If there's one thing I learned while I was married, it's that relationships are never balanced evenly." She turns and steps over the fallen branch, continuing along the root snaking between the tall brush. "Robbie wrung me dry and tossed me aside. I will never allow that to happen to me again." The venom in her voice is painful to hear. Even Beanie whines from where he rests in the crook of my arm.

"I would never treat you that way," I say softly.

Suzanne does an about-face and glares. "No, you won't, because we're not in a relationship. I just told you I will never allow that to happen again."

Everything I know about her now clicks into place. I understand why she's been avoiding me. Much of her life has been spent in service to a man who didn't deserve her. I'm certain I've found my second-chance mate, but she may be too wounded to recognize me as hers. I sigh and bow my head. "I see."

"Good." Pivoting, she continues walking.

I follow slightly behind, full of questions but concerned they might make her angry. Finally, I decide to ask about plants again. "Do you ever intend to resume your studies?"

She glances over her shoulder toward me, eyebrows raised. "I told you my grades suck."

"Your grades don't matter, as long as you're learning something you love."

Her steps slow, allowing me to draw up beside her. "Actually, I start classes at the community college when I get home."

I smile. "Excellent. Perhaps you can take samples home with you from here."

"That would be fun, though I wouldn't want to introduce an invasive species."

We continue to talk about horticulture on her planet as we follow the path of broken foliage. Beanie scouts ahead of us, running back to check on us now and again. Eventually, we reach a mass of splintered roots and branches laying haphazardly over a deeply carved trench in the forest floor. A ragged piece of the shuttle's purple hull lays half buried in the dirt.

"Look." I point toward a vacant escape pod poking up from the brush. "There's another pod." Beanie is already sniffing around the trench.

"Hello!" Suzanne calls.

Nobody answers our shouts. We follow the gouged landscape until we reach the nose of the shuttle butted up against a tree. Another empty escape pod rests nearby—a single that can only be from inside the cockpit.

I poke my head inside what remains of the shuttle's cockpit. "Tazhio? Anybody here?"

There's no sign of my friend, just damaged control panels and crumpled hull plating. Worry coils inside me, but there are no bodies, so I take it as a good sign.

"Tamara was with the pilot." Suzanne stands next to me and looks inside. "Do you think they're okay?"

"I don't know, but Tazhio will do everything in his power to keep your sister safe."

"Assuming their pods didn't malfunction too."

I swallow thickly and nod. "That was unusual. Let's hope they just went in search of the other passengers."

Her brow is furrowed, and I want to offer better comfort, but after what happened in the cave, I'm not sure I should. Usually, my *Iki'i* gives me an edge in my personal interactions, but Suzanne's inner conflict poses an uncertainty I'm at a loss to resolve.

She takes a step inside the destroyed cockpit. "Any chance we might find food or water in here? I'm starving."

My stomach has also been complaining. I glance around hopefully, but recalling the way the cockpit looked before we left the *Romantasy*, I think it's safe to assume there isn't. "I doubt it." Taking her arm, I gently pull her back out of the cockpit. "I think we're going to have to find something local."

We climb the other side of the trench, loose dirt and branches giving way under our hands and feet. When we reach the top, Suzanne points to a spot farther along the edge. "That area looks like it's been trampled."

We navigate over and around debris to reach it. Broken branches and fallen leaves cover the ground, and the edge looks sloughed, as if someone had difficulty climbing it. Small yellow orbs covered in spikes litter the ground. Suzanne picks one up. "This looks like a large grain of pollen. Ouch!" She drops the orb as if it burns, rubbing her fingers against the front of her pants. "Shit, don't touch those. Might be poisonous. My fingers are tingling."

I frown, looking up at the branches high above us. "They may be falling off the trees. Let's move."

She nods, and we slide back down to where Beanie has been sniffing along the wall of the trench. Suzanne picks him up, but as we walk away, he squirms free and takes off barking. In the blink of an eye, he's up the trench wall and disappearing into the brush.

"Beanie, come!" Suzanne yells, climbing up after him. "Beanie!"

I hurry to follow but pause at a churned spot of dirt. There are indentations that look like paws. Not small ones like Beanie's—human-sized. With claws. I frown. Could it be a Kirenai? I try to think of any beings that might leave these tracks, but I know of none that have six toes.

I glance up at where Suzanne and Beanie have already disappeared in the brush.

"*Kuzara,*" I say, vaulting up the side of the trench. Suzanne is heading straight toward whatever made these prints.

11

SUZANNE

eanie moves quickly through the brush ahead, dodging beneath the understory with ease. My slit-leg pants are definitely not made for bushwhacking, catching on everything as I crash through the dense brush after him, and my exposed skin stings with scratches. I push past a glowing fuchsia plant with multi-lobed leaves and nearly trip over what looks like an azure sea fan. This planet reminds me of a coral reef, only without the water or any lively fish darting among the plants. In fact, other than the enormous creature that attacked us at the pond, we've encountered no animal life at all, which seems strange.

But that isn't my concern right now. I can't afford to lose track of Beanie. He must've picked up Tamara's scent. Behind me, I hear Kiozhi rustling and cursing. "Suzanne, wait. We don't know—"

"I think he smells something," I shout back.

Beanie has climbed up onto another root path and is circling with his nose to the ground. I don't know how he got up there so quickly, because I need a minute to pull myself up behind him. I hope my sister stayed on the trail from here on.

Kiozhi joins us, grabbing my arm. "We need to slow down. I saw clawed footprints back there."

I hadn't even considered that Beanie might be chasing something besides Tamara. "Well, crap." I pat my thighs with both hands. "Beanie, come here!"

The dog darts away as I approach, gleefully ignoring me.

"Come back here, you little rat-chaser!" I take off after him.

Kiozhi pulls me up short. "Stop. Whatever he's chasing is at least as big as we are, and there may be more than one."

My chest tightens. "My sister will be devastated if anything happens to her dog." I pat my thighs again. "Beanie, want a cookie?"

I think he knows I'm lying about the cookie because he gives me a disdainful look before trotting down the trail with a jaunty twitch of his rump.

"Dammit, Beanie!"

Kiozhi moves ahead. "Let me go first. If we encounter danger, run."

I pause to pick up a hefty branch I can use as a club. For better or for worse, Kiozhi and I are in this together, and I don't plan to abandon him now, no matter what he says.

We chase the dog for a while without incident. I'm starting to think Kiozhi's fears are unfounded when suddenly Beanie yelps.

Ahead of me, Kiozhi comes to a sudden stop, and I lean sideways to see around him. A ten-foot-tall bush with enormous, fleshy, arrowhead-shaped maroon leaves and thin, curling tendrils covered in what look like dangling yellow berries looms over the trail about thirty feet away. Beanie stands facing the plant, baring his teeth and growling.

I grip my club and raise it like a baseball bat, expecting some sort of monster to burst from the shrubbery.

Instead, the plant's tendrils lash out. Beanie yelps again, dancing out of the way while continuing his barking.

"Oh, shit!" I try to push past Kiozhi, but he's already moving forward.

The tendrils whip toward the dog again, and this time one of them loops around Beanie's middle. He struggles, but the vine lifts him into the air. One of the fleshy maroon leaves splits open like a six-petaled flower. Except it's not like a flower at all, but more like a mouth, dripping saliva and making sucking sounds. The tendril swings the wriggling dog closer, trying to position him over the flower.

"Beanie!" I scream.

Kiozhi reaches Beanie and grabs him by his hind legs. With a swift jerk, he snaps the tendril, freeing the dog. He steps backward, but before he can move out of range, a vine shoots out and captures his ankle. His feet are yanked out from under him. He crashes backward onto the trail. Beanie's small form tumbles from his grip and rolls off into the brush.

I halt about ten feet away from Kiozhi. My heart thunders against my ribs. How the hell do you fight a carnivorous plant? I need a torch or a machete, not a useless stick.

Another flower opens, much bigger than the one that tried to eat Beanie. The tendril around Kiozhi's ankle jerks him along the ground, ever closer to the pulsing flower mouth as he struggles to unwrap himself. Now that I can see inside the flower's maw, I notice what look like hundreds of tiny teeth, each dripping what I suspect are digestive juices.

It's an alien version of a Venus Flytrap—a huge, man-eating version.

Kiozhi frees his ankle, but more tendrils have wrapped around his wrist and other ankle. For every one he breaks, two more ensnare him.

I move closer and extend my club, praying I'm not in range of the plant's lashing vines. "Grab the stick. I'll help pull you free."

"You need to run," he says, ignoring me as he tears through another vine.

"Come on, before it drags you any closer."

With a frustrated grunt, Kiozhi breaks his wrist free and rolls over onto his belly, taking the end of my club in one hand. His bound legs are useless, but his free hand claws the path, dragging himself forward as I lean back to add my weight to the pull. He now has at least five tendrils around his legs, and the plant has bent over toward him, flower mouth wrapping around his foot. It makes disgusting slurping sounds, and I have the horrible mental image of it stripping the flesh off Kiozhi's bones.

"Hold on!" I grunt, putting every fiber of my being into holding onto the club. The rough bark stings my palms, but I refuse to let go. I feel like I'm playing tug-of-war: heaving, heaving, heaving.

Kiozhi's teeth are bared with effort. We seem to be evenly matched with the plant. In a moment of terror, I realize the plant is slowly climbing up the trail after us.

"Kiozhi!" My eyes are wide on the monster.

Glancing back at the creature, Kiozhi returns his attention to me. "Save yourself," he says through clenched teeth. "Run."

I know what he's about to do, and I can't bear it. Not just because I don't want to be alone, but because Kiozhi doesn't deserve this. He's a good man. I grit my teeth. "No. Fucking. Way."

Beanie pops out of the bushes, growling. He clamps his teeth around a tendril and tugs. The tendril shudders and releases its grip on Kiozhi. More tendrils whip toward the dog, but Beanie lets go in the nick of time, dashing away.

It's enough of a distraction for Kiozhi to jerk one leg free of the free of its remaining tendril. He pulls his knee under him and strains forward, still gripping the club with one hand. *"Kuzara,"* he groans. "Keep pulling. I have an idea."

His trapped leg flexes and thins, seeming to flow upward toward his body. The flower mouth clamped around his foot snaps shut, pulsing in a strange, gulping motion. Kiozhi grunts in pain and lurches forward.

Without his foot.

"Oh, God!" I yelp, helping him crawl several yards away. "What the hell just happened?"

"I sacrificed part of my matrix."

"Jesus," I breathe, understanding why the plant looked like it was swallowing. "Did that plant *eat* a part of you?"

"Yes."

I stop and let him sag to the ground, both of us panting. His foot and leg have reformed, but his shin and calf look raw, seeping a blue-tinged liquid. "How bad are you?" I ask. My concern is like a boulder inside my chest. "I thought you said Kirenai are impervious to most damage."

He's breathing in heaving gulps, and his face looks ashen beneath his blue skin. "Yes, unless we're in our amorphous state. Then I'm pretty helpless."

I grab one of my pant legs and tear a strip free so I can bind his injured leg. I'm not even sure that will help, but I have to do something.

Beanie emerges from the bushes and joins us. He's panting, and a large patch of fur is missing from one hip. The skin looks raw but not bloody. Kiozhi reaches out and strokes his head. "Thank you, little man. You saved my life."

I glance behind us toward the plant and gasp. It's slowly shambling onto the trail after us.

"Shit. That plant's still after us. We need to get away from here." I put a shoulder under Kiozhi's arm and help him stand.

He wobbles and sags against me.

Supporting as much of his weight as I can, I help him limp in the direction we came from, trying not to trip over Beanie, who's apparently decided it's better to stay close to us. We have to stop and rest several times, but at least we seem to have left the plant behind. I really hope it can't track us.

During one rest break, I notice a dark spot at the base of a trunk just off the trail. I squint through the dim light cast by the glowing plants. "Is that a cave?"

Kiozhi seems to be having trouble keeping his eyes open. "We should go see."

My heart races as we step off the trail. So far, this planet has given us nothing but danger, and I'm not sure how much more we can take.

12

───

SUZANNE

I stumble under Kiozhi's weight. He leans on me more and more as we struggle through the brush toward the cave until I'm almost dragging him along. I examine the foliage ahead as we move. The light from the pastel-colored foliage is murky at best, making me feel like I'm in a sci-fi horror movie.

We reach the tree, but my heart falls at the sight of the darkened bark. "Shit, this isn't a cave. Just a discolored part of the trunk."

Kiozhi lets out a grunt I think is disappointment and sags to the forest floor. His body feels hotter than I remember, and he closes his eyes with a sigh as Beanie climbs tiredly onto his lap.

I stand up straight to stretch my aching back. I should be sweating up a storm after our walk, but my skin is papery and dry. My mouth feels like cotton, and my stomach is so empty I

312

feel like I'm about to turn inside out. We need to find water, but Kiozhi's in no condition to search with me.

"Stay here and rest. I'm going to find water," I say, looking around. After our initial encounter, the thought of approaching a pond by myself is terrifying, but I don't see any other choice.

"Wait." Kiozhi points to the right. "You hear that?"

It sounds like something dripping. I follow the sound and find a bank of turquoise vines hiding what looks like a three-foot-high hole beneath one of the massive roots. Nervously, I push the vines aside to reveal an underground cavern. The same golden moss I noticed in the other cave covers the walls, giving the space the same gentle light as the surrounding forest. Intertwining roots and vines form a lattice I think we can climb to get in and out.

Better yet, there's a thin trickle of water running down the wall on the far side. It forms a tiny pool before streaming away under the spongy gray leaves covering the floor. "It's a cave!" I call back to Kiozhi. "And there's water too. I'm going to check it out."

"Not without me," Kiozhi says as I swing my feet over the lip. He tries to sit up but ends up sagging onto his elbow. His face is pinched with agony, and he shakes his head. "Maybe not. But at least take a weapon."

He has a good point. I pick up a hefty branch, then swing my feet over the edge and drop inside.

The cave is about twelve or fifteen feet in diameter and seven or eight feet high. It slopes downward toward the back where the stream runs along the wall. There are a few spots of round fuchsia leaves growing in the corners near the ceiling, but they don't seem to be moving. I don't see any other cracks or openings leading to other caves.

Stepping carefully across the floor in case the dead leaves hide pitfalls, I move toward the spring. The air here is sweet, like a ripe peach, full of life yet layered with the subtle scent of decay. I scoop a handful of water from the pool and smell it. There isn't any foul scent, so I take a tiny sip. The cool water coats my parched tongue, and I suddenly want to drop to my knees and lap up the water like a dog.

I take a bigger gulp. The water hits my empty stomach like a brick, and my gut heaves. I gasp, remembering all those spaghetti westerns Dad used to watch where people who've been wandering in the desert throw up after drinking too fast. Guess that part wasn't fiction.

Swallowing back the nausea, I go back to the entrance and call for Kiozhi to climb down. He hands Beanie to me, then I hover behind Kiozhi as he clumsily descends. The instant his feet hit the bottom, he drops to his knees and flops over so he's half propped against the wall. "I'm sorry."

"Don't apologize. You're hurt. Let me bring you some water." I head for the pool.

Beanie is already there, lapping greedily. It's only two feet in diameter, so I wait until he's done, then empty my purse and rinse it out before filling it—not the most sanitary container, but it works. I return and offer it to Kiozhi. "Not too much. We can't be certain it's safe."

"I don't care at this point," Kiozhi says between gulps. The water runs down his forearms and drips from his elbows, glistening as it hits his muscular chest. I don't understand how he can be so sexy at a time like this, but even injured, he's beautiful.

I return to the pool, glad to see the spring has already refreshed the water. Ignoring my own warning, I drink until my stomach aches with fullness, then scrub water over my face and arms, glad to feel cleaner. "I can't believe how lucky we are to have found this place."

Kiozhi sits with his back against the wall, Beanie once more curled on his lap. His fingers toy with the small dog's ear. The two seem to have developed a bond, which I have to admit is sort of cute.

"Come, sit." Kiozhi pats the leaves beside him. He still looks tired, but the water seems to already be making him feel better.

I shake my head. "I should go find food before I'm too tired to look."

"Let the water rejuvenate you first." He lifts an arm, inviting me to snuggle against him.

I know I said we aren't a couple, but the temptation to accept his comfort is too great. We've been through a lot together—I can forgive myself for wanting to be close. And it seems he's incapable of holding a grudge.

I settle next to him, resting my cheek on his pecs. My eyes immediately want to drift closed. The glowing moss on the wall behind us is plush and velvety, and the floor of leaves is as plush as my pillow-top mattress back home. I sigh. No more words pass between us, and I don't know how much time has passed before I open my eyes again. Kiozhi's breathing is steady under my cheek, his arm warm around my shoulders, but his skin no longer seems feverish. I smile with relief.

My stomach is a gnawing ache that won't let me sleep, so I ease myself out of his embrace. I thought I saw a plant with things that look like berries not too far from here, and it should only take me a couple of minutes to gather some.

Beanie opens one eye to look at me, then closes it again as if to say, "You're on your own."

I rub his head, then go take another long drink of water. My phone, sunglasses, and lipstick are still scattered next to the pool, so I shove them back into my purse before I scale the wall and exit the cave.

I can see the mint-green bushes with clustered raspberry-shaped fruits down in a hollow next to a decaying log. Despite how close they are, my pulse races as I move toward them, trying to keep my footsteps as quiet as possible. I feel like I need eyes in the back of my head. I brush my anxiety aside. Kiozhi is injured and needs food to recover—I'm the only one capable of finding it.

When I reach the bushes, I glance around to be certain nothing is stalking me before picking a berry. It's soft and very juicy. I squeeze it until glowing green juice coats my fingers. There don't appear to be any seeds, and it smells sweet and citrusy.

I chew the inside of my cheek. My girls earned a badge for wilderness survival, and I remember how to test the edibility of wild plants, but these are alien. They glow in the dark, for heaven's sake. Do the same rules apply?

My stomach grumbles loudly, prodding me to touch the tip of one juice-covered finger against my tongue. My eyelids twitch at the sour taste and my mouth puckers. I like lemon flavor, but this is downright acidic, like drinking raw vinegar. I swallow again and again to clear my palate, wishing I had some water. At least I haven't gone blind or keeled over on the spot. I smack my lips. No numbness or stomach cramps yet. Still, these are too sour to consider palatable, at least until I'm out of other options.

I toss the berry aside, wiping my fingers on some nearby leaves as I look around the edges of the hollow.

On top of a root near the trunk of a tree sprawls a mat of dull yellow foliage covered with golden brown nodules the size and shape of kiwi fruit. They look promising.

I glance over my shoulder again, making sure I can still see the cave. The trunks all look alike, and it would be easy to lose my way. The last thing I want to do is to get separated from Kiozhi. I shake my head at the irony. On the ship, I worked so hard to evade him—I was downright mean when he sat next to me on the shuttle. Yet if he hadn't joined me, I'd probably be dead right now, drowned in the pod or digesting inside the belly of the centipede monster. The longer I'm with him, the more I realize I've grown to like him. He's a good guy, not at all selfish like my ex. He even stepped in when the Venus Flytrap tried to eat Beanie, and what does the little dog offer in terms of survival?

I climb up onto the roots next to the yellow plant and open my cross-strap purse to retrieve my lipstick, using it to mark the nearby trunk with an arrow pointing toward the cave. The pale pink isn't startlingly visible, but I should be able to find it again if I look.

Bending down, I grasp one of the kiwi lookalikes and tug.

Like I just pulled a lever, the matted leaves sweep up and engulf my hand. I scream and pull free. My entire hand is covered in something sticky, and my skin burns.

I need to wash this stuff off *now*.

13

KIOZHI

Something startles me awake. A noise? I'm aching and disoriented. The air smells sweet and fruity, almost like regeneration fluid, but I'm not in my resting state. And I'm definitely not in my resting pod. A small wet tongue flicks against my face, and I open my eyes to a small quadruped hardly bigger than my head licking me. *Beanie.*

Everything comes back in a rush. I push myself to sitting, and the dog wriggles onto my lap, whining softly. His poor skin looks mottled and bruised where he lost fur during the attack, but he seems to be recovering. I scratch behind his ears. "Good boy."

I look around the small cave for Suzanne, but there's no sign of her. Where did she go? I frown at Beanie, who whines again. My stomach tightens with worry. *Perhaps she just stepped outside to relieve herself.*

"Suzanne!" I shout, voice loud in the cave.

No response.

I stand and test my weight on my injured limb. The water and rest have rejuvenated me considerably, though the fabric tied around my leg is stiff with blood. I haven't been wounded like this since I was a small child, before I learned to harden my form. My friends and I were trying our hand at carving, and I still remember my parents' distress when I stumbled home dripping blood.

Limping over to the opening, I peer outside. I can't see much beyond the veil of vines. "Suzanne? Are you out there?"

Still only silence.

My worry turns to dread. She should've woken me so I could at least be on standby. I might be weak, but I'd give my life to protect her, even if all I can be is a distraction so she can escape.

I grasp the lattice when a yip reminds me that Beanie can't get out by himself.

"All right, little man. Come on." I pick him up and put him outside.

Just then, Suzanne stumbles into view clutching one hand against her chest. I step back so she can get into the cave. She drops to the floor with a thud, not even bothering with the lattice. She's breathing hard, and my *Iki'i* thrums under her fear.

"What happened?" I ask. "Are you all right?"

She extends her right hand to show me raised red welts covering her delicate skin. "I found another carnivorous plant."

I grasp her undamaged arm, guiding her toward the pool. "You shouldn't have gone out alone."

"I just wanted to find food, and I didn't plan to go far."

"I can't lose you, Suzanne. Don't do that again. Please."

Sluicing water over her hand, I gently rub away some sort of slippery substance coating her skin. She flinches at first, then relaxes as I wash the back of her hand, her palm, between each finger to be certain I don't miss a spot. It's totally the wrong time and place, but touching her makes my balls ache.

"Kiozhi." Suzanne's voice is a little husky. "I think you got it."

I snap my gaze to hers, realizing I'm now washing up to the crook of her elbow, well beyond the welts covering her hand. Yet she doesn't pull away. Her lips are parted, her breathing quickened.

It would be so easy to bend down and kiss her. To take her again. *Kuzara*, I could claim her right now. But that would only create a shell of a relationship. I want her to embrace our bond, not resent it. So I pull back and reluctantly release her hand.

"Better?"

"Yes, thank you."

Beanie barks from outside, and she goes over to help him down. He snuffles her, then trots over and nudges my injured leg.

"I'm all right, little man." I pat his head. For such a small creature, he has a lot of empathy. "Thanks for checking."

"How's your leg?" Suzanne pulls aside one edge of my bandage. Dark spots on the fabric show where I've started bleeding again.

"The bandage helps." I'm feeling better, though not completely healed.

She makes a doubtful noise before gently unwinding it. "This looks terrible."

I lean over to look at the abraded skin. "As long as the blood is mostly clear, I'm okay."

"But there's dirt in the wound. Even you could be vulnerable to infection." Tearing off a fresh strip from her pant leg, she washes and re-bandages my leg, then sits back on her heels to review her work. "Are you okay to walk again? We should try to find food."

"Yes, if we take it slow."

We exit the cave again, and she finds me a branch I can use as a crutch. Though I enjoy having an excuse to touch her, she needs to be able to run without worrying about me. Plus, it would be good to have a weapon in hand.

We move along the trail, and she points to a matted yellow plant. "That's the thing that tried to eat my hand."

I nod. "We need to approach every single thing here as dangerous."

"Yes," she agrees. "Though I'm getting hungry enough to bite back."

I chuckle, and we continue looking for plants that could be edible. Beanie scouts ahead, but not as far as he did earlier, and Suzanne's usually perky movements have grown more lethargic. Each step I take feels leaden. Without food, none of us will be able to carry on much longer.

Suzanne keeps track of our path by marking the trunks with a waxy pink color stick she stores in her purse. I may be driven to protect her, but without her, I'd probably end up wandering around in circles on this hostile planet—or worse.

We pause to rest along the trail. Suzanne sighs. "I wish we had a way to carry water."

"What about your purse?" I ask.

She shakes her head. "It leaks."

Suddenly, Beanie lets out a joyful yip and darts off into the bushes.

"Not again," groans Suzanne. "I swear that mutt has no regard for danger."

I suppress a smile, thinking of how she went off to find food by herself, but refrain from making the comparison out loud.

The dog returns and lowers himself on his front legs, yipping again as if expecting something.

I focus my *Iki'i*. There's a sense of joyful anticipation about him. "I think he wants us to follow."

Suzanne sighs. "Why not?"

We step down off the trail.

"His barking is going to attract more trouble if he doesn't stop," I say.

Then his barking does stop, and we hear a faint female voice calling, "Beanie, come!"

Suzanne grabs my arm. "That sounds like Tamara!"

14

SUZANNE

I pull Kiozhi's arm around my shoulder, helping him hurry through the tangled bushes. My heart beats faster with each step, and I smell what I hope is campfire smoke.

"Tamara!" I shout. "Tamara, it's me!" I don't think she can hear me over Beanie's yapping.

We round a tree, and I nearly run straight into Jennifer.

Kiozhi drops his arm as my sister throws her arms around me. "Oh my God, Suzanne! I knew you'd find us!"

Shocked and delighted, I clutch her back. Tears of joy flow down my cheeks, and when Tamara joins us seconds later, I grab her in a bear hug too. "I'm so glad you're both okay!"

Crying, all three of us simply hold each other.

When I regain control of my sniffling and break away, I see the shuttle pilot, Tazhio, helping Kiozhi to his feet. Tazhio wears a one-piece flight suit with the top half hanging around his hips, leaving his blue chest and arms bare. "How'd you get injured?" he asks Kiozhi.

"I'd like to say it was your terrible landing," Kiozhi says with a smirk. "But I'm embarrassed to admit I was nearly consumed by a hostile plant."

Jennifer tugs at my purse. "Where's your phone, Suzanne? I need it."

"Seriously, Jennifer?" I jerk my purse away and glower at her. "Is astronomy the only thing you think about? I almost died out there. More than once."

She scowls back. "We've all almost died. And this isn't about my thesis. I'm making a rescue beacon."

My indignation dissolves. If anyone can cobble together technology for a beacon, it's my brainy little sister. I sigh and retrieve my phone from my purse. "Here. But it got wet. It's dead."

She takes it and walks away, head bent over the dark screen. That girl has a one-track mind.

"We have food and water," says Tamara. "But before we go back to camp, we need to know if you encountered any monsters? Flying monsters, specifically?"

My heart skips a beat. I thought the gargantuan centipede and carnivorous plants were horrible enough. "Shit! Are there flying monsters on this planet too?"

"Yes. You haven't seen any?"

"No, nothing like that."

"Oh, thank God." Tamara loops her arm through mine. "Come on."

Tazhio helps support Kiozhi as we push through more bushes, emerging into a clearing next to a small pond. A cheery fire burns on the shore, and several more passengers rise to greet us —a red-haired Fogarian, a small, gray Hage in a crew uniform, and a Kirenai in a yellow Speedo.

Another Kirenai with a bald head and muscles like an ox sits propped against a nearby tree trunk—Nazhin, the porter who was with us on the shuttle. Jennifer's already sitting next to him, setting our phones in a line on the ground. He raises a hand and plays with a strand of her hair. She smiles back at him in a way I haven't seen her smile since, well, ever. I raise an eyebrow. *I knew there was a vibe between them back on the shuttle.*

On board the *Romantasy*, I thought the Kirenai looked like clones, and I'm surprised to realize how different the four here appear now. Tazhio with his large eyes, Nazhin with his bald head, the Ken doll Kirenai in a Speedo, and Kiozhi, who's developed a more hardened GQ look since we crashed. His cheekbones are sharper, his nose more Roman. Even injured, he's sexier than any man I've met before. Or maybe it's *because* he's injured; it's hard to resist a self-sacrificing hero.

A booming voice near the fire startles me. "Greetings!" The Fogarian beams at me and fluffs a stack of leaves next to him. "My name is Erud, and I would be honored to have you sit beside me."

"Oh, that's um, thank you, but I'm good here." I sit next to Kiozhi—the devil you know, as the saying goes. I definitely don't need more aliens trying to gain my attention.

Erud's crimson mustache droops, but he doesn't say anything else.

"I'm called Ubi, and this is Hanzu." The Hage in the crew uniform gestures toward the Kirenai in the yellow Speedo. "Would the two of you care for some food?" He offers us something that looks like purple golf balls.

"God, yes, please," I say, reaching for one.

He shows us how to twist a ball in half, revealing a juicy center. The pulp tastes like ambrosia, and I'm thrilled when it turns out they have an entire basket to share.

Tamara sits with Beanie on her lap, feeding him something that looks like a long white French fry. She offers me one, too. It crunches like a carrot and tastes like cardboard, but it's somehow satisfying enough that I take a second one. Kiozhi devours several sticks and twists open golf balls in rapid succession, handing me an open half almost before I've finished the half I have.

I look around the rest of the sparse camp. "Are we the only survivors?"

"We haven't found everyone yet," says Tazhio somberly.

There's a strange tenseness in the air, as if nobody wants to say more. "What?" I ask.

Tamara takes a deep breath. "We did find one other human. A woman named Sophia. She…" She lets out a shaky breath. "She was infected."

"Infected?" I'm suddenly no longer hungry and lower my half-eaten cardboard stick to my lap. "With what?"

Tazhio scratches behind one ear. "There's a parasite on this planet the locals call a Gloor. It hunts fertile women to lay its eggs in them. When the eggs hatch, the spawn eat their way out of the host's body and attack anyone nearby. The locals, they call themselves Sheeghr, keep their females perpetually pregnant to stave off the parasite. They recognized that Sophia was infected and…" he tapers off to glance at Tamara.

I stare at him. Impregnated by an alien parasite? The more I learn about this planet, the more I feel like I've been dropped into a horror film. "What happened to her?"

He presses his lips into a tight line. "We couldn't keep her here with us. The Sheeghr took her."

I can't even breathe, let alone speak. Kiozhi says what I'm thinking. "To do what?"

Tamara's lip trembles, and tears fill her eyes before she looks away. "Put her out of her misery."

Tazhio puts an arm around Tamara as she cries softly, and his voice has a gravelly edge to it. "There wasn't anything we could do to help her, not without advanced medical technology. We couldn't risk keeping her with us, especially since we don't know when or if we'll ever be rescued."

Everyone else stares morosely at their hands. What they've told me is too horrible to even imagine. Then I realize. "Wait—when or if we're rescued? What do you mean? Surely people are looking for us?"

Tazhio takes a deep, pained breath. "Sensors and signals can't penetrate this planet's ionosphere. That's why a special license is required to fly—"

Tamara lifts her cheek from his chest and gives him a hard look. "Not your fault, Tazhio. And we mustn't give up hope. Jennifer thinks she can get a signal through."

The food I just ate churns below my ribs. Jennifer's brilliant, but if aliens who can build starships haven't already figured out how to make a rescue beacon work here, I doubt she's going to be able to create one using a bunch of smartphones. It sounds to me like we're stuck here permanently.

"I hate this fucking planet." I clutch my arms tightly around my ribs, thinking about giant centipedes, carnivorous plants, and now a flying parasite. "How are we going to keep ourselves alive?"

Tamara's worried eyes meet mine. "The Gloor is only attracted to fertile women. I'm already pregnant, and Jennifer's birth control protects her."

I frown. "You haven't had a boyfriend in years. How can you be pregnant?"

She laces her fingers with Tazhio's. "That's a story all by itself. The short version is that Tazhio and I are now mates."

I open my mouth to argue that they just met, that getting pregnant so quickly is impossible, then snap my jaw shut. I was only with Robbie a few weeks in high school before I got knocked up. It's totally possible. "But how could you possibly *know* you're pregnant? We've only been here a few days."

"The Sheeghr can sense it," she says.

I want to argue again, but I've never seen my sister glow like this, full of confidence and contentment. I want to be happy for her, yet icy dread is slowly creeping through my veins. My tubal ligation means I can't get pregnant, yet I still have hormone cycles. *Technically fertile.* There is no protection for me. "What if neither of those are an option?" I say hoarsely. "You know I can't have kids anymore."

"Yes." She takes my hand. "We've all agreed to set up a watch, and Erud will dig burrows women can sleep in for extra protection."

"Dens," the Fogarian corrects. "I would never relegate a female to a mere burrow."

Much as I appreciate his attempt to redefine comfort, a burrow or den sounds like fucking hell. I'm still processing everything when Jennifer moves over to join us. "I think I can get a signal out," she says. "But we need to take the beacon as high in the trees as possible."

Nazhin gets to his feet behind her and shakes out a massive pair of bat wings. I only recognize it's him because he still has a bald head and silvery eyes. He's sprouted a crown of small horns, and a long tail twitches behind him.

"Do any of you have experience flying?" he asks, flapping his wings once and lifting slightly off the ground.

"No, but I'll try if it means a chance for Suzanne to escape this planet." Kiozhi climbs wearily to his feet. He's been silent during the discussion about the parasite, but he's rubbing the back of his neck as if agitated.

"No need. I was just hoping for advice," Nazhin says. "You stay and protect the camp."

Everyone watches Nazhin practice flapping around above the camp, shouting advice while Kiozhi and I remain near the fire, finishing our food. My attention keeps drifting to his bandaged leg. He's injured because of me and Beanie. If I remain in camp, I'm a risk to him and everyone nearby. The last thing I want is someone dying while defending me. I look toward the wall of brush surrounding the camp, realizing that I only have one choice. One thing I can do to keep my sisters and the others safe.

I have to leave.

15

KIOZHI

I watch the expressions flit across Suzanne's face, my *Iki'i* reeling under her rapidly cycling emotions. Anxiety, uncertainty, despair.

My own feelings mimic hers. This parasite sounds formidable. "Don't worry. I'll die before I let anything hurt you."

Her shoulders are hunched, and she has a sadness in her eyes that cuts me to the core. "That's what I'm afraid of."

Shame fills me, but she has reason to doubt. I couldn't even overcome a carnivorous plant without losing part of my matrix. "I'll be on better alert. I promise."

She smiles tightly and turns her attention to Nazhin, who's careening above the clearing with ungainly flaps of his wings. If I was stronger, I'd join him as backup for this rescue plan. I've never tried to assume a flying form before, but I understand how awkward it can be learning to use unfamiliar muscles and limbs.

Once he seems to get the hang of things, Jennifer and Nazhin leave for the treetops with the beacon. The rest of us settle around the fire with more food. Tamara and Suzanne chat about what's happened so far, but I'm too exhausted to keep up. My eyelids drift closed.

When I wake, Suzanne is no longer beside me. Hanzhu and Erud are also gone, and Tamara and Tazhio are asleep, snuggled together on the other side of the fire with Beanie curled contentedly against Tamara's belly. Only Ubi is awake, cooking something yellow and rubbery-looking jabbed on the end of a stick over the flames.

"Did you see where Suzanne went?" I ask the Hage crewman.

"I believe she followed Hanzhu and Erud." He pulls the stick toward him, pokes a finger at the yellow lump, then returns it to cooking. "They went to gather firewood."

I look toward the surrounding brush. Is Suzanne considering a mate other than me? My stomach feels full of acid. It would make sense for her to choose someone who isn't injured to protect her.

I pull the bandage from my leg. My skin looks less raw, and I don't think I need the covering anymore, but when I stand, I still feel weaker than I should. Though my stomach is roiling with uncertainty, I grab a handful of the starchy white stems; more nourishment will help me recover. "Which way did they go?"

Ubi points toward a narrow gap next to some glowing violet bushes with round leaves. "If you find any more of these mushrooms, please bring them back." He pulls the yellow lump from his stick and shoves it into his small mouth, speaking around his bulging cheeks. "They are quite satisfying."

The last thing I'm thinking about is mushroom hunting, but I nod and head toward the trail. I haven't traveled very far before I meet Hanzhu and Erud returning with armloads of wood. I scan the forest beyond them. "Where's Suzanne?"

Hanzhu tilts his head. "We haven't seen her."

My heart thumps harder against my ribs. "Ubi said she followed you."

Erud drops his sticks, hopefulness lighting his features. "She did?" He turns to look around the glowing brush. "We did not encounter her."

I release a shaky breath. I have a sneaking suspicion Suzanne didn't go in search of either of these males. And if she's lost, it's because she wants to be. I turn in a slow circle, searching for any sign of her. She could be anywhere in this vast forest.

"Go back and tell the others she's missing," I say. "I'm going to look for her."

"Going alone isn't—" Hanzhu begins, but I cut him off.

"I'm aware of the dangers. Go tell the others." The longer I delay, the farther away Suzanne gets.

They sigh and hurry back to camp. I step up onto one of the many root paths snaking through the understory. If I were her, I'd try to go back to the cave with the spring in it. She marked our path with her waxy pink stick. If I can find the spot where we met her sisters, I should be able to pick up the trail.

I wander over the roots and through the bushes. Everything looks too similar. Then I see a trampled area I'm pretty sure was where the sisters stood hugging. I pick up the pace, finding Suzanne's color stick wedged in a V between two roots. When I unscrew the cap, it's empty.

She must have used it all to mark her way to this spot. I closely scan the nearby brush. *There.* A pale pink smudge is barely discernible on the purplish bark of a tree trunk ahead. All I have to do is look for the next mark.

Now that I know what I'm looking for, I reach the turquoise vines covering the entrance to the cave easily. Standing outside, I call softly, "Suzanne?"

Her pale face appears between the foliage, and alarm flicks my *Iki'i.* "What are you doing here?" she asks.

I push the vines aside and drop down next to her. "The better question is, what are you doing here?"

"You know what I'm doing. I'm a liability. A danger. You need to go back."

I move to the spring and kneel for a drink. "Nope."

"Kiozhi, I can't ask you to risk yourself for me."

"You're not." Moving over to the far wall, I plop down on the thick leaves with my back against the velvety moss. "Come, sit with me."

She hesitates, but then shakes her head and moves toward me. "You're an idiot, you know that?"

"Possibly." I smile wryly. "But I already lost one mate. I refuse to lose another."

She stops mid-step and stares at me. "What do you mean, you lost a mate?"

Talking about Nanaia is still painful, but if I ever hope to have Suzanne in my life, I have to be open with her. "She died in a collision. An intoxicated driver had turned off the guidance system in his vehicle. Neither of them survived."

I've imagined her death a million times, and the weight of it presses in on me again now. I only realize how tightly my fingers are clenched when Suzanne's soft fingers slide over my knuckles. "I'm so sorry. What was her name?"

"Nanaia." Saying her name out loud seems to release a dam inside me, and I keep talking, turning my hand up to lace my fingers with Suzanne's. "Kirenai mate for life, and after she died, I thought I was doomed to a long, lonely existence knowing what joy was but never finding it again. I spent tens of cycles in therapy, tried to find purpose in building my investments, even turned to pleasures of the flesh in an attempt to feel something besides pain. People called me a playboy, but inside I was dying every day." I lift my eyes to meet Suzanne's face and see her green eyes glazed with tears. My own eyes prickle, and I lift my free hand and cup her cheek. "Then I heard you laugh at the party, and it was like I'd just been rescued from a black hole."

Her fingers tighten around mine, and I watch her swallow. "Don't put that burden on me, Kiozhi. Please." There is pain in her eyes. "I have my own baggage. Half my life has already been lost chained to someone else's needs. I can't save you."

I gently stroke her cheek with my thumb. "You already saved me. And I have no desire to put you in chains. But I will always choose to remain near you in whatever capacity you'll allow."

Emotions play out on her face, her indecision like a thousand tiny wings beating against my *Iki'i*. Her eyes dart from my eyes to my mouth and back before she swallows hard and answers. "I'm not done exploring what it means to be me. What if I want to see other men?"

Jealousy flares in my chest, crowding out all other emotions. *She doesn't understand the mate bond.* "If we become mates, neither of us will want another person. That's how the mate bond works."

"But if I do?" she insists.

I run my tongue over the front of my teeth thoughtfully. Then I lean closer until we share the same breath. "Tell you what. If I ever fail to measure up to your expectations, then you can seek affection elsewhere."

She narrows her eyes, a smile quirking her lips. "Really? Because I'll hold you to that."

A matching smile twists the corner of my mouth. "You have my vow."

She shakes her head. "I must be an idiot. But…" Sighing, she leans forward and seals that vow with a kiss.

16

SUZANNE

Kiozhi's mouth on mine feels like something out of a dream, surreal and too good to be true. I have no idea if this arrangement will work, but he pushes all the right buttons to make me crave him. We've made love before, but right now, I want to melt into him. To become one with him in a way I've never felt before. I don't want to admit it, but the idea of being his and his alone feeds something inside me I didn't know was hungry.

His tongue slides over my lips, parting me to his caress as his fingers move to my neck, holding me close.

I moan softly into his mouth. "Why do I want you so much, Kiozhi?"

He kisses the corner of my mouth, then slides his lips down the column of my throat, sending shivers of delight through my center. "Because I belong to you. Weren't you listening?"

We sink to the leafy floor of the cave, our bodies pressed close together as he runs his hands over my body. He lifts my shirt and bra, taking a nipple into his mouth. It tightens at his touch, and I whimper softly, arching up as he nips and sucks one breast before moving to the other.

Kissing his way down my stomach, he kneels between my legs, removing my pants and panties. His hands roam up between my thighs to stroke the outer folds of my pussy. I shudder and widen my legs, yearning to feel him inside me. He dips a finger into my channel, and I groan, tightening around him. He finds my G-spot with practiced ease, stroking with increasing intensity as I writhe. Before I tip over the edge into orgasm, he pulls free and replaces his finger with the thickness of his cock.

I gasp and buck up to meet him, my orgasm exploding like fireworks behind my eyes. He stays there, pulsing inside me, but I don't think he came yet.

Lowering himself to cover me, he holds me tight and begins to thrust again, building me into another frenzy. We move together, our bodies slick with sweat and lust. Something prods my ass, and he growls against my ear, "Are you ready, *kikajiru?*"

I'm gasping, Kiozhi's cock deep in my body, the beginning of another climax thrumming through my veins. "God, yes!"

I wrap my heels behind his ass, pulling him closer. I'm so wet, there's little resistance, just sensation as he penetrates and fills me. The double sensation tips me over the edge and I scream, back arching in ultimate pleasure.

He pounds into me, driving my climax to impossible heights. Then he bellows and thrusts forward, filling me with heated jets of his seed.

Collapsing above me, elbows supporting the bulk of his weight, he breathes against the side of my neck. My heels are still locked behind him, and I loosen their hold, letting my legs fall like lead weights to either side. Limp and boneless, we lay there together, simply soaking up each other's essence.

I kiss the warm skin of his shoulder, tasting his salt. "That was… different than before."

"Better, I hope?" He rolls off me and pulls me over onto his chest.

I nod against his skin, trying to process all the feelings inside me. I hadn't really believed him when he said the mate bond would change me. Sex and love had always been something I wanted to be synonymous, but until this moment, I didn't understand exactly what that might feel like. Now I do. It's like a blanket fresh from the dryer, warm and irresistible. Or having someone hand you comfort food after a stressful day. A perfect sensation I will now crave forever.

"Will it always feel this way?" I ask.

"Yes." His voice rumbles under my cheek. "We are true bonded mates. You are my everything. I love you, *kikajiru.*"

I'm dizzy with the knowledge of his words. In a whisper, I reply, "I love you too."

We rest and make love again before Kiozhi convinces me he should let my sisters know I'm okay. I'm worried they will insist on dragging me back, but he promises he won't let that happen. I sit with my back against the wall facing the entrance, a makeshift spear at my side. If something tries to get in, I want to be ready. While I wait, I think about my girls, my parents, my other sister, Bethany, who's still on the *Romantasy*. Will I ever see any of them again? Am I going to spend the rest of my existence basically trapped in this cave on an alien planet?

By the time Kiozhi returns, I'm teary-eyed with a full-on pity party.

He pads over and sits down next to me. "Everything okay?"

I nod and swipe angrily at my cheeks. "How'd my sisters take it?"

"They're not happy," he says, "but they believe me when I tell them you're alive."

"Did Jennifer set up the beacon?"

"Yes. Now all we can do is wait. I'll check back every day to see if a rescue ship has arrived."

I sigh and lean my head on his shoulder. "I'm already out of my mind with boredom."

He puts a hand on my knee and slides it up the inside of my thigh. In a low voice, he says, "I can think of a few things to keep you occupied."

17

KIOZHI

We fall into a routine of me going to the camp while Suzanne remains in the cave. Food and rest have brought my strength back, though regenerating my full matrix will take longer. We have no way of knowing day from night, and I don't know how much time passes this way. There is no talk of the future. We just live in the present.

At the camp, I learn what plants are edible, and though I'd prefer to gather them and bring them back to Suzanne, she insists she'll go crazy if she's cooped up in the cave all the time. I grudgingly agree she can accompany me to forage, but we both carry sharpened sticks with us.

We've just finished gathering purple fruits when she runs her fingers over the thick, toothy spike of a flaming orange plant. "This is shaped exactly like an aloe plant from Earth." She glances around. "I wonder how many of these plants might have medical uses? I wish I had a notebook or something so I could keep a record."

"You could use my ICC." I lift my arm and bring up the interface. "I'll have to operate it, but just tell me what to record and when we get back to the ship, we'll transfer it to your media."

Her eyes light up. "That would be amazing."

I show her how to run the interface and then hold my arm steady so she can document the plant. She uses both hands on my arm to aim the camera implant, her hair covering part of her cheek as she takes the picture. She moves us around the plant, positioning my arm for each individual picture, then breaks off the tip of one spike, photographing the inside. "Too bad we can't preserve actual samples."

A sibilant noise echoes between the trees, and she jerks her head up and looks around. "Was that my name?"

"I'm not sure." I scan the depths of the dim forest with my *Iki'i* but can't detect anyone.

"Sussssuuunnnn." The sound comes again.

A prickle races along my spine. I drop my arm, letting my ICC go dark. "I don't think that's human. We need to go back to the cave."

We both grab our spears and retrace our steps, but before we've taken twenty paces, a woman's scream splits the air. Suzanne spins around and looks at me with wide eyes. "That was human."

I grit my teeth. I already know she's going to argue that we need to go help. "We don't know that for sure."

"It was. And if it was me out there in trouble, you'd want someone to help, right?" She turns back toward the sound.

"*Kuzara*," I grumble. "At least stay behind me, okay?"

We cautiously make our way through the forest toward the sound. The screaming continues, accompanied by the sibilant buzz and some strange chittering.

Skirting the base of a tree, we emerge on a scene that makes my jaw drop. Six or eight furry bipeds with banded purple fur are locked in battle with a flying creature that's larger than I am. The creature has one biped trapped in its long legs and is trying to lift the kicking, screeching being from the ground. The sound of Suzanne's name is coming from its flapping, gossamer green wings.

"I think those furry beings are Sheeghr," I whisper, grabbing Suzanne's arm to pull her back out of sight. I've never met the local tribe, but these beings match the descriptions Tamara and Tazhio gave us.

The Sheeghr on the ground clutch their captured comrade's limbs and stab the flying creature with crude spears.

"Look, in the middle," Suzanne whispers.

A human female with golden brown hair huddles on her hands and knees in the center of the commotion, trying not to get trampled or stabbed. It looks like her hands and feet are tied.

"We have to help." Suzanne steps forward. "They're going to kill her."

One of the Sheeghr spots Suzanne's movement and looks straight at us. He chitters something in a language my universal translator doesn't understand. My *Iki'i* can't decipher any emotions beyond the maelstrom of hostility, but I think he may be asking for help. I frown at the bound woman in their midst but recognize now isn't the time for questions. She's in danger, and we need to help.

I grab Suzanne's arm and make her look at me. "Wait here. If things go wrong, promise you'll run back to the cave."

"I'm not—"

"I can't have my attention divided if I'm going to save that woman. Promise, or I take you back to the cave myself."

She scowls at me, but nods. "Fine."

Gritting my teeth, I raise my spear and move toward the fray, hardening my matrix so I don't get damaged—I've learned my lesson the hard way with the beasts on this planet.

The bound woman spots me, her cheeks dirty and stained with tears. "Oh, thank God! Help me, please!"

I'm a head taller than the Sheeghr, but the winged creature is still barely within my reach. I pull back my arm and hurl my spear. It bounces uselessly off the creature's carapace, but the impact distracts it enough to let the pack drag their friend from its grip.

The flying creature rises, obviously posed to strike again. Then, as if changing its mind, it swivels.

And heads straight for Suzanne.

Her eyes widen, and she spins, tripping through the brush to get away.

I pelt after them, weaponless and furious. I knew it was a mistake to leave her side. Sheeghr race past me, bounding forward on all fours. But the winged creature is faster. It catches up to Suzanne, long pointed legs stretching down to grab her.

She screams and drops to the ground. The beast zooms past over her head, feet brushing the leaves along the trail. Suzanne scrambles upright and turns back toward us, running for all she's worth. Behind her, the winged creature has veered around and is coming back for her.

The pack shrieks and chitters, already circling up around her. By the time I reach them, one of them has dragged the other woman along, and she lays curled in a ball on the ground, sobbing. They lob more yellow stones into the air. The winged beast weaves and sways, its flight looking drunken under the onslaught, but it persists in coming forward.

It catches hold of another biped and successfully takes to the air. But instead of flying away, it rises several stories into the air and drops the screaming Sheeghr. The being's screams are cut short on impact with the ground.

Suzanne gasps beside me.

The beast buzzes around and dive-bombs us again. There is no stopping this thing, not until it gets what it wants, which appears to be the women. It's going to pick us off one-by-one if we don't find a way to bring it down first.

I plant my feet wide and wait for the next time it approaches. If I can just get hold of a leg or two, I might be able to use its own momentum against it. Suzanne stands next to me, spear gripped in both hands. "I'm going to try to drag it toward me," I say. "Be ready."

The creature swings a crooked path overhead, dodging yellow missiles. But eventually, it comes within reach, aiming for Suzanne. The moment it's in range, I grab its legs and yank downward.

At the same moment, Suzanne lets out a feral scream and jabs upward with her spear. The pointed tip skitters over the carapace before lodging in the crevice between its thorax and abdomen. The creature lets out a horrible grating noise, its momentum driving the shaft deep into its body. It careens into Suzanne, laying her out flat on the forest floor.

"Suzanne!" I grab the creature by a spasming wing and heave it off her.

Suzanne is looking up at the sky with unblinking eyes. A trickle of crimson blood drips from her nose, bright against her ashen skin. I kneel next to her, my heart refusing to beat. She can't die. Surely fate wouldn't be this cruel. "Suzanne?"

She blinks slowly. "Is it dead?"

Heart jolted back into rhythm, I laugh and gather her into my arms. "Yes, my love. The beast is dead."

Her fingers claw against my chest, her gaze turning toward the surrounding Sheeghr. "Now what about them?"

I glance up and realize the Sheeghr are all leering at us. And every one of them has a prominent pink phallus poking from between his legs.

18

SUZANNE

$\mathcal{M}$uscles tense, I glance beyond the surrounding Sheeghr toward where the blonde woman remains huddled on the ground. She's sobbing incoherently. "Untie her," I demand.

The Sheeghr purr and chitter, but make no move toward the woman. They seem to have completely forgotten her now that I'm here. My stomach roils when one of them grabs his dick and brandishes it toward me.

Kiozhi lets go of me and stands, surprisingly unaggressive. His modesty shield is gone, revealing a huge blue erection jutting like a shelf from his crotch. "I'm fairly certain they mean no harm," he says without looking at me. "Your sister said the Sheeghr establish status based on the size of their penises."

To my utter surprise, the Sheeghr turn away as if satisfied by his show of masculinity. They move to their fallen friend, emitting small, high-pitched squeaks as they arrange his body.

I feel sorry for them, but I'm more worried about the woman. Climbing unsteadily to my feet, I stumble to her and fall to my knees I try prying apart the knots around her ankles, but my hands tremble, and I can't seem to get a decent grip on the vine.

"Let me," Kiozhi says, taking over.

I glance at the Sheeghr. Several are now carrying their friend away into the brush, while the rest have begun slicing the downed creature into pieces with crude knives. One of them tucks the severed wings into a pack on his back, the gossamer green blades fanning above his head like an otherworldly peacock's tail.

A shudder rolls through me. The beast looks a lot like a giant dragonfly. I might've even considered it pretty if it hadn't been attacking us. Turning back to the woman, I realize how young she is—not much older than my daughters. "What's your name, honey?" I ask.

"A-amy," she says between sobs. "Those ferret aliens threatened to rape me. When I fought back, they hog-tied me like a dead animal. Then that flying thing attacked—" she chokes and throws her arms around me. "I thought I was the only one from the shuttle left alive."

I cringe, feeling all my new bruises. "It's okay." I stroke her hair and give her a squeeze, feeling homesick for my children. "That creature is dead. You're safe now."

Not that I believe my own words. That flying thing had to be the parasite, and I'm not sure we could've killed it without the help of the Sheeghr.

The furry aliens appear to be arguing over the monster, showing off their penises to each other. One turns toward Kiozhi, as if inviting him to take part, and I realize Kiozhi remains standing on full display. He purrs back, and the Sheeghr turns away.

Amy is gawking at him, and he turns so his back is to her.

I smile appreciatively. *That's my guy.*

Several of the Sheeghr approach carrying body parts. They bow and chitter, offering dripping bits to me and Amy.

Amy buries her face against my shoulder. I shake my head and hold her tighter. "No, thank you."

Kiozhi says something that sends them away, then looks over his shoulder at us. "They want to escort us back to the survivor camp."

"You can understand them?" Amy asks.

"Just a few words," he says. "They call themselves Sheeghr, and others in camp have interacted with them."

I'm less concerned about understanding the Sheeghr and more about returning to camp. "I can't go back to camp. That parasite was definitely attracted to me."

Kiozhi shrugs. "The Sheeghr aren't going to let us traipse off alone. I think we have to go with them, at least for now. "

I count five Sheeghr still with us. I doubt we can run and hide from them. With a resigned sigh, I stand and help Amy to her feet. My adrenaline rush is fading, and my muscles feel weak as we follow the Sheeghr through the brush. I can't breathe through my nose, and when I lift my fingers to my upper lip, they come away sticky with blood.

Thankfully, we don't have to walk too far before a familiar barking greets us and Beanie comes racing out to greet us. The tiny dog dances around Kiozhi, insisting on being picked up.

"Still best buds, I see." I smirk at him.

He just smiles back and rubs Beanie's head before setting him back on the ground.

The Sheeghr seem in awe of the little dog, muttering among themselves and keeping a respectful distance. I hear my sister calling for him, and a moment later, Tamara appears. She rushes forward. "Suzanne!" She halts and gives me a startled once-over. "You look like you've been through hell."

"You have no idea," I say, wiping dried blood from under my nose.

The Sheeghr insist on leading us all the way back to camp, where Erud and Hanzhu fawn over Amy. While the Sheeghr engage in a chittering conversation with Tamara and Tazhio. I glance over the assembled people, noting that the camp has grown. There are at least fourteen survivors here now, including another human woman.

"How many people are still missing?" I ask Jennifer.

"According to Ubi, this is everyone."

"No sign of a rescue?" I ask, glancing upward as if a shuttle might magically appear.

She shrugs. "We won't know until one arrives. All we can do is be ready."

I press my lips together and nod, but a sick feeling has settled in my stomach. It's been days since she set the beacon, and even more since the crash. If rescue teams haven't figured out where we are by now, I doubt they ever will.

Kiozhi puts an arm around my shoulders and guides me toward the fire where Erud is twisting open a purple fruit for Amy. It looks like she's already eaten one or two based on the discarded hulls in front of her, and she listens with rapt attention as Erud talks to her.

I'd prefer to leave, but doubt I'll be allowed while the Sheeghr are still hanging around, so I sit. Jennifer offers me a leaf that's been folded into a cup. It contains water, and I suck it down gratefully. It tastes musty and herbal, nothing like the fresh water from our cave, but I'm grateful.

"How are you?" Kiozhi asks, dabbing at my chin with a scrap of damp cloth.

"My nose is throbbing, but I'm okay." I take the cloth and scrub my upper lip. What I wouldn't do for some ice right now.

Tamara and Tazhio us, and I glance toward where the Sheeghr are departing into the trees. "That thing you fought was a

Gloor," Tazhio says. "The Sheeghr's name for the parasite. I guess defeating it was quite an accomplishment."

"Yeah, we were lucky." I glance toward the sky.

Tamara nudges me with an elbow. "They were impressed that you killed it. I hope you don't mind we let them keep all the trophies."

I'm in no mood for humor, though. "I need to leave." I stand and look at Kiozhi expectantly. "The longer I stay, the higher chance I might draw another of those things."

"Wait," says Jennifer, moving to stand in front of me. "Amy says she has an IUD."

I frown. "So?"

"Like you, she's fertile but can't get pregnant."

The thought of another person joining me and Kiozhi in the cave sounds unpleasant—not to mention we'll lose the privacy we've been enjoying—but what else can I do? "She can come with us."

"I'm not going anywhere," Amy says. Her hair's tangled and her skin and clothes are so dirty I can't even tell what color they're supposed to be. "The rescue is coming here, so this is where I'm staying."

I scowl at her. "You saw how dangerous the parasite is. If you stay, you'll just draw another one to the camp and get everyone killed."

She looks around at the assembled survivors. "There are enough of us here to fight it off."

"One of the Sheeghr died protecting you," I remind her. "Are you willing to let more people die like that?"

"Going off alone only divides our forces." She takes one of Erud's clawed hands. "The more people we have to fight, the better chance we have to survive. Right, Erud?"

His red mustache curls up into a grin. "I will keep you safe no matter what."

Kiozhi puts one hand on my knee. "They're right. There is strength in numbers."

"Staying is irresponsible," I say, pressing my mouth into a hard line. I can't believe he's taking their side.

His gaze is soft, and he squeezes my knee gently. "Suzanne, it's time you allow others to share responsibility. You don't need to be the one always sacrificing yourself to take care of someone else."

I ponder that for a moment, thinking about all the times I've bemoaned my responsibilities. Taken on everything myself so that others weren't inconvenienced. "This is different," I insist. "This is literally life or death."

"Doesn't that make it even more important?" He raises his eyebrows. "What would you do if one of your sisters was in your place?"

Dammit. It's not fair that he's right. I chew my lip, then huff, "Fine."

Tamara leans over and hugs me, and Jennifer comes over to squeeze me from behind. I lean into them with my eyes closed, praying, *God, please don't let me doom them all to a horrible death.*

19

SUZANNE

"I feel like an unwilling contestant on a reality TV show," I complain, picking at a splinter in my thumb. I'm trying to weave a basket out of vines while Jennifer fiddles with electronics salvaged from the shuttle. "I'm just waiting to be voted off."

Jennifer snorts. "If only it was that easy. That would mean you get to go home."

I glance upward for the billionth time since agreeing to stay in camp, listening for the whisper of wings through the trees. Wisps of pale smoke float lazily through the darkness from the leaves we're burning to keep the Gloor away. The entire camp smells like burning socks, but I'm not sure the smoke is working. Twice now Amy and I have fled to one of Erud's tiny burrows when a shadowy form was spotted above the camp.

Despite everything we're doing, I'm not sure Amy and I should stay. There are so many people I care about here, people who are in danger because of me. And with Tamara pregnant, she counts as two. Kiozhi and I were doing well on our own—

Kiozhi plops down beside me. "Don't even think about it."

I glare at him. I both hate and love that he knows me so well. "You're really annoying, you know that?"

He just smirks in response and cracks open a purple fruit, offering me half. I decline, returning to my basket weaving.

"Is she thinking of running away again?" Jennifer asks.

Irritated that she's talking about me like I'm not listening, I say, "I'm right here, you know."

"I know," Jennifer says with a smile. "But sometimes your selflessness is actually a little selfish."

My blood heats with ire, and I thrust my basket aside. How dare she call me selfish? Even before I had kids of my own I was helping Mom take care of my three younger sisters. "What the hell is that supposed to mean? I've given everything for the people I love."

She lowers the nest of wires she's holding to her lap. "Yes, you have. Even when you shouldn't. And I'm not saying it's unappreciated. But accepting from others can be a gift, too."

I clench my teeth about to retort, but Jennifer thrusts her palm out. "Just listen. Remember when you were in the hospital after your appendix burst? You were in so much pain and scared out of your mind. Mom and I were by your side the whole time, but we couldn't do anything to help you. All we could do was watch as you suffered."

"Yeah, I remember." I lower my head, feeling the weight of those memories bearing down on me. Mom missed her vacation because of me.

"Then when you were discharged, you refused to let us come home with you, even though the nurses said you would need someone to help. You pushed us away and insisted on going through it alone. And I get why you did. You're strong and independent, and you didn't want to burden us. But it took you three months to recover when it should've only taken one."

My throat constricts, and I have to swallow hard before I can speak. "I hate feeling weak and helpless. I also hate letting others see that side of me."

She nods solemnly. "I know. And it's okay to not want to show your vulnerable side to others. But you need to realize that you can't do everything yourself. We're family, and we all help each other no matter what. We can help you stay alive on this planet."

"It's different—"

"Is it? Or is it even more vital we act as a team?" Jennifer spears me with her gaze. "You're not the only one allowed to sacrifice for someone. How do you think we'll feel if you die out there all alone? We'll always wonder if there was something we could've done to save you. Or what if something else attacks the camp and we need your help to fight it off?"

I press my lips together and stare at the uneven weave on my basket. "God dammit," I mutter. She's right. Yet how can I surrender my fear? If they die because of me, I may as well die, too.

Kiozhi takes my hands. "I know you're scared," he says gently. "But asking for help from others can be a strength, not a weakness, and our forces help them as much as they help us."

My heart aches but I nod, squeezing his hand back. "I just hope a rescue arrives soon."

Nazhin joins us, settling next to Jennifer. One of his huge wings circles protectively around her back and he poked a clawed finger at the wires in her lap. "Find anything useful?"

"Not yet," she says, picking up the tangle.

I tilt my head, examining the horns on his forehead. I thought Kirenai are supposed to look like a member of their mate's species once they bond, but although he and Jennifer say they're mated, he's definitely not human. "Nazhin, why do you still look Khargal?"

He shrugs. "I haven't tried to shift back to human yet because we might need my wings."

Jennifer gives Nazhin a sly wink. "Plus, I find this form sexy."

He smiles at her, his silver eyes glinting. "Oh, really?"

I roll my eyes, but I'm also smiling. I enjoy seeing my sisters with mates they obviously adore and who adore them back. My attention slides over to Kiozhi to find him smiling softly at me.

I'm about to say something when a throaty buzzing interrupts me from the trees. *Sussshuuu sussshuuu.*

I jump to my feet, heart about to explode. This doesn't sound like one Gloor coming in to attack.

It sounds like an entire flock.

~

KIOZHI

Suzanne darts toward one of the dens, shouting, "Are we under attack?"

I stand, searching the sky and poised for action. The sound isn't like the Gloor's wings. It's more powerful, a grumble rather than a buzz. I know that sound.

"It's a shuttle!" Tazhio shouts. "Come on!"

The entire camp surges into motion. I dart after Suzanne and grab her hand, keeping pace with the others as we hurry through the dense forest with our eyes on the canopy. Something sounds like it's crashing through branches far overhead, and the rumbling is growing louder.

Branches and leaves start raining down on us, and bright green light spears down from the sky. A fierce wind rips down through the trees. We crowd up near the base of a trunk, trying to avoid getting hit by debris. Overhead, I spot a shuttle coming in fast, engines straining as it dodges the largest of the limbs.

"We're saved!" someone shouts.

I'm not so sure. The vessel wobbles, and for a moment, I think it's going to retreat, then it drops with a heavy thud to the forest floor.

A cheer rises from the group, and everyone rushes forward, cowering as debris continues to fall from above. The wind drives leaves and branches against us, and Suzanne's hair whips around her face like it has a life of its own. Ahead of us, Nazhin raises a wing over Jennifer like an umbrella. I envy his ability, but I'm still recovering from the loss of my matrix, and holding a human form has been challenge enough.

The shuttle's purple hull is scratched and dented, and the pointed nose is bent to one side. I'm impressed it's in one piece. Its hatch rolls open, and a brown spiny G'nax in a dark blue uniform stumbles out onto the ramp. Yellow blood stains the collar of his uniform.

Tazhio reaches the ramp first. "Eraj! I should've known you'd be the one to come for us."

Eraj is clutching a small box in one hand. "We received your transmission." He staggers and Tazhio offers a supportive shoulder. Gesturing toward the green light spearing down through the trees, Eraj continues, "I used the first available window through the storm, but I'm afraid the shuttle took some damage. We need to go before the window closes, but I'm not sure I can fly."

The branches overhead are whipping like tentacles, and it's hard to take a full breath in the blasting wind. I lean into it, trying to provide a shield for Suzanne against the brunt of the storm. Streaks of angry red and purple arc down from the green sky.

Tazhio motions to two people from camp. "Take him in and see to his injuries. The rest of you, on board now." He grins. "I'm flying us home."

Clutching Suzanne's hand, I scramble up the ramp with the others. This isn't a luxury shuttle with plush seats that transform into safety pods. It's a military ship with basic personnel harnesses lining the walls. I strap Suzanne in before taking the spot next to her.

The ramp rolls closed, leaving us in near darkness except for the dim glow through a pair of viewports near the door to the cockpit. At least we're now sheltered from the wind. We all wait in silence, the sour stink of fear filling the cabin.

"Are we going to take off?" Amy asks, both arms clutched over the straps on her chest.

A few minutes later, the shuttle deck hums and gravity tilts as we wobble up off the ground. We jerk sideways then shoot upward.

From the cockpit, I hear, "Waaahooo!"

I stare that direction, praying my friend really is as good a pilot as he always claims to be.

It feels like we're spinning, and the floor shakes until my teeth are rattling. The light from the viewports shifts from sickly green to a vibrant yellow. A moan courses through the ship, rising in pitch until it sounds like an opera soprano. Pink sparkles fill the air, coalescing into globs that drift and flow like drops of water in zero gravity. Then the turbulence stops.

I lean forward, trying to see through one of the small viewports. It looks dark. Someone is sobbing, and another person whispers, "He did it."

My heart fills with hope. I stretch my hand out and take Suzanne's. A disbelieving smile lights her features. Across the cabin from us, Jennifer is grinning like a fool, her hand gripping Nazhin's. "My beacon worked!"

20

SUZANNE

We step off the shuttle onto a dull gray deck full of armed guards in dark blue uniforms. "This isn't the *Romantasy*," I say, clutching Kiozhi's hands. "What's going on?" I can't help thinking of all the sci-fi movies I've seen where people end up on dissection tables after being exposed to alien pathogens.

He squeezes my fingers. "Guess they brought out the big guns to find us. These are imperial soldiers."

I gulp. "Are they afraid we're dangerous or something?"

"I don't know." He draws me closer to his side as we're escorted down a nondescript hallway.

The entire group of survivors shuffle into what appears to be a medical facility, much like the ones I've seen in Sci-Fi movies. There's an exam table and a few beds, and everything's made of metal. The walls are a shiny silver color and the machines and equipment stand like vaguely threatening sentries. The doctor is a bright pink alien who reminds me of a monitor lizard wearing a long black skirt held up by suspenders.

"My name is Dr. Egwan," he says in a soft, nasal voice. "I'll be seeing to your health before we transport you back to the *Romantasy* for your journey home. Who would like to go first? Are any of you injured?"

I'm actually surprised at how few of us are hurt. After more than a week stranded on that hostile planet and all the creatures we fought off, you'd think we'd be in worse shape.

I push Kiozhi forward. "Have your matrix checked."

"But your nose—"

I shake my head. "Is nothing compared to what you suffered. Go."

Sighing, he follows the doctor into another room. While the rest of us wait our turns, a crew member offers us nutrient bars. They taste like cardboard but might as well be ambrosia as I wolf mine down.

Kiozhi comes out and I push Tamara forward. "Go get that baby checked out. I want to know how Kiozhi's exam went."

She nods gratefully and takes Tazhio's hand. "Come with me."

They follow the doctor, and I had Kiozhi a nutrient bar. "How'd it go?"

He tears open the package. "He offered me time in a regeneration pod, but I prefer waiting until we get back to the

Romantasy. It'll take a day or two for full recovery, and I don't want to keep us stuck on this ship."

"Which of you is the owner of Demod Industries?" someone calls. A slender alien with skin white as snow and raven hair braided in several rows over her head stands at the med bay door.

Nazhin steps forward, still in Khargal form. "That'd be me."

"We assume you're the one who sent a signal from the surface," the slender alien says. "Nice job. We'd like to have a chat with you once you're done here."

"It wasn't me." Nazhin takes Jennifer's hand and pulls her beside him. "It was Jennifer."

My sister is smiling so broadly, I swear every one of her teeth show. She extends her hand toward the woman. "Jennifer Bloom."

The woman tilts her head as if confused, then takes Jennifer's hand. "A human? Now I'm even more intrigued. Are you willing to discuss this technology with us?"

"Is the Confederation willing to lift restrictions on sharing technology with Earth?" Jennifer asks.

"Ah." The woman bows her head respectfully. "A wise question. I believe the Senburu will consider it. But I will verify before we proceed."

"Thank you," says Jennifer.

The woman leaves, and my sister shoots me a satisfied smirk.

"Well played," I say, smiling back.

"I know, right?"

Tamara emerges from the exam room holding Tazhio's hand. Beanie trots beside her, the missing fur on his rump now fully restored. She joins us, looking somewhat shocked.

"Is everything okay?" I ask.

She nods, a dumbfounded smile on her face. "I—"

"We've just been told we're going to have twins!" Tazhio puts an arm around her shoulders. He's grinning as he looks at Kiozhi. "Can you believe it? Twins!"

I blink for a moment. For some reason, Tamara's pregnancy never seemed real to me. It seemed impossible in such a short time. But I guess a lot of impossible has happened to us on this trip. I laugh and wink at Tazhio. "Twins run in our family. Boy, are you in for a ride."

Tamara smiles nervously. "And one is a boy, so he'll be a shapeshifter. I'm going to need all the help I can get."

"You know I'm always here for you." I hug my sister.

"Me too." Jennifer joins the hug. "But I'm handing them back if they get fussy."

Kiozhi pushes me toward the doctor. "You're next."

I follow him to a small room off the main medical bay. Panels on the walls scroll with green alien symbols. The plain metal exam table hovers in midair.

"Lie down here please," the doctor instructs.

I'm not sure what to expect, but at least he didn't ask me to undress, so I don't think it will include any awkward probing. I lay back on the hard metal while he waves a handheld scanner over me from head to toe.

"Can you do anything for my nose?" I ask. Though it no longer throbs, it's still stuffy, and I'd hate to have lasting damage.

"Of course," he says. "Let me look at your scan first."

He turns and reads the scrolling data on a nearby panel. I can't help staring at the scales on his bright pink tail. I've met so many aliens recently, but he's the first lizard-like one.

After a few minutes, he says, "Oh, dear."

I sit up, looking at the panels as if I'll suddenly be able to read them. I haven't seen myself in a mirror yet, but I suddenly worry my nose will be crooked forever. "Is it unfixable?"

"You have a minor blockage in your reproductive system."

Oh, shit. Bile rises into my throat as I imagine my stomach filled with parasite eggs. This is way worse than a bent nose. "What kind of blockage?"

He pulls the arm of a nearby machine toward me. "Scar tissue is preventing the passage of gametes into your gestational organ. An easy fix—"

"Wait!" I put up my hands to ward him off. My heart is beating too fast. I'm pretty sure he's talking about my tubal ligation. "That scar tissue is intentional. I don't want it fixed." When I'd requested the procedure all those years ago, the doctor had been a bit of an asshole, making me establish evidence that I really wanted the surgery, so I feel a need to add, "I already have two children."

His lizard face has no expression that I can read, though he tilts his head as if confused. "I see." He scratches under his chin. "Your scans show the genetic markers of a Kirenai mate bond. Is he aware of your condition?"

Kiozhi and I never talked about whether or not he wants children of his own. When I agreed to be his mate, it never came up. But he does know I can't get pregnant because it was the entire reason I had to stay away from the camp.

I nod firmly. "Yes, he is."

But my gut is churning as I return to the others and sit next to Kiozhi. What if he assumed I'd get the procedure reversed when we got back to civilization? The doctor made it sound like an effortless task. Now that we're no longer stranded on that planet, will Kiozhi try to convince me to have more kids? If I refuse, will he regret taking me as a mate? I swallow, realizing how wrecked I'll be if he does either of those things. But I raised two kids already. I sure as hell don't want to start all over again.

Sensing my mood, he puts an arm around me. "Is everything all right?"

I sigh and stare at my hands folded in my lap. "I'm worried you're going to regret taking me as a mate."

"Why would I regret it?"

I sit in silence for a moment before answering. "The doctor just offered to make me able to have more children."

He remains perfectly still. "I thought you didn't want more."

I turn to look at him. "I don't."

His features soften. "I promised I'd never ask of you anything you didn't freely offer."

"But don't you want kids?"

He cups my cheek. "I'm blessed enough to have you."

Relief makes me want to melt, and I wrap my arms around him, loving that he hugs me back tightly and without an ounce of doubt. "I love you, Kiozhi."

"And I love you, Suzanne. With every molecule of my matrix."

I grin. It took crash landing on an alien planet to find my perfect mate, but now I could never imagine life without him. I don't have a clue what that life is going to look like, but I'm totally going to rock this next adventure.

SUZANNE

Full fanfare greets our return to the *Romantasy*. I think every passenger on board has crammed into the shuttle bay to see us, and a band plays a processional march as we stride across the red carpet to a raised platform. All I want to do is take a shower, call my kids, and fall asleep in an actual bed, but the captain insists on making a speech.

"Thank you all for coming to celebrate the safe return of fourteen of our esteemed guests." The captain is a spiny alien that reminds me of a bug. He stands behind a podium with his arms rigid against his sides, and the spines on his head move when he talks. "On behalf of the Intergalactic Dating Agency, I would like to offer you all free passage for life. And for those whose lives were lost, we will pay restitution to the families."

I frown, wondering if someone died trying to save us. If so, this is the first I'm hearing about it, and I think it's rather shitty to gloss over such a heroic loss. Sophia's death was dreadful enough, and thinking about how devastated her family will be makes my throat feel tight.

Thinking of family, I look for Bethany among the crowd. Why isn't she front and center, demanding to be let on stage to hug us? Perhaps the captain is insisting on making it part of this god-awful ceremony. I yawn, hoping it'll be over soon, and lean into Kiozhi.

The captain comes along the line of survivors on stage, making a strange alien salute to each person. When he reaches me and my sisters, he bows deeply. "I cannot adequately express my grief over your loss." He extends a green piece of plastic the size of a poker chip. "I know this cannot bring your sister back, but I hope it will help ease your pain."

I blink at him, unsure if it's exhaustion making me hear things or what. "Bring my sister back?" I look at Tamara and Jennifer, who appear to be just as confused as I am. "We're all here, though."

"I speak of Bethany. She didn't return with you."

"Of course not," I say. "She wasn't on the excursion with us." Nausea clenches my stomach, and I look out over the audience, shouting, "Bethany? Where are you? Come up here."

The audience murmurs, but my baby sister doesn't appear. Jennifer and Tamara move to the front of the platform and start calling into the crowd. "Bethany!"

My legs tremble and the roar of the crowd increases, people shouting Bethany's name to help locate her. Where is she?

The cruise director scrolls through a document on his ICC. "Her name is on the manifest," he says. "And she hasn't accessed her cabin or used any of the ship's amenities since your shuttle left. Is it possible you didn't realize she was on board with you?"

I round on him. "There were only fifteen fucking people on there. One of us would've noticed her."

"Ubi, you said all the passengers were accounted for, right?" Tamara asks, clutching Beanie against her chest.

The small alien looks frightened but nods. "Yes."

"She wasn't on the shuttle," Jennifer insists. "I would've seen her on my app."

I add, "She was too focused on getting that chef to join her cooking show to join us."

"Ch-chef?" the cruise director stutters. He turns to the captain. "Sir, one of our Kirenai chefs went missing around the same time as the shuttle crash. We've been unable to locate him and simply assumed he's been hiding among the guests."

The captain's spines stand straight up around his head and shoulders. "Why was this not reported immediately?"

"With everything else going on, we—"

"I don't want excuses." The captain slices a pincered hand through the air. He steps close to the cruise director and mutters, "Put this ship on security lockdown and verify the identity of every person on board immediately."

"Yes, sir." The cruise director scurries off, and crew members clear the riled-up crowd from the bay.

Tamara loops one arm through mine, pressing herself close. "What's going on?"

I grip her back, barely able to breathe. "Why would one of the crew hide among the guests? Are you suggesting he's some sort of serial killer?"

"I'd be surprised if he means her any harm," the captain says, but his spines are now laying flat against his head in a way that makes me think of a dog that's afraid of getting beaten. "Let's wait and see if they're just holed up somewhere on board."

Kiozhi clears his throat. "How many ships have docked with the *Romantasy* since she disappeared? Humans are big business on the black market."

My knees threaten to give out. I don't know if the black market is better or worse than being murdered by a serial killer. "You think that's what happened to her?"

"I don't know," he says, his face somber. "But we won't stop searching until we have her back."

"I've ordered the latest bio-scanners from my company," Nazhin says. "They should be here soon to help search the ship."

Kiozhi opens his ICC. "I'll reach out to my contacts at the shipping hubs and have them keep their eyes open for any unusual traffic."

"Great idea," says Tazhio. "I can do the same with friends in the shipping lanes."

"Thank you." I take my sister's hands. The same the terror gripping my heart is reflected in their eyes. With more conviction than I feel, I say, "We're going to find her."

"And she's going to be fine." Jennifer lifts her chin. "Out of all of us, Bethany is the most stubborn, most determined, and the most likely to survive despite the odds."

Tamara adds, "If anyone will be okay, she will."

I smile tightly. "Damn straight."

I thought that escaping the planet meant we were finally safe, but it seems our tribulations aren't over yet.

ear Reader,

I hope you enjoyed visiting (and escaping!) the Singing Planet with Suzanne and Kiozhi. But how horrible to come home and find out baby sister Bethany is missing! We'll wrap up the cruise by finding out what happened to her and her grumpy chef in the next book, Izhima

An alien cook convinces a snooty human with amnesia that she's his mate. How long can he keep up the charade before everyone discovers the truth?

Keep reading for a sneak peek!
Love, Tamsin

SNEAK PEEK OF IZHIMA

I HAVE NO MEMORY OF A MAN IN MY LIFE, LET ALONE GETTING MARRIED TO AN ALIEN. BUT HOW CAN I BE CERTAIN WHEN I DON'T EVEN RECALL MY OWN NAME?

BETHANY

I grip the stem of a glass holding what passes for alien champagne in one hand while I pace near the service elevator on the *Romantasy's* observation deck. The strange spicy scents coming from the nearby hors d'oeuvres tables would usually intrigue me, but tonight I need to stay focused. My entire career could hinge on this slightly underhanded scheme, but it's not like I have a lot of options.

Overhead, the domed ceiling reveals a glowing yellow planet surrounded by multi-colored rings, while an alien orchestra plays a lively tune from a circular stage in the middle of the room. Nearby on the dance floor, I catch the familiar laugh of my oldest sister, Suzanne, as she waltzes by in the arms of a blue-skinned alien. At least she's having fun. I've lost track of my other two sisters, but I'm sure they're here too, as we're required to attend these nightly meat-markets as part of our free cruise package.

A winged alien with gray skin and horns sprouting from his forehead catches my eye and angles toward me, but I cross the edges of my pashmina over my chest and level my best resting bitch face in his direction until he changes course. I probably should've opted for something less sexy than my elegant black evening dress and stilettos, but there's a chance I'll need to shoot some selfies this evening, and I want to look my best.

I'm not on this cruise to have fun. My primary focus is the food —more specifically, the chefs. It's been two weeks since my producer threatened to cancel my baking show if I don't come up with a plan to improve ratings, and I was at a loss about what to do until my sister won tickets to this luxury space cruise. Aliens are all the rage since the galactic prince married a human last year, and hosting a real-life alien chef on my show could send ratings sky-high. My producer sure was salivating at the idea.

Yet here I am, three days in, and I have yet to even meet a chef in person. Apparently, the Intergalactic Dating Agency has a policy against staff mingling with guests, and no matter how much I protest, plead, or pout, the cruise director keeps denying my request. Everyone acts like I intend to jump the chef's bones on sight or something. The best I could do was commission one chef to bake my birthday cake as a demo.

I've bribed a steward to smuggle me into the kitchen so I can capture footage of the chef at work. I think the chef's Nebula Chef credentials will impress my producer, but the show is about more than just the food—the guests need camera appeal, and the only way to prove that is to capture footage of the chef in action. Once I have that, I can focus the rest of the demo on the show-stopping presentation and taste test. I can't afford to let this plan go sideways or I'll lose my show for sure. And I don't lose.

As I'm searching for my guide but trying not to be obvious about it, I notice a young woman with gorgeous black skin searching the buffet. Her eyes are red and glistening with tears, and her arms are crossed tightly over the front of her bronze cocktail dress.

"Are you all right?" I ask, checking behind her in case some creeper is trying to follow her.

Her breath hitches. "Do you know if there's any club soda around here?" She uncrosses her arms to reveal an ugly magenta stain on the neckline of her dress. "I need to get this out before it sets."

"No, I'm sorry." I grimace. "But club soda doesn't really work for stains, anyway."

She bites her lip, chin wobbling as if she's about to cry. "This is my only cocktail dress..."

I move closer to get a better look at the smudge. I can't tell what it is. "They probably have some sort of alien technology on board that can remove that for you by morning."

"Maybe. But I was hoping to clean up now." She smiles weakly. "It's not easy to flirt when you look like a slob."

Although I'm not here to meet alien men, most of the women on board are, and I feel bad for her. I remove my black silk pashmina and hold it out. "Here. See if this will cover it up."

She shakes her head. "I can't take your shawl!"

"It's fine, really. You need it more than I do." I drape it across her chest and let the long ends hang down her back like a dupatta. "See? Now nobody can see the stain."

She smiles with relief. "Thank you so much. How do I get it back to you?"

"I'm having a birthday party tomorrow in the restaurant on the lower deck." I've used a sizable portion of the show's marketing budget to book one of the ship's small restaurants for my birthday so I can showcase the alien chef's cake, and even invited the galactic crown prince, Arazhi, and his new human bride. Go big or go home, right? "Come to the party and you can return the shawl."

"Oh, wow! Happy birthday!" She hugs me. "I'll see you tomorrow. Thank you again." She heads back to the dance floor with a bright smile.

I watch her disappear into the crowd before once more searching the vast, crowded room. Where is my contact? I've been standing here since the party began. It's impossible for him to miss me.

Chewing my lip, I check the time on my phone for the tenth time in as many minutes. I paid in advance, so that little alien better not stand me up. Though if he does, I'm not certain I can tell one short gray alien from another enough to ream him out…

The elevator cycles open for what feels like the hundredth time tonight, and my pulse quickens. A thin gray alien wearing a white crew uniform steps into view. He looks like something straight out of the Roswell books, with an oversized head and huge dark eyes, and he hurries straight toward me. *Finally.*

"Are you ready, miss?" The alien glances nervously from side to side. "The corridor will be vacant for a brief span of time while the servers ready the next courses. We must be quick."

"Not a problem," I say and follow him to the circle on the floor. The lift descends with dizzying speed, making my already nervous stomach lurch. Maybe I should've avoided that drink. I'm still reeling as we come to a stop in the middle of a corridor intersection.

"This way." My escort hurries me down the passage. Unlike the ornately decorated guest areas of the ship, the walls and ceiling of this wide corridor are a featureless gray, though the deck is painted with symbols I can't decipher. If I didn't have the alien leading me, I'd be utterly lost down here. I pause to snap a photo of the symbol on the floor so I can get back on my own if I need to.

When I look up again, the alien is already several yards away. I run to catch up, my stilettos clicking against the hard deck. Ahead, the familiar bustle and clank of working kitchen staff echoes from an open hatch on the left. We slow as we approach, and my guide says, "We need to pass by here quickly." He peers around the corner, then beckons to me and whispers, "They're not looking. Hurry."

I tap the record button on my camera and aim it inside as I scurry past, barely daring to breathe. Three or four alien cooks move around stainless steel counters, too focused on their work to notice us. I'll take a better look at what I filmed them doing when this is all over. Maybe I can work some of it into the demo film.

We turn down another hall, moving past hovering carts of neatly folded linen before coming to a stop at a closed hatch. The small alien gestures toward it. "Chef Izhima is in here."

I hand him several of the credit chips we use onboard as tips, thinking it might be good to reinforce the bribe. "Thank you."

The alien grins, small mouth displaying what looks like glistening gray gums instead of teeth, and presses the door control. "Enjoy yourselves."

He scurries away as the door shushes quietly open. Music emerges from inside, a soprano voice singing in a language I can't understand.

Taking a steadying breath, I slip into a half-lit kitchen.

IZHIMA

I squeeze another artful loop of green frosting onto the stack of golden-brown funnel cakes when the sound of someone clearing their throat draws my attention.

Annoyed by the interruption, I glare over my shoulder. A human with auburn hair pulled away from her pale cheeks stands just behind me. She wears a black dress that hugs the curve of her waist and hips, slit to expose a considerable portion of her thigh. My heart cramps in my chest, and I suddenly understand why we're restricted from interacting with the humans; with her watching, I don't think I could concentrate enough to make a dumpling, much less cook for the entire cruise ship.

"You're not supposed to be in here, *tekina*," I say, using the galactic word for human. I can't afford to be distracted, but I also can't seem to take my eyes off her.

"I'll leave in a minute." Her pink lips spread in a winsome smile that makes my groin tighten. "I only need a few seconds of footage for the show."

My eyes narrow. The cruise director told me the human who ordered the cake is some sort of video celebrity on her planet. I glance at the order on my ICC to read the name I'm supposed to scrawl across the surface of the completed cake. They gave me the words in a dialect called English, and I sound out the phonetics as best I can. "Are you Beth?"

She ignores me, her gaze drifting to the stack of funnel cakes I've assembled. Her bright smile withers to a frown. My heart sinks. Though the confection isn't complete, I'm proud of how it's coming along. The whipped green frosting I concocted has a perfect balance of rich and sweet that won't overpower the delicate flavor of the cakes.

"Is that... my cake?" she asks. She's staring at it as if it's a delivery of three-day-old fish.

My *Iki'i* is overwhelmed by the itchy feeling of her dismay, yet I don't understand why. I set the piping bag aside and turn to face her fully. "Is this not what you expected?"

"Absolutely not. Where did you find the recipe for this... this... whatever this is?" Her annoyance feels like a flame thrower.

My own indignation rises. Perhaps I was wrong about why the crew is restricted from the human guests. This female is quite abrasive. I lift my chin. "I searched our database on human cake extensively to formulate this recipe. This will please the human desire for both fat and sugar."

"Oh, my God. You have no idea what you're doing." She strides past me and the island counter toward the appliances on the far wall as if she owns the kitchen.

"Now hold on—"

"We need to fix this. Fast." She glances around, veering toward the big door next to the garbage chute. "I need butter, eggs, sugar, flour—"

I hurry after her and grab her arm, my irritation barely in check. "This is my kitchen, and you're not supposed to be in here. Just tell me what's wrong, and I'll fix it."

She jerks away, her brown eyes flashing. "There's no way you can salvage this on your own. All of it's wrong. I'm not leaving this up to chance. Now where's your cooler?"

Before I can stop her, she reaches up and hits the button for the garbage chute.

"Wait, don't—" My words are sucked away as the door irises open and a hurricane of wind and flying utensils sweep through the kitchen. Normally, the chute opens to a repository that is ejected through a secondary airlock. An airlock which is apparently stuck open.

In less than a breath, we're swept out into black, empty space with the rest of the kitchen's contents.

I barely have time to assemble my wits, hardening my matrix to protect myself against the cold vacuum of space. But then I see Bethany spinning next to me, her face a mask of terror. The whites of her eyes are turning red, and crystals of frost are creeping across her skin.

Kuzara. She might be a pain in the ass, but if I don't do something, she'll be dead in mere moments. I stretch out a hand and pull her against me, encapsulating her in my matrix before hardening again. I've just cut my survival time down exponentially, but I've more than doubled hers. On my own, I can survive space quite a while in a state of hibernation, but maintaining oxygen and warmth for her will drain me quickly. I can only pray someone on board the *Romantasy* notices what happened before it's too late.

This damn female is going to be the death of us both.

Get your copy of Izhima to keep reading now!

GLOSSARY

Ahen - an opiate-like drug.

Amai wood - a rich golden brown wood sought after for its buttery texture and sweet scent. The resin is used as an aphrodisiac on the planet Hy.

Ayabe - slightly astringent fermented leaves humans might think resembles cole slaw.

Bacca - a game that resembles frisbee golf

Bareshi - brilliant one.

Burendo - a Kirenai who excels at shapeshifting and is able to not only assume the form of other species, but coloration as well.

Damma - the Kirenai word for mother.

Fogarian - aliens with red hair and sideburns who live on a rocky, mountainous planet.

G'nax - a species that uses light to communicate attraction and arousal. They also have a symbiotic relationship with an eight-legged insectoid.

Hage - bald, wide-eyed alien that looks much like the iconic alien humans have circulated.

Happa trees - blue fronds resembling palms.

Hypawa - species with magma colored eyes.

ICC - Integrated Circuit Chip - an embedded chip that is an alien version of a holographic smart phone

Ijin'en - four legged herd animal raised for meat and well known for its stupidity.

Iki'i - empathic power.

Irn - a unit of measure. One planetary rotation around the Kirenai's sun.

Itoshi - beloved. Term of endearment.

Jiro - a unit of measure equivalent to approximately two Earth hours.

K'ogai - the town near the palace on Kirenai Prime.

Kazhitu - nuts that look like sticky buns when baked. High in sugar, buttery and fruity.

Khargals - gray horned aliens with stone-like skin and wings from the planet Duras ;)

Khensei - a toxin that causes Kirenai to denature into their resting state.

Kikajiru - my distracting one - a term of endearment.

Kirenai Prime - the Kirenai home planet. Purple and blue with swirling white clouds.

Klen - aliens who communicate via scent.

Kuro - a type of bitter, very black tea.

Kuzara - shit, damn, fuck.

Kryillian death swarm - tiny insectoid creatures that can kill a man within seconds by sucking his blood.

Lensoran bubbly - alien champagne

Lonala moth - fragile insect native to Hypawa

Lukulio - purple worm-like insects usually consumed while alive.

Malila flowers - fragrant, night-blooming flowers popular in conservatories across the galaxy

Matrix/cellular matrix - the term for a Kirenai's cellular mass.

Nezumi - a small downy animal with a stumpy tail and floppy ears found on most space stations.

Nilgawood - a tree used to make resin.

Oritsu - An expression of awe.

Popotan - the plant used to line ship interiors that provides oxygen, recycles water, is highly resistant to radiation, and can regenerate itself if damaged.

Qalqan - a species known for their healers. Good bedside manners due to their resistance to emotional fluctuation.

Resting state - a Kirenai's amorphous shape, like nakedness to humans, it is shown only to family or trusted friends.

Senburu - a galactic conglomeration of merchants who oppose the emperor's rule. Individual members are called *Senbur*.

Sheegr - a hyper-sexual, weasel-like species native to the Singing Planet.

Sireta Prime - a popular party planet.

Sowain - tastes like chicken!

Supo cloth - smart fabric for clothing that doesn't need buttons or zippers.

Tekina - the galactic word for human.

Teozhisa - a cart to carry people.

Tolonovone - a device that creates lighted markings on the skin. Used by G'naxians as part of their mating rituals.

Ukimi ice - beloved dessert with cool, spicy flavor like sweet mint.

Urru - purple egg-sized fruits from the Singing Planet that taste like cantaloupe

Vatosangans - species with alabaster skin and blue or green hair who tend to be stocky or rounded. Planet is called Vatosang.

Zhikegi - morning stimulant drink.

Zhinku weed - common in the popotan fields.

Kirenai are an all-male species of shapeshifters with a natural form (resting state) like an amoeba who usually assume a bipedal shape to interact with other species. Until the discovery of humans, Kirenai required a permanent pair-bond with a female of another species to produce offspring. All Kirenai traits are dominant and located on the Y chromosome; male offspring are fully Kirenai, while female offspring are fully of the mother's species.

Birth rates have been historically low, and over the ages, the population has dwindled. Human females are exceptionally receptive to impregnation, and do not require formation of a pair-bond to conceive, which has made Earth a target for black market slave traders who deal in "breeders." The Emperor is making attempts to protect the population.

Regardless of the shape a Kirenai's matrix is in, he cannot change his skin or hair color. The most common color is blue, although hues range anywhere from mint green to lavender. Rare individuals, called *burendo,* can vary coloration outside this range. Kirenai blood is clear or slightly milky unless infected, when it grows murky to almost solid white.

All Kirenai have empathic abilities called *Iki'i* which make them capable of reading emotion and desire, and also enables them to identify individuals within their own species regardless of shape. This is the only Kirenai trait sometimes passed on to female progeny. The ability also makes the species consummate lovers because they can take actions and form attributes their partner finds most appealing. Bonded mates assume a permanent form pleasing to their mates; rarely can they force themselves into an alternate shape after bonding.

The average Kirenai life-span is approximately eight hundred human years. When a pair-bond is formed, a Kirenai passes a small genetic market to his mate that mitigates the aging process, giving the mate a lifespan to match his own.

Qalqan – A pink, lizard-like race who are innately skilled at medicine. They have more than two genders and change genders as they age, which makes reproduction rather complex. It also means means they rarely pair-bond with Kirenai. In addition, their emotions are hard to understand for others and unreadable by Kirenai *iki'i*.

Hypawa – A race with large, expressive eyes, smooth luminescent skin, and luscious hair on their heads and eyelashes; considered by many to be the most beautiful race in the galaxy. Their origin is a mystery - even their supposed world of origin doesn't seem to be their homeworld. Their economy is dependent on tourism and entertainment.

G'nax – A spiny, bug-like race that can breathe a variety of atmospheres. Biologically they are inclined to be traders and have senses that let them navigate through hyperspace. They use light to communicate attraction and arousal. The females have a symbiotic relationship with an eight-legged insectoid which secretes dew used to feed G'naxian infants.

Khargal – A horned, gray-skinned race that can enter a hybernating state where their body becomes stonelike. The number of horns indicates the amount of royal blood in them. Honor is more important to them than anything. They have wings and claws and resemble gargoyles of Earth mythology. Their planet of origin is a barren world that has two moons and is known for having some unusual ore deposits and relatively few life forms.

Fogarian – A burly, thick-skinned race with crimson hair, claws, and fangs. They come from a high-gravity planet rich in crystalline gemstones and excel at digging. The females usually bear litters of two to four offspring, and are favored mates for Kirenai. Fogarians tend to be very straightforward and keep their promises, even if it means death.

Vatosangan – A small, slight race with alabaster skin, rounded features, and blue to black hair. As the most common race to pair-bond with Kirenai, some say they actually control the galactic empire behind the scenes. They seek any alliance, technology, or advantage that will benefit them, and their current government is a meritocracy.

Klen – A green-skinned humanoid race with eyes on extendable stalks. Their tongues can act as prehensile limbs, and they have the ability to withstand a wide range of temperatures. They are a race of scavengers and can modify some of their bodily secretions to become various useful substances.

Hage – Short, bald, gray-skinned aliens with large heads. They were the first to make contact with humans. Though their scrawny frame doesn't suggest it, they are addicted to the pleasures of taking nutrition, and their cuisine is spectacular. A past war obliterated their homeworld, and they now live scattered among the other races, usually employed in a service capacity.

Sheeghr – Not advanced enough to be admitted to the Galactic Confederation. A matriarchal, ferret-like race native to the Singing Planet. Known for hypersexuality, the females maintain a constant state of pregnancy to ward off a native parasite called a Gloor. Any female who refuses or who cannot get pregnant is killed. The males determine rank based on the size and color of their phalluses.

Human – New members the Galactic Confederation. This bipedal race has not yet homogenized into a single language, culture or appearance. The species has skin tones that vary between black and alabaster, with shades of brown in between. The females are capable of reproducing with many other species throughout the galaxy, and have become a target for illegal slave trading.

INTERGALACTIC DATING AGENCY

Looking for more out of this world romance? Your local Intergalactic Dating Agency can help! These strong, smart, sexy aliens are on the prowl for mates, and humans like you are exactly what they're after. Jump in with Book 1 of any standalone trilogy from our crew of rock star SFR authors and make steamy first contact! Warning: abductions may or may not be included!

Grab more hunky alien action here:

http://romancingthealien.com

ALSO BY TAMSIN LEY

SCI-FI ROMANCE

Galactic Pirate Brides series

Kirenai Fated Mates (Intergalactic Dating Agency) series

Khargals of Duras

FANTASY ROMANCE

Mates for Monsters series

PARANORMAL ROMANCE

Alaska Alphas series

AUDIOBOOKS

BOX SETS

BOOKS IN GERMAN

Gefährten für Monster

Alphas in Alaska

POST APOCALYPTIC SCI-FI written as Tam Linsey

Botanicaust series

ABOUT THE AUTHOR

Once upon a time I thought I wanted to be a biomedical engineer, but experimenting on lab rats doesn't always lead to happy endings. Now I blend my nerdy infatuation of science with character-driven romance and guaranteed happily-ever-afters. My monsters always find their mates, with feisty heroines, tortured heroes, and all the steamy trouble they can handle. I promise my stories will never leave you hanging (although you may still crave more!)

When I'm not writing, I'll be in the garden or the kitchen, exploring Alaska with my husband, or preparing for the zombie apocalypse. I also enjoy crocheting while binge watching Netflix, playing video games, and enjoying family time during our weekly D&D session.

Interested in more about me? Join my VIP Club and get free books, notices, and other cool stuff!

www.tamsinley.com